ROSE COTTAGE

OLIVIA CLAIRE HIGH

Olivia Claire High

Fireside Publications
1004 San Felipe Lane
Lady Lake, Florida
www.firesidepubs.com

Printed in the United States of America by
SPS Publications
POB 787
Eustis, Florida
www.spspublications.com

This is a work of fiction. Names, characters, places and incidents are either the product of the author's imagination or are used fictitiously, and any resemblance to actual persons living or dead, events, or locales is entirely fictitious.

ISBN: 978-1-935517-53-5

OTHER BOOKS BY OLIVIA CLAIRE HIGH

An Angel Among Us

(Nonfiction)

The Crystal Angel

(Romantic Suspense)

Olivia Claire High

Dedication

This book is dedicated to my husband, Joe, with all my love.

Acknowledgements

Many thanks to all my faithful readers.

Olivia Claire High

PROLOGUE

Summer Gabriel lay among a cluster of tall weeds crying out her grief. She'd fled to the abandoned cottage because it had been a happy place in her childhood. Shabby after twenty years of neglect, her love for the old house remained untarnished. She hoped she would find the peace she sought here.

People weren't supposed to die when they were only thirty-two, not if they had two little kids who needed their mother, not like her sister-in-law, Rebecca. Cancer. She had loved Rebecca as she would a sister.

Nightfall crept in. The moon shimmered, a bright globe of light surrounded by stars twinkling like fireflies dancing in attendance. The call of a night bird calmed her. She closed her eyes, inhaling the potpourri of scents: damp earth, pungent weeds, and the sharp tang of pine from the nearby woods.

A sudden sensation that she was no longer alone rippled through her. Scrambling to her feet, her heart pounding, she peered into the darkness. She frowned at the nearby barren rose bushes, catching the unmistakable scent of roses where it had not been before. A hot bubble of fear rose to the surface, as slender fingers touched her tear stained cheek and words sounded inside her head urging her to be strong for her brother and his children. Terrified, Summer spun around and ran to her car, a silent scream lodged within her throat.

Olivia Claire High

Chapter One

Ted walked into Summer's bookstore exactly six months to the day after Rebecca's death. His timing produced such an unexpected jolt, she felt her pulse leap. Studying him, she thought he looked pretty good for a man who'd been walking around for months with an empty space where his heart used to be. Trapped in grief and burdened by the yoke of sorrow, at times he'd looked so achingly sad Summer had wept with helplessness. She gave herself a mental shake and smiled at him.

"What are you doing wandering around this time of day?"

"I knocked off early." His eyes scanned the empty store. "Do you have a minute?"

She shoved aside the stack of books she'd been sorting. "Sure. What's up?"

"I have a favor to ask. A big one," he emphasized and leaned on the counter.

"I'm not dressing up like a Playboy Bunny to serve drinks to your poker buddies."

His grin made him look boyish. "It does have to do with males, but nothing that sexist. Buster's gotten it into his head that he wants to go to Disneyland for his birthday. He and Teddy have been doing some serious nagging."

"And?"

"And, I'm hoping you will come along and help me with the boys."

She blinked in surprise and moved back from the counter. "You want me to go to Disneyland with you and the kids? That's the big favor you were talking about?"

He nodded. "That's it. It'll be my treat. Will you go?'

"Disneyland," she said, savoring the word. "The place is a virtual Mecca for a storyteller like me. Why wouldn't I jump at the opportunity to tag along?"

"I wasn't sure if you would be able to get away."

"I just have to check to see if Sandy's free to watch the store."

"Tell her it's for Buster. You know what a big softie she is when it comes to kids." He shoved his hands into his pockets and looked down at his feet for a moment. "I just wish Bec could..." He cleared his throat. "Anyway, I think it'll be fun; don't you?"

Summer hadn't missed the sudden huskiness in his voice and the flash of pain. It slid into her too, squeezing like a hard fist, but she forced herself to smile at him. "Are you kidding? We're talking Disneyland here, bro." She leaned toward him again and grinned. "I'll bet you a set of Mickey Mouse ears we're going to rock the place."

Stepping off the plane, it was difficult to tell who was more excited, the adults or the children. At the hotel, Ted insisted they all go for a cooling swim before exploring the mysteries of Magic Kingdom. Feeling hot and sticky, Summer was more than willing.

A large aqua rectangle rimmed with dark blue tiles, the hotel pool beckoned. A bright egg yolk yellow sun beamed down enveloping everything with its warmth. The odor of chlorine drifted through the air mixed with the scent of jasmine vines climbing along a chain link privacy fence. Several children and adults splashed or swam in the pool while others stood or sat in scattered groups along the perimeter.

Summer liked the hubbub of laughter and playful shouts. These were happy sounds. She reminded herself that happy was what they'd come looking for. She hurried after Ted and the boys as they tossed their towels onto empty loungers and kicked off their shoes. She took charge of Buster in the shallow end while Ted let Teddy talk him into going further away and before long they were splashing around like playful otters.

Summer aimed the biggest splash she could manage right at Buster. He saw it coming and ducked under the water just in time to send most of the water flying onto the sleek body of a woman sunning herself beside the pool.

She sprang off the lounger, brushing frantically at the drops of water as though someone had thrown acid on her.

Buster's head popped up from the water and she faced him quivering with open fury. "Look what you've done, you stupid little boy!"

Buster's bottom lip began to tremble as he reached for Summer. She gathered him close. "Hey! Lighten up. I'm the one who splashed you and if you didn't want to get wet, you shouldn't be so close to the water."

Despite being irritated with the woman, Summer realized she had set a bad example for Buster and taking him by the arm hustled him to the other end of the pool where Ted and Teddy played.

"Is everything okay?" Ted frowned at Buster. "Was that woman yelling at you:"

Not wanting to spoil Ted's day, Summer answered before Buster could launch into an explanation. "He's fine. She's just some Hollywood type blowing off steam."

They left soon after and hurriedly dressed for their first visit to the park. With so much to see and do, they spent several minutes looking at the map before they could decide where to start. Beginning with rides and ending with a parade of colorful characters nodding and shaking hands with the delighted boys as they passed by. The long, exciting day finished with a spectacular fireworks display.

Summer loved it all. She gazed around with an eye for the fanciful and the carefree soul of a dreamer. A pleased little sigh escaped her. She was truly in her element and she intended to enjoy every minute of it. The illusion of magic and fantasy where whimsy was the order of the day appealed greatly to her storyteller's heart.

Reading and crafting her own stories was an important part of her life and being here in this environment encouraged inspiration for future creations. It made her think of her early days at Rose Cottage where she'd first discovered what wonderful worlds a person could invent using imagination. Because of the strange feelings she'd experienced during her last visit, she hadn't been back but now, standing here with this magical world all around her, she had an irresistible urge to return.

They practically inhaled breakfast the next morning in their anxiousness to rush back to the park. They sampled rides, took in another parade, gobbled down hotdogs for lunch, and went on more rides.

"What do you say we take a break, fellows?" Ted said.

Summer felt as though she'd walked miles, which now that she thought about it she had. She treated them to ice cream cones and they found a patch of grass where they sprawled out to enjoy the creamy confections. Buster's eyes began to droop and she nudged Ted. "Looks like this one's ready for a nap."

"He's not the only one. My batteries could use a recharging. How about you? Ready to go back to the hotel?"

She felt a trickle of sweat dribble down her back and looked up at the sun. "Ready, but I think I'll do my reviving with a swim."

Summer changed into her simple one-piece swimsuit and headed for the hotel pool. She kept a sharp lookout for the wicked witch of the west and spotted her on the same lounger. She rolled her eyes thinking, some people never learn from their mistakes. Having no desire to tangle with the lady again, Summer skirted the area giving her a wide berth.

She was so intent on avoiding the woman that she pulled off the mother of all bumbling stunts. She hadn't realized her towel was dragging behind her on the ground. When she tripped over it, rather than a simple fall at the side of the pool and a possible skinned knee, she toppled into the water like a baby taking her first steps and landed on a man just coming to the surface.

She sent them both to the bottom and by the time they came up for air, they were both coughing up water and gagging. They faced each other among thrashing arms and legs. He didn't look happy and she couldn't blame him. Summer braced herself for the tongue lashing she knew she deserved.

"What the devil do you think you're doing?" he ground out

6

while shoving a thick wave of dripping hair away from his forehead.

Summer wiped water out of her eyes and rushed to apologize. "I'm so sorry. I didn't mean to fall on you. It was an accident. I tripped on my towel. Are you okay?" His hair was black with the sheen of wet seal skin. Smoky gray eyes flashed with obvious annoyance. There seemed to be an awful lot to him, but no sign of flab. All muscle and bone put together in a ruggedly handsome package. She decided he could bawl her out anytime he'd like.

He treated her to a hard stare. "I am, but it's fortunate I'm not a child, who might have had more to deal with than coughing up a chlorine cocktail."

She looked around at all the children swimming nearby. "Oh God, I know."

"Did you hurt yourself?" The steel in his eyes and tone had softened.

Relieved that he didn't seem as angry, she concentrated on the sound of his deep voice and experienced an odd little ripple in her belly. "I'm terribly embarrassed, but fine, really. Are you sure you're all right?" She wouldn't mind kissing anything that hurt.

He nodded. "I'll live. You tripped on a towel?"

"That's right. I'm afraid I wasn't watching where I was going. That's it." She pointed toward the offending piece of colorful terrycloth draped over the edge of the pool, one end still dangling in the water.

"If I were you I'd remove it before someone else comes along and trips."

She bobbed her head up and down like one of those novelties you sometimes see in cars. "Right." She supposed this was his way of politely letting her know he'd like her to go away. The sound of a child's voice broke into her thoughts.

"Daddy! Daddy! I want to go swimming with you now."

They turned together and the man smiled. Summer sucked in her breath when she realized the child was with the golden goddess of mean and they were heading her way. It was time to make a hasty departure. She took one last look at her rescuer's excellent physique.

"Well, bye and thanks for being so understanding." She scrambled out of the pool, retrieved her towel, and dashed for the nearest exit without daring to look back. But Summer had little doubt the woman was boring holes in her back when she heard the unpleasant sound of that shrill voice questioning the man.

"What were you doing with that woman?"

"Water aerobics," he said, as he watched Summer hurry away.

CHAPTER 2

As soon as she was in her room Summer leaned back against the door struggling to catch her breath. She lifted a hand to push the wet hair out of her eyes and realized she was trembling. Was her reaction the result of the unexpected fall or the sexy man? Probably a combination.

She looked at the soggy towel in her hand wondering how on earth she could have let herself trip on the thing. It was as though someone had actually wanted her to fall at the exact spot where that man swam in the pool. She shook her head. Using fanciful thoughts to rationalize her clumsiness wasn't going to work.

She sighed. How disappointing that such an attractive man should be married to such an unpleasant woman. Their little girl was cute though with her father's dark hair and eyes.

"Not my problem," she muttered pushing herself away from the door. She doubted she'd be seeing them again and even if she did they'd probably avoid her. Why would he want to get near someone who tried to drown him?

By the time she'd showered and changed Teddy and Buster were knocking on the door and calling to her.

"What are you two monkeys doing out here in the hallway on your own?" She looked over their heads. "Where's your dad?"

"He said we could come get you. He's kind of sick," Teddy offered.

"But not throwing up or anything," Buster added helpfully.

Summer frowned and grabbed her purse. "Let's go take a peek, shall we?"

The room was dim with a sliver of light coming from beneath the bathroom door. Ted was lying on the bed with a washcloth over his eyes. Summer rushed over to him. "What's going on, Ted?"

"Migraine," he mumbled. "Would you mind taking the kids

9

to dinner and back to the park? I'm going to try to sleep this off."

"Of course not. Are you sure you'll be okay?" She knew his headaches had been frequent and rather severe in the first weeks following Rebecca's death, but had gradually lessened over time. That didn't mean she wouldn't worry. "I don't like leaving you."

He lifted the cloth and winced. "It's just a headache. No brain surgery required." He looked at the boys. "Behave yourselves or there'll be no Disneyland tomorrow."

Two little heads nodded solemnly.

Knowing Ted needed the serenity of a quiet room, she hustled the boys out the door and straight downstairs to the hotel's coffee shop.

They'd barely settled themselves at a table when she saw the man from the pool approaching with his little girl. There was no sign of his wife, but she might be in the restroom.

Summer smiled. "Hi there." Her pulse did a nervous flutter when he smiled in return and her brain slid into a fantasy of how it would be to kiss his sculpted mouth.

"Well, hello again. It looks as though our paths are determined to cross today. Would you and your sons mind if we joined you?"

"My what?" she mumbled, shaking herself free of her self-induced daze. "Oh, they're not . . ." she started to explain when the boys chose that moment to begin arguing. "Excuse me while I deal with these two." She turned to the boys. "What did your father say about behaving?"

They instantly slumped silently back in their seats, glowering at each other.

That settled, Summer gestured at their small table. "Um, I don't think this is large enough," she said knowing the whole place wasn't big enough if she had to share it with his wife.

He let go of his child's hand and grabbing the table next to hers pushed them together. "That should work," he said looking pleased with his effort.

Summer wasn't sure if she approved of his audacity, but his daughter had already climbed onto a chair next to the boys.

"Looks like it," she mumbled.

He settled himself on a chair opposite her. "We haven't been properly introduced. I'm Marcus Brennan and this is my daughter, Sasha."

Summer looked over his shoulder. Apparently his wife wasn't coming. She relaxed the mental shield she'd been building up. "I'm Summer Gabriel and these two rowdy characters are Teddy and Buster."

He shook her hand. It was nice, but it couldn't quite compare with the sizzle she'd felt having his bare wet flesh slapping against her in the pool. She studied him wondering if he was thinking about that encounter, but there was nothing in his expression to give her a clue.

They spent the next few minutes studying the menu and coaxing the kids into ordering something besides ice cream. The room was filled with the clatter of dishes, a baby crying, snippets of conversation, and an occasional burst of laughter. Summer wrinkled her nose at the smell of fried food and strong coffee. By the time the waitress arrived to take their order she didn't have much of an appetite and opted for soup.

"None the worse for wear after today's dunking?" he asked in a friendly voice.

"I should be asking you that. You're the one who got torpedoed."

"Not a problem given your size, but I do want to apologize for my rudeness."

She shook her head. "You weren't rude and you had every right to be angry. I'm just lucky you didn't shove me back under in retaliation."

His smile was slow and his eyes held a touch of wicked looking humor. "Too many witnesses. But I didn't mean to chase you off when I mentioned getting your towel."

She couldn't very well say she was running away from his wife. "You didn't."

Their food arrived, but the boys barely touched their toasted cheese sandwiches. All they could talk about was going on more rides. Summer gave up trying to appease them. She turned to Marcus. "Dinner was obviously not on their to-do list."

He frowned at his daughter's nearly full plate. "Yes, I see what you mean."

He signaled for their bills and Summer wasn't prepared when the waitress handed them both to him. He waved her money away when she reached into her purse.

"I didn't expect you to pay for our dinner."

"It was worth it having the boys entertain Sasha."

"Well, thanks." They left the café and fell in step together.

"How old is she?"

"Five. We're here to celebrate her birthday."

Had she mistaken that quick shadow that suddenly moved over his lean features?

She tucked that away to think about later. "What a coincidence. Buster's just turned five and this is his birthday trip, too."

"Interesting name."

She smiled. "It's a nickname. His given name is Bernard after his grandfather and Teddy is Theodore after his dad."

"Their father didn't come with you?"

"He did, but he's back at the hotel with a migraine."

"I'm sorry to hear that. Miserable things, migraines. I hope he feels better soon. It would be a shame to spoil your family vacation."

The hint of sadness in his voice was unmistakable. Perhaps he and the glamour queen had had an argument. She was about to mention her relationship to the boys, but was stalled when they arrived at the park and the kids pushed their way through the turnstiles.

Sasha tugged on her father's hand. "I want to go on rides with Teddy and Buster."

"Honey, I'm sure they already have their own plans."

The corners of her mouth drooped downward. "But Daddy."

Summer took pity on the child's obvious disappointment. "Hey, we don't mind. Right, guys?" She raised her eyebrows at Teddy and much to her relief he responded.

"You want to go on the Pirates of the Caribbean with us?"

Sasha's eyes lit up and she gave Marcus a beseeching look. "Please, Daddy."

He looked at Summer. "Are you sure? We've already intruded on your dinner."

"It's no big deal. You had to eat and so did we. Let the kids have their fun."

They went on rides and settled down on a curb just before dark for the evening parade. Marcus bought the children glow-in-the-dark wands from a passing vendor.

"I can't let you keep paying for everything," Summer protested.

"Are you afraid your husband will object? We're not doing anything wrong here."

"No, it's not that." It was time to end the charade. "There's something I need..."

A burst of music rent the air cutting her off. "Looks like they're starting," he said.

They made the mutual decision to skip the fireworks and take a shuttle back to the hotel when Sasha fell asleep with her head resting on Marcus's shoulder and the boys had begun to snip at each other again.

"Would the boys mind spending some time in the pool with Sasha tomorrow?" Marcus asked, as they entered the hotel's elevator.

Although she was certain mommy dearest would nix the idea, Summer didn't air her thoughts. "I don't see why not. We usually go in the afternoon."

"Hopefully we'll see you there, then."

"I promise to watch where I'm going this time."

He smiled. "If not, I'll be happy to break your fall. Thank you for an enjoyable evening. I hope you'll find your husband feeling better."

"He's not . . ." The elevator stopped and the doors slid open. The boys dashed out leaving Summer no alternative but to bid Marcus a hasty goodnight and hurry after them.

Ted was up watching television. "How's the head?" she asked going over to him.

"Down to a dull ache. How'd everything go?"

"Okay." Summer didn't think it was necessary to mention they had shared the evening with strangers, but Teddy didn't have any qualms and told all.

Ted looked at Summer. "Where was the guy's wife?"

She shrugged. "I don't know. Back at the hotel I guess. I didn't ask. I wondered if they may have quarreled. He seemed kind of down at times."

"Are you talking about Sasha's mommy?" Teddy wanted to know.

"Yes, we were wondering if maybe she didn't feel well."

"She's in Heaven like our mommy."

Summer exchanged a quick look with Ted. "I think you're mistaken, sweetie, because I saw her at the pool today."

He shook his head. "That's not her mommy. Sasha told me," he insisted.

Summer shrugged. Who was she to argue? Maybe Sasha's mother really was dead and this was her daddy's girlfriend tagging along on a trip. But whatever the case, Summer didn't want to be responsible for exposing the boys to someone else's problems. They'd had enough to deal with on their own the last several months.

Summer wasn't a psychiatrist, but she was sure about the hint of sadness she'd sensed in the man. It made her want to offer comfort, especially to his little girl. The poor child had seemed almost desperate to spend time with them.

She helped Ted get the boys settled for the night before going to her own room.

She undressed and crawled into bed and lay there staring at the ceiling. She thought about Marcus. Maybe he was still mourning his wife's death and had brought the blond icicle with him to ease his loneliness.

"And maybe I should mind my own business," she muttered and after punching her pillow into a more comfortable shape, closed her eyes.

CHAPTER THREE

Despite the boys' anxiousness to hurry to the park, Ted insisted they take time to enjoy a more leisurely breakfast. Summer made a quick study of the coffee shop as they walked in wondering if they'd run into Marcus again. He wasn't there, but that didn't keep her from darting anxious glances at the door every time someone came in.

No doubt he'd automatically assume that Ted was her husband. She wanted to clear up the misconception about her being the boys' mother, but it could turn out to be awkward and embarrassing, especially for Ted. She gave an inward groan, as her conscience continued to gnaw at her like sharp little teeth. Summer breathed out a sigh of relief when Marcus hadn't shown up by the time they were ready to leave.

They headed for the park where the boys wanted to go on the big Mark Twain paddle boat. They piled onboard and by tacit agreement immediately climbed to the uppermost deck. The extra height gave them an unexpected behind the scenes view of the park. It allowed Summer to see the reality of what was on the other side of the many carefully constructed wooden facades.

She knew if she looked long enough it would spoil some of the lovely illusions she'd been harboring; so she pulled her eyes away and focused her attention downward, as the boat cut a wide swath through the pale brown water. She smiled at several small ducks swimming alongside the vessel with daring ease poking yellow beaks at any scraps floating on the water's surface.

She leaned her elbows on the glossy wooden railing and clasped her hands in front of her while tilting her head back to enjoy the delicate rays of the morning sun. A light breeze ruffled her hair teasing a few wispy strands against her cheeks. She heard Ted laugh and knew instinctively that it was a small piece of time she wouldn't forget.

The afternoon sun was glowing high in the sky when Ted hustled them back to the hotel for a dip in the pool. Thoughts of seeing Marcus and his significant other made Summer want to hide in her room. Maybe she'd get lucky and Marcus wouldn't be there, but of course he was. At least his wife, girlfriend, mistress, or whatever title she went by, didn't seem to be anywhere around.

Sasha spotted the boys and ran over to them with Marcus following close behind. The children didn't bother wasting precious time getting reacquainted. They'd jumped into the water before the adults barely had a chance to kick off their shoes.

Summer sat with the men on the edge of the pool at the shallow end. She dangled her feet in the water while they watched the children. She sat next to Ted, but was keenly aware of Marcus on the other side of him. She did her best to contribute to the small talk the men had initiated, but was barely aware of what she was saying.

Her reaction mystified her. She'd been worrying about seeing him and now she had trouble tearing her eyes away. She kept sneaking peeks, taking a renewed inventory of his body while trying not to be too obvious. Her eyes traveled past his broad shoulders and muscled chest to narrow hips and flat stomach before moving down to his powerful looking thighs making her ache to touch the sun bronzed flesh.

With such erotic thoughts roiling around inside and the way her body was heating up, she was going to have to slip into the water to cool off. But Teddy ended the idea by picking that moment to announce he had to go to the bathroom.

Ted stood up and grabbed a towel. "Okay, climb out. How about you Buster?"

"I don't have to go. I wanna stay here and swim with Sasha."

"You go on, Ted. I'll keep an eye on him," Summer offered.

Marcus shifted closer to her as soon as Ted walked away. "Why didn't you tell me you weren't the boys' mother?"

She couldn't stop the quick rush of color that rose in her cheeks, but lifted her chin in self-defense. "Well, that didn't take long." She wiggled her left hand in front of him. "It's not like I'm wearing a wedding ring."

"Which we both know doesn't always mean a whole lot these

days."

"I did try to tell you, but I kept getting interrupted. I don't have an ulterior motive if that's what you're thinking. Besides, I wasn't sure I'd be seeing you again."

"Is that a polite way of saying I'm interfering with your family vacation?"

She stared at him surprised. "Not at all. As far as I'm concerned it's fine if Sasha plays with the boys and I'm sure Ted feels the same."

"That takes care of my daughter. But I want to know how you personally feel?"

"It's not up to me." He arched a dark brow making her squirm. She pointed to the children splashing in the water hoping to draw his intent gaze away from her. "We're here for the kids, remember? Sasha seems to be having a great time."

He stared at her for a few more seconds before letting his gaze slide back to his daughter. "She's fascinated by the boys. She rarely plays with children."

"Really? Why's that?"

He shrugged his shoulders and brushed against her. It was no more than a light touch, but enough to make Summer feel as though someone had released a net full of butterflies inside her stomach. "It's just the way things have worked out."

"That sounds more like an evasion than an answer to my question."

"Does it?"

He was obviously going to make her work for information. It wasn't that she was nosy she told herself. She was just trying to make conversation. "That's another sidestep. I'm not with the CIA in case you were wondering. Is it all right to ask where you live?"

He smiled showing even white teeth. "Las Vegas. Where do you call home?"

She told him and he showed no sign of recognizing the area. "You wouldn't have heard of it. It's a small town up north that barely earns a blip on most maps."

"Does your brother live there, too?"

"Yes. We were all born and raised there." Since he obviously didn't have any reservations about asking her questions, she decided to plod on with her own inquiries. "Is this Sasha's first trip to Disneyland?"

"Her second, but she's having a better time, thanks to the boys." He paused a moment. "Ted told me about his wife. I'm sorry. It's a very difficult thing to go through."

Was he just being polite, she wondered or was that hint of grief in his voice genuine? "Yes it is. She was a wonderful person with the soul of an angel. Everyone loved her. It's so unfair that she had to die when she had so much to live for. I'm still angry that her life was cut short. I thought God was supposed to answer our prayers."

"He does, just not always in the way we'd like. My wife, Diana, died of breast cancer two years ago. The sorrow while not always overt is deep-rooted. You find yourself existing in small manageable increments of time trying to get through each day and sometimes a day can seem more like a month."

So she'd been right about those fleeting moments of sadness. The sound of his unveiled pain and the sudden bleak expression shot straight to her heart and without thinking Summer laid her hand on his arm. "Oh Marcus, I'm so sorry. I thought the woman I saw with Sasha at the pool was your wife."

"She's my wife's stepsister. Their widowed parents married when the girls were in their teens. I asked her to come because I thought it would be better for Sasha to have a woman along, but it was a mistake. She hated it here. I sent her home this morning."

"I can't imagine anyone not liking Disneyland, but that's only my opinion. Does she live in Las Vegas, too?" She hoped not. Summer wasn't going to examine her reason right now, but she didn't like to think of them being too near each other.

"Yes, she does."

Summer realized she was still touching him and reluctantly pulled her hand away. Ted returned at that moment squelching any further private conversation. She had mixed emotions when she heard him invite Marcus to join them that evening. She'd come here to have fun, not to get all tangled up with hot sexual urges, but there was no denying she felt a definite surge in her blood pressure whenever he was near.

They ate at a pizzeria near the hotel and walked through the gates of the park once more where the adults indulged the children in their choice of activities. It didn't take long for Summer to admit it wasn't so bad having Marcus along. It was just good family fun. Maybe that's what was lacking in his and Sasha's lives. They'd lost...what did he say his wife's name was? Diana. They were without the important third person that made up the family triad of father, mother and child. She knew what a big gaping hole that could leave. She'd witnessed Ted struggling to fill that break in harmony, but liked to think she had made a difference in helping him cope. She hoped Marcus had someone else besides his sister-in-law to ease his emptiness.

It pleased Summer when they were able to stay for the fireworks again. She bent her head back and watched the explosion of bright colors and patterns as they fanned out against the night sky. At one point she turned and saw Marcus staring at her.

She grinned. "I love this stuff. I guess I'm a big kid at heart." He didn't say anything, but the look he gave her caused her pulse to race and her face to flame.

Later, as they walked back to the hotel the men asked the kids if they'd like to go to a sea aquarium. They let out a chorus of enthusiastic yelps of approval before Buster had the adults choking back laughter when he asked what a "quarium" was.

They squeezed into the elevator taking them up to their rooms and Summer found herself pressed next to Marcus. She breathed in his clean male scent and tried in vain to get the image of envisioning him naked out of her head.

She'd never been this attracted to a man so quickly. It was as though some invisible force was pulling her toward him. Summer was afraid if she wasn't careful she could end up rushing into something she wasn't capable of handling.

Ted glanced at her, as they left the elevator and the boys ran on ahead toward their rooms. "I hope you didn't mind that I invited Marcus and Sasha to join us without asking you first."

"Of course not. This is your trip and you don't have to ask my permission for everything you want to do, Ted."

"I know, but I don't want you to feel uncomfortable."

"It was fun, especially for them I think."

"Yeah." His eyes clouded over for a moment. "Did he tell you he lost his wife?"

She nodded. "Yes he did."

"It makes me feel a certain affinity with him. He understands how it is." He shoved his hands into his pockets." You know, the feeling that you've lost a vital part of yourself."

Hearing the vulnerability in his voice and remembering the pain she'd detected from Marcus earlier made her squeeze his arm. "I'm sure he understands perfectly."

CHAPTER FOUR

The telephone rang, shattering the morning quiet making Summer fumble for the instrument, as she struggled to sit up. "Hello," she muttered trying to smother a yawn.

Sorry Sis, I didn't mean to wake you."

She blinked sleep out of her eyes and peered at the bedside clock. "It's okay, I should be getting up anyway. Is something wrong, Ted?"

"It's Buster. He's complaining of a bellyache and he keeps saying he feels like he's going to throw up, so I think I should keep him here."

"That's probably best. I'll sit with him while you go to the aquarium."

"I'd take you up on that, but he's being all clingy and Daddy's boy. I think I should stay with him, but I really hate to disappoint Teddy. Would you mind taking him? I've already talked to Marcus and he suggested it."

She sat up very straight, fully awake now. "He did?"

"Yes. He'll meet you in the lobby. He suggested breakfast before you go," Ted quickly added. "What do you say? He's waiting for me to call him back."

She didn't miss Teddy's pleading in the background. "Give me twenty minutes."

Summer hung up feeling like a gawky teenager going on a date with the class stud. On the other hand, spending the day with a good looking man shouldn't be too much of a hardship. Fortunately she'd have the children to help keep her raging hormones in check in case she slipped and did something stupid like patting him on his very fine looking butt.

As soon as she and Teddy stepped out of the elevator, Sasha rushed forward and hugged Summer around the waist. Surprised,

21

but charmed by the uninhibited display of affection, she hugged her back and caught a glimpse of Marcus watching them with an enigmatic expression.

He laid a hand on Sasha's shoulder and she stepped back. "I'm glad you came."

Despite what she'd been thinking earlier, she didn't want to give him the impression she was here for his company. "I didn't want to disappoint Teddy."

"No, I didn't think you would." Their eyes met for a millisecond before she looked away. "Would you mind if we ate someplace other than the coffee shop today?"

"Whatever is easiest," she said with a nonchalance she was far from feeling.

As soon as they started across the wide lobby Summer realized several pairs of female eyes were focused on Marcus. She wasn't surprised. Dressed in a navy blue knit shirt and jeans that showcased his rugged build, he exuded sizzling sex appeal. By the time they reached the entrance Summer felt like she should have run a serpentine pattern to dodge all the blatant arrows of womanly lust hurling his way.

She could hardly blame them when she'd been panting after him herself. She just didn't like the idea of running with the pack. She had the childish urge to turn around and tell them he was with her now and they'd have to wait their turn.

A valet delivered his black Mercedes SUV to the curb in front of the hotel. After they settled the children in back, Marcus held the passenger door for Summer while she climbed in front. The inside smelled of new leather and a hint of sunscreen.

The restaurant he chose was stylishly elegant and Summer thought the setting suited Marcus more than the hotel's noisy café. The place was certainly more chic than anything she or Teddy were used to, but Teddy took the unfamiliar surroundings in his stride and without his brother to argue with, conducted himself like a little gentleman.

They ate mostly in silence enjoying their food, the quiet, and the excellent service.

Marcus set his coffee cup back on its saucer and looked at her across the table. "Am I correct in assuming you would rather not have come without Ted?"

Was she so obvious? "This is his vacation and I hate to think of him being stuck at the hotel, especially since he was laid up last night. I'm also upset about Buster."

"There is that, of course. But as you pointed out, you're here with me because of Teddy. Why is it that you find the idea of spending a few hours with me so daunting?"

Quick color rushed into her cheeks. "I don't know what you're talking about."

He lifted a brow. "No? Now who's being evasive?"

"What difference does it make?" she mumbled, staring down at her plate.

"Hopefully you'll have a favorable answer to that by the end of the day."

The aquarium was a fascinating place and Summer found herself almost as excited as the children flitting from one huge tank to another marveling at each new discovery. But concern for Buster eventually had her looking for a payphone.

"Forget your cell?" Marcus asked and reached into his pocket. "Here, use mine."

"I don't have one," she confessed taking it from him. "Thanks."

He raised his eyebrows. "You're not serious. How do you survive?"

Because he made her feel embarrassed, Summer answered him more sharply than she'd intended. "Quite nicely and in case you've forgotten people did manage to function before cell phones came along."

"They also did without electricity, but life is definitely a lot easier with it. Do you boycott computers, too?"

"I didn't say that." She saw his mouth twitch in a smile. "I'm glad I amuse you."

"I'm sorry. I didn't mean to sound condescending. It's just that I don't know of anyone who doesn't carry a cell phone around with them like an extra appendage. But I imagine life is different in your small town compared to large cities."

"Yes, I suppose it is, but we're getting more sophisticated all the time. We even have indoor plumbing now," she snapped.

He lifted a brow. "Prickly little thing, aren't you?"

She wasn't sure if he was teasing her or not, but pride made her treat him to a defiant glare. "I happen to like the pace of my town. That's why I still live there."

"You're lucky. A lot of people spend years looking for their ideal place."

His tone made Summer wonder if he wasn't happy living in Las Vegas now that his wife was dead. He walked over to stand by the children leaving her feeling as though she'd reopened an old wound. She made her call and handed his phone back.

"Thanks." She cleared her throat. "I'm sorry I snipped at your before."

He waved her apology away. "I shouldn't have teased you. How's Buster?"

"Better. I suspect he just needed a little one-on-one with Ted."

"You're probably right. Ted told me you've been a tremendous help with the boys since his wife's death. He's very fortunate to have you."

There was no mistaking the loneliness in his voice. She'd heard it too many times from Ted not to recognize it. It made her want to reach out and soothe the deep lines that suddenly framed his mouth. For a moment everything around her fell away and all she could hear was a soul crying out before he seemed to take control of himself again.

"I do what I can. Ted and the boys are all the family I have. I need them just as much as they need me, so I try to be with them as often as my work allows."

"He said you own a bookstore."

She nodded. "I do. I sell and trade gently used books."

"I hope you don't mind, but I asked him if you were seeing anyone."

The unexpected statement had her heart doing a couple of quick thumps. She supposed she could tiptoe around his startling confession, but decided to see what he had in mind. "Did you? So, are you just window shopping or actually interested in buying?"

"That depends."

Narrow eyebrows lifted. "On?"

"You. I'd like to get to know you better, but I should warn you that I have a tendency to try things out while I do my looking."

Summer stared at him with what she hoped was a composed expression while her heart continued to skip dance inside her chest. It was one thing to flirt and feel a quick flash of heat whenever he was around, but to actually have him talking about starting up a more serious twosome had her teetering on uncertainty.

She wanted to go carefully for both their sakes. He was reaching out and she didn't want to offend him by slapping that hand away. Neither, however did she relish doing anything that might put her in an awkward position.

"Thanks for the heads up. I'm flattered you want to see me, but I don't see how it'd work since we live pretty far apart."

"Not that far when you consider today's air travel. In the meantime, if you wouldn't mind giving me your telephone number I'd like to call you."

At least Ted had left that option up to her. She wished she had more time to think about it. "My phone number?" Seconds passed while she wrestled with her indecision.

"If you'd rather not have me pursue this you have only to say so. I have no intention of forcing myself on you, Summer. I've enjoyed your company and thought we could be friends. Was I wrong in thinking you might be interested in the same thing?"

God knows she'd been imagining more than that between them. "No, I'd like that, too." She pulled her business card out of her purse and jotted her home number on the back. "It's usually easier to catch me at work during the day and home in the evenings."

He reached into his wallet and gave her his card, but the children came running up before she had a chance to look at it. Teddy began tugging at her hand and she quickly shoved the card into her purse before allowing herself to be led away. They spent the next couple of hours wandering around until the children began to complain that they were hungry.

Marcus snapped his fingers. "I have an idea." He led them

back to the car and stopped at a delicatessen where he picked up sandwiches, soft drinks and small bags of potato chips before driving to a public park for a spontaneous picnic lunch.

Despite her protest Marcus paid for everything. "I do have money, you know."

"I'm trying to impress you with my gentlemanly manners."

She laughed. "It's working."

"Good, but I haven't even begun yet. One of these days I'm going to take you out to a proper meal without having the children along as chaperones."

"That certainly gives a girl something to think about." She could only hope her voice sounded calmer than she felt.

As soon as they finished eating, the children ran to the swings. She watched them and shook her head. "I sometimes wonder where they get all that energy."

Marcus chuckled. "It's called youth. Tell me about your childhood."

She supposed it was his first step toward getting to know her better, so she began a rambling description of her years growing up. She looked at him ready for him to reciprocate. "What about you? What were you like as a boy?"

He shrugged. "A shorter version of what I am now."

She didn't bother to hide her annoyance. "I've just spent the last five minutes rambling on about myself. I think I deserve something in return."

But before he could reply Sasha suddenly cried out and they shoved off the bench to rush over to where she lay on the ground holding her knee. Teddy scrambled off his swing and stood darting nervous glances at the adults, as they knelt by Sasha.

"I told her she was pumping too high, but she said she wanted to beat me."

After running his hands quickly over her body, Marcus gathered his sobbing daughter in his arms. "You're all right, sweetheart. It's just a scrape on your knee." He held her close and stroked her hair, but she continued to cry.

Galvanized into action by the child's sobs, Summer took leftover napkins, wet them in the water fountain, and handed them to him. "This might help take the sting out."

He pressed them gently against the slightly bloodied kneecap bringing fresh tears from Sasha. Summer leaned down to the whimpering child. "I have a magic Band-Aid in my purse. Would you like me to put it on your owie?"

Sasha nodded and Marcus lifted his brows. "You carry Band-Aids in your purse?"

She dug the bandage out and pulled back the outer wrapping. "You never know when you'll need one when you're with kids," she said laying the strip carefully over the injured knee.

Sasha looked at it and then at Summer. "Is it really magic?"

"Only if it makes you feel better and I hope it does because the fairies and I don't like to see you crying. So what do you think?"

Sasha gave her a teary smile. "It only hurts a little bit."

"I'm glad." Now that the small crisis had been smoothed out, Summer looked at her watch. "It's getting late. I should be getting back. Ted could probably use a break."

"When are you going home?" Marcus asked as they walked to the car.

"The day after tomorrow. How about you?"

"In the morning. Will you join us for breakfast before we leave?"

"I should warn you that I have a tendency to doze off in my food before 6:00."

He chuckled. "Not to worry. I was thinking more along the lines of 9:00."

"Would that invitation happen to include Ted and the boys?"

He slanted a brief look at her. "If you'd like."

Neither his expression nor the tone of his voice gave her a clue as to whether or not he was pleased with her request. But he was friendly enough as she stepped out of the elevator and they said their goodbyes,

"Thank you for inviting me today. I had a good time."

"Don't sound so surprised," he said in a voice that matched the smoky depths of his eyes.

CHAPTER FIVE

Summer told Ted about breakfast. "I accepted for you. It'll give you a chance to tell Marcus goodbye. I'll stay here with Buster if you don't think he'll be up to it."

"He'll be fine. I have a feeling he was just tired from all the excitement."

"Not surprising when you consider we've been hitting Mouseland pretty hard and swimming in the afternoons, too." She twisted the strap of her purse. "Um, Marcus said he asked you if I'm seeing anyone."

"Yeah. I think he's a good guy, so I told him the field was clear." He grinned at her. "Are you going to take a strip off of me for suggesting it without asking you first?"

She shook her head. "No, but I may not be what he's looking for, Ted."

"You shouldn't underestimate yourself."

"I'm trying to be realistic. If I haven't been able to snag a man locally, what makes you think a long distance romance will make a difference?"

"Because I happen to believe that Marcus is a lot smarter than the guys back home and he knows a fine woman when he sees one."

"I detect a little nepotism brother dear, but thanks for the compliment." She walked to the door and stopped. "He may want more than I'm capable of giving. I don't want to hurt him. Seriously, what if I don't turn out to be what he needs?"

"We're not talking marriage. You've just met. Why don't you try the friendship on for size and enjoy what you have while you can? What do you have to lose?"

"My virginity?" she said feeling impish and had to laugh at his strangled gasp.

Thinking of Marcus made her dig his business card out of her purse. The title named an electronics company, but it was the letters CEO after his name that got her attention. The confidence she'd felt from Ted's compliment and advice deflated like air whooshing from a balloon. Summer couldn't picture herself fitting in with the VIP of a big city company. Sighing, she tore the card into little pieces and sprinkled it in the trash.

But that didn't keep her from wondering what it would be like to be with a man like Marcus. He may cover himself with a respectable façade, but he literally radiated an animal magnetism that had her girlie parts on high alert and she wasn't the only one who noticed. All those women ogling him in the lobby had been proof of that.

Summer had a feeling he'd be quite capable of giving her a whole lot of pleasure without too much effort. He barely touched her and she felt singed. Thinking what it would be like to make love with him made her insides feel all quivery.

She thought about his wife. She had a feeling there was probably still a lot of love there. If he were to have an affair would it stir feelings of guilt in him? Had he had other women since her death and if so, did her memory intrude if they shared his bed?

She thought about his sister-in-law. That tigress already had her possessive claws clamped on him and obviously wasn't about to share her prize. Slumping down onto the bed, Summer decided it would be best if she skipped breakfast. No sense dangling a carrot if you didn't intend to give the man a bite. She'd call Ted in the morning and tell him she had a headache.

She was at work a few days later when Marcus phoned. "Hello, Summer."

"Marcus?" Did that squeaky sounding voice really belong to her?

"Am I calling at an inconvenient time?"

"I'm pretty busy with customers at the moment. Would you mind if I called you back tonight?"

"All right. I look forward to hearing from you."

She hung up feeling terrible knowing she had no intention of contacting him. She spent the rest of the day trying to convince herself she was doing the right thing, but no matter what argument she used, Summer couldn't ease the guilt that warred inside her.

The need to focus on something else before she went home that night made her decide to drive out to Rose Cottage. Thinking about her strange experience the last time she'd been there caused little beads of sweat to dot her forehead, but she had to go. While at Disneyland she'd promised herself she would. She missed the place and needed to know if it could still offer comfort to her.

Summer pulled up in front of the cottage and sat in the car. After several minutes, when all remained quiet, the tension drained out of her body. Her eyes looked at the house and did not notice the decay, but saw it with a heart that remembered the beauty of long ago. It may not be Disneyland, but in its own way it was still a magical place to her.

She decided that whatever she'd thought had happened before had probably been the result of the grief she'd been suffering at the time. There was nothing to make her believe anything unusual was going on now.

That is she could believe it, as long as she didn't consider the empty rose bushes and still acknowledge the strong scent that suddenly seemed to surround her.

Summer had just nodded off in front of the television the next evening when the phone rang jarring her to alertness. She groped for the receiver and mumbled into it.

"I'm sorry, did I wake you? It's Marcus."

She pushed herself up while trying to ignore the sudden leap in her pulse. "Not quite," she said pulling in a breath. "But I was about to zone out in front of the TV."

"I waited for your call last night."

Although there wasn't any censure in his tone, Summer shifted uneasily in her chair. "I'm sorry, but I've been kind of busy trying to catch up since I got back."

"I thought as much."

She wished he'd be more of a jerk, so maybe she wouldn't feel so lousy about lying. "How's Sasha?" she asked, hoping to ease some of her guilty conscience.

"Well enough, but she keeps asking when she can see all of you again."

"She's very sweet."

"She was quite taken with you and your family. I thought I'd call Ted and set up a time when it would be convenient for us to visit."

Her heart did a quick flip flop. "What?"

"When I mentioned to Ted at Disneyland how much Sasha was enjoying the boys, he invited me to bring her for a weekend visit."

"He did?" She knew she sounded like an idiot, but the thought of facing Marcus made her feel panicky. Maybe if she knew when he planned on coming she could be out of town. "Better give him plenty of time to prepare. You'd be surprised how busy his life is trying to fill the role of both parents."

"Oh, I think I have a pretty good idea of how that goes."

She wanted to smack herself in the head. Of course he'd understand. "Oh right," she mumbled. "Um, did you and Sasha have a good drive home?"

"We did. Thank you for asking. How was your flight?"

"Not bad, if you don't count the water Buster spilled in my lap. I walked off the plane looking like I'd wet my pants." She groaned. "I can't believe I said that."

His laugh sent tiny shivers quivering through her belly. "It must have been quite a sight."

Summer searched for something to say to steer the conversation away from herself. "Did your sister-in-law make it home okay?" Like she cared.

"Yes."

She waited for him to say something else, but when he didn't she plunged on in an effort to fill the silence. "I suppose she had to get back to a job like the rest of us."

"She doesn't need to work. Her late husband left her very well off."

"Must be nice." She couldn't quite keep the sarcasm out of her voice.

"Personally I think she'd be happier if she had something more to do. She has a flair for interior decorating. Diana tried to get her to open her own shop, but she never took to the idea."

"It's a lot of work running a business. I suppose she didn't want to tie herself down to such a commitment, especially when she doesn't need the money."

"You'd certainly understand the workload involved. How long have you had your bookstore?"

"I started working for Sandy, the previous owner while I was in high school. She sold the business to me five years ago, but helps out when I need her."

"Do you have any old limited editions?"

"I get a few now and then, but the bulk of my inventory is made up of more current books in paperback. I like to carry a good variety of children's books and I have a lot of romance novels because that's what sells best here."

"Romance novels," he repeated sounding amused. "Soap operas without music."

She couldn't tell if he was being critical or not. "I suppose you could call it that, but they provide inexpensive entertainment. What's the harm in that?"

"Nothing I suppose, except it seems a bit pathetic to have to enhance your love life through the pages of a book."

She felt an instant burst of aggravation knowing how often she'd gotten a mild sexual kick herself from reading a steamy love novel. "Fortunately for my business my readers don't share your opinion. What's wrong with indulging in a little escapism? Real life isn't all sweetness and flowers, you know."

"No one understands that better than I."

Summer closed her eyes wishing she could take back her impulsive statement. "I'm sorry, Marcus. I didn't mean to minimize what happened to your wife."

"I realize that. I was merely responding to your observation. You don't strike me as the kind of person who goes around deliberately trying to hurt people."

Her heart sank. He was being so nice there was no way she could continue her pretense. "You may not think so when I tell you I had no intention of returning your call." She held her breath wondering if he'd hang up or say a few choice words.

"May I ask why?" he said after a few seconds.

"Nerves I guess."

"I see. Is that why you didn't join us for breakfast the day I left Disneyland?"

She sighed. "Caught me. I had a feeling you wouldn't buy the headache thing."

"Are you feeling better now?"

"Yes, but before you let me off the hook you should know that I tore up your card with the phone number. I'll take it now if you'd be willing to give me another chance."

"Are you sure that's what you want?"

"A pen's in my hand as we speak and, just so you'll know, the hair-shirt I'm wearing has become rather uncomfortable." It was a relief to hear him laugh.

"Well, we can't have that." He gave her the number and she repeated it back. "Do you know what the best part of the Disneyland trip was for me?" he asked.

"This is just a wild guess, but was it riding in a cup and saucer?"

His chuckle was warm and friendly. "Meeting you."

She shivered at the instant dash of pleasure that raced through her. "You were an unexpected bonus too, Marcus."

"That's nice to know. We'll talk again soon. Goodnight Summer, pleasant dreams."

CHAPTER SIX

Their telephone conversations over the next couple of weeks were friendly enough to make Summer rule out skipping town. By the time Marcus set up a date to visit, she willingly agreed to clean house for Ted.

She had just put her feet up when he phoned.

"How's it going? Finding everything you need?"

"I had to pick up some floor wax when I was at the store."

"You're going to too much trouble. The floors look fine with a good mopping."

"Now they look better. Aren't you supposed to be leaving for the airport soon?"

"Yeah, but I'm waiting for a call I have to take and it's going to be a while. I won't be able to get away in time. Would you mind meeting Marcus's plane?"

She frowned. "Oh Ted no, that hour and a half drive is a long way for my car."

He let out a derisive snort. "A mile and half would be too much for that clunker. You can take my car. I hate to dump this on you at the last minute, but I'd feel lousy making him rent a car after I said I'd be there."

Despite having talked to Marcus on the phone, Summer wasn't sure if she was ready to see him on her own, but she knew Ted was right about someone meeting Marcus. "I'll go, but do you mind if I take the boys with me?" she asked on a sudden inspiration.

"Are you kidding? They love airports."

"You're going to owe me big time for this."

"I know. Think of something really disgusting to get even."

"Don't think I won't," she warned.

In addition to having them act as a buffer between her and

Marcus if things did prove to be awkward, some of her earlier apprehension eased, especially when she saw how excited the boys were at the prospect of going to the airport.

Summer parked the car and they hopped a shuttle to the terminal area. They were a bit early, but the boys were happy to wait while they pressed their noses against the huge windows watching planes landing and taking off.

Ted had given her so little notice, Summer had rushed when she changed. She hoped her pink sweater and tan slacks looked more presentable than her shabby coat did. She could have worn a nicer one, but it had been a case of vanity vs. practicality. It was cold out and this jacket was her warmest. When she reached into her closet, practicality had won out.

She spent the next several minutes keeping an eye on the boys and checking her watch before she spotted Marcus and Sasha coming down an escalator. There was no denying the sensual pull tugging at her midsection. His black jeans, black turtleneck sweater, and black leather jacket gave a whole new meaning to what she thought of as sexy male attire. She forced her eyes away from him and called to the boys.

Sasha rushed over as soon as they stepped onto solid ground and Summer bent down to accept her hug. But her breath stalled in her throat when Marcus leaned over and brushed his lips across her cheek. "It's wonderful to see you again." He shook hands with the boys. "Sasha was hoping you'd be here to meet us."

"We like the big airplanes," Buster blurted out making Marcus chuckle.

Summer shook her head. "So much for a welcoming committee. Ted's sorry he couldn't meet you himself, but he got bogged down at work. He'll be waiting at home."

Marcus smiled at her. "How could I mind when he sent such a lovely substitute?"

Her pulse jumped like drops of water on a hot griddle. Dragging her eyes from him, she pointed to the sign directing them to the luggage carousels. "Do you have any bags to collect?"

He held up a large zipped carryall in his hand. "No, we're all set."

"Oh, okay. Well, I guess we should go catch the shuttle to the parking lot. Unless you'd rather wait here with the kids and I'll bring the car. It's kind of windy out."

He shook his head. "The fresh air will do us good."

Summer asked if he'd prefer to drive when they reached the car, but he assured her that he had every confidence in her. His comment made her so flustered she missed the exit and had to circle back.

"Sorry. I don't come here often," she mumbled gripping the wheel.

"Airport parking lots are tricky. Some of them can make a person feel like they're trying to find their way out of a labyrinth."

Grateful for his understanding, she began to relax. "I take that to mean you've seen your share of airports."

"A few."

She had a feeling he was being modest about that, but before she could comment a burst of giggling came from the back. "The boys are happy to see Sasha again."

"She talked of little else once I told her we were coming." He looked out the window at the passing scenery. "It's quite different here than the desert, but appealing in its own way."

"I think so. We have a nice variety of vegetation and wildlife. Our lakes and rivers have enough fish to keep most fishermen happy and you can practically taste the changing seasons. The hills are beautiful in the spring when all the wild flowers carpet the ground. Fall here doesn't have quite the spectacular hues that you see on the east coast, but there's enough color to make a person want to grab a paint brush and try to capture it. I'm thankful developers haven't come into the area and changed everything by adding housing tracts and condos."

"Then you might want to be more careful with your enthusiasm."

She gave him a quick puzzled frown before turning back to the road. "Why?"

"You just sounded like a very good PR spokesperson for the local chamber of commerce describing a virtual country paradise. Keep that up and those dreaded developers just might show up with their bulldozers."

Summer wasn't sure if he were mocking her or not, but she

couldn't keep the irritation out of her voice. "I'm not ashamed to admit I'm proud of where I live."

He lifted a brow. "Seems to me we've bumped up against this kind of misunderstanding before. I meant it as a compliment, Summer, not a slur on your town."

She pulled her bottom lip between her teeth. "Sorry. I guess I'm a little nervous seeing you again and it's making me edgy."

"I see. I thought you'd gotten beyond that. You always sound relaxed enough when we talk on the phone."

"It's not the same as seeing someone in person."

His eyes raked over her. "No, it certainly isn't."

Thankfully he turned his attention to the outside again and eased some of the tension by asking questions about the area and before Summer knew it she was pulling into Ted's driveway. She helped the kids out of the car while Marcus went to the trunk to retrieve his bag. Ted met them at the door and the two men shook hands.

"Can we show Sasha our room, Dad?" Teddy asked, as soon as they'd all gathered in the living room.

"Okay, but try to keep it looking good for at least five minutes. Aunt Summer spent a lot of time mucking it out." The kids scurried away and Ted turned back to Marcus. "Let me show you where you can dump your bag."

"I'll start getting things ready for dinner," Summer volunteered and walked away.

"I do a fairly decent barbecue, but Summer's agreed to round out the rest of the menu," he told Marcus, as they walked down the hallway.

Marcus smiled. "Sounds good."

Summer had put baked beans in the oven before she'd left for the airport and their maple scented aroma filled the room while she put together a green salad and Ted grilled steaks. She'd picked up a pie at the bakery and had ice cream to go with it for dessert.

Ted served wine with the meal and although she rarely drank, Summer allowed herself a glass hoping to relax. She told herself she wouldn't need false courage if Marcus would stop staring at her. Every time she looked his way his eyes were on her making her squirm in her chair, especially when Ted grinned.

As soon as the children had wolfed down their food they raced back to the bedroom to play. But when Ted heard the boys yelling at each other he excused himself.

"I'd better make sure no blood is being shed."

Summer scowled at Marcus as soon as Ted had left. "Please stop doing that."

He cocked a questioning brow.

"Don't pretend you don't know what I'm talking about. You've been staring at me as though you'd like to take a bite out of me."

She stood up and began to gather dirty dishes hoping to put some distance between them and steady the shakiness she felt. But Marcus picked up a couple of plates and followed her to the kitchen which caused her tension to build even more.

"Maybe I do. You look pretty delectable and I wouldn't mind a sample. You intrigue me, Summer. You're such an interesting mixture of emotions; sassy, witty, shy, and I suspect very sexy underneath it all. I've wanted to know more about you since the first moment I saw you."

She set the dishes down and spun around to face him. "You couldn't have," she sputtered. "I practically drowned you."

He set the plates he'd been carrying aside and crowded her against the sink pinning her there with a hand on either side of her body. "There's more than one way to drown a man," he said in a husky voice.

She could have sworn the air surrounding them crackled as though it had been charged with a jolt of electricity. He was so close she could feel his breath brush against her forehead. "I . . ." She swallowed and her eyes darted around the room. "I don't think this is a very good idea, Marcus."

"Probably not, but it's not going to stop me from helping myself to that taste," he muttered, as his mouth covered her lips smothering any further protest.

CHAPTER SEVEN

The silverware she'd been holding slipped from Summer's hands and landed with a loud clatter on the floor spinning out around their feet. She had meant to push him away, but somehow her fingers were digging into his sweater urging him closer. Heat roared through her body and she began to tremble like someone caught in a powerful maelstrom.

He toyed with her mouth, teasing, nipping, and coaxing her lips apart. When she felt his tongue slip inside, sparks of awareness shot through her leaving her tingling all over. Her body tightened in resistance for a moment and then went soft and pliant.

His hands cupped her face and continued along the sides of her neck to rest on her slender shoulders. Summer moved her arms around his waist and clung while murmuring his name in a voice gone hoarse with desire, her blood whipping through her veins. Marcus moaned into her mouth and fisting his hands in her hair, deepened the kiss.

"They were..." Ted came to a halt in the doorway. "Oh, jeez I'm sorry!"

Summer couldn't have been any more shocked if she'd had a bucket of ice water dumped on her. She immediately pushed Marcus away and ran a trembling hand over her hair struggling to regain a semblance of composure.

"We were just..." she trailed off feeling helplessly mortified.

Marcus came to her rescue. "I apologize. This is my fault, Ted."

"No, no I shouldn't have barged in like that. I'll leave you two alone."

Summer pressed her hands to her flaming cheeks. "I want both of you to go," she said in an unsteady voice. "I'll stay here to finish cleaning up."

Marcus looked at her and frowned. "Summer, I'm sorry."

She shook her head at him. "Please just go away."

He reached out a hand toward her. "Let me . . ."

She glared at him. "Not here, not now." She turned back to the sink.

Ted tapped him on the arm. "I think this might be a good time to start getting the kids ready for bed."

Marcus gave Summer one last troubled look before turning to follow Ted from the room.

Her hands shook when she began picking up the silverware. She set the pieces in the sink and turned on the water. What had she been thinking allowing Marcus to kiss her like that here in Ted's house?

The kids easily could have walked in and seen them. It was bad enough having Ted witness them practically sucking on each other's faces. She started loading the dishwasher. But it wasn't as if she'd done anything so terrible, she consoled herself. They'd kissed. What was the big deal? She let out a long, low sigh. Whom was she kidding?

She'd felt Marcus's aroused body when he pressed against her. It was obvious he wanted more than a kiss. But despite his phone calls and coming here to visit, he hadn't clarified his relationship with his sister-in-law and there was no way Summer wanted to get involved in a triangle with her.

She had to start showing more restraint with the man until she could get a clearer picture of where this was going. Marcus seemed to be ready to take things to the next level, but he was moving too fast for her. She couldn't deny that she was physically attracted to him, but she'd be darned if she'd end up being his weekend roll in the hay.

She had just finished loading the dishwasher when Ted poked his head around the door. "Everything okay in here or should I be waving a white flag?"

"It is if you don't count the fact that I feel like a complete idiot." She shook her head in self-derision. "I'm so embarrassed."

"I'm the one who's embarrassed. I shouldn't have barged in on you like that."

"Why not? This is your house." She heard the impatience in her voice and took a deep breath. "Don't mind me. I'm a little rattled, but I shouldn't take it out on you."

"Do you feel like reading to the kids? It might help to calm you down."

She always read to the boys when she was here at bedtime. She enjoyed the ritual as much as they did. For a moment she thought of begging off, but realized it wasn't fair to penalize them because she was feeling unsettled.

"I could use the distraction."

Marcus was standing in the hallway outside the bedroom when Summer walked by. She made it a point to avoid looking at him. Teddy had chosen a familiar book, which was probably a good thing given her state of mind. But once she began reading her natural love of storytelling took over and her earlier stress slowly began to ease away.

Ted flung an arm over her shoulders when she finished and they walked out of the room. "I've heard you read that story a dozen times and you can still draw me in."

"It was amazing," Marcus added, clearly impressed. "I've never seen Sasha so enthralled and I myself have never thought a children's story could be so fascinating."

Summer felt a nice glow from the compliments. "I'm glad you enjoyed it."

"It looks like those trips to Rose Cottage with Mom paid off," Ted remarked.

Marcus looked from one to the other. "What's Rose Cottage?"

Summer shrugged. "Just a place my mother took me to when I was a little girl. The old woman who lived there used to tell wonderful stories."

"What happened to her?"

"She died and the cottage is empty now, but I still go there sometimes."

"It sounds like a very special place."

"It is to me." She looked at Ted. "I've got to go. I have a couple boxes of books at home I want to go through before I take them to the store in the morning."

41

As Ted handed Summer's jacket to her, Buster called for a drink of water. He rolled his eyes toward the ceiling. "Duty calls. I'll see you tomorrow, Sis."

Left alone with Marcus, Summer felt her pulse shoot up a couple of notches. She mumbled a quick goodbye and hurried outside hoping he'd stay behind, but he followed.

"Are you leaving because of a simple kiss?"

Did he say simple? It had been more like a torrid dance of tongues. "No, I have work to do." She hoped her voice sounded steadier than she felt.

"You, Ms. Gabriel, are running away," he said quietly contradicting her.

The image of their bodies locked together and the taste of his mouth came back in a vivid replay. She rubbed her forehead. "I wasn't prepared for what happened."

"Nor was I, but you'll have to admit you weren't exactly fighting me off and I certainly am not going to stand here and deny that I enjoyed every bit of it. I've made no secret of the fact that I want more than phone conversations with you, Summer. I realize you're busy with your store and helping your brother, but I hope you'll find time to fit me into your agenda."

She pulled in a shaky breath. "I don't know. I'm a little confused right now. I need to think about what happened tonight. I have to go now, but I'll see you tomorrow."

She started to turn away, but he grabbed her hand. "You can count on it."

The intensity of his stare and those all-observant eyes bore into her, mesmerized her until she tugged her fingers free. She scrambled into her car and prayed the old girl would start on the first try. The car gods were with her and the engine fired to life.

Summer put the car in gear and carefully backed out of the driveway. She glanced back and saw Marcus watching her. She gripped the wheel so tightly her hands hurt. She was running away, just like Marcus said. She felt like a scared rabbit. She guessed that compared to the women he knew, she must seem ridiculously gauche.

She swung out into the street and drove away as fast as she dared, needing to put as much distance between them as quickly as

42

possible. The man had certainly stirred her up. It wasn't as though she'd never been kissed before she reminded herself. She'd locked lips with plenty of guys and most of those episodes had been pleasant experiences.

But with Marcus it felt like dynamite going off inside. It didn't matter that they barely knew each other. He'd brought out needs Summer wasn't sure she was ready to explore with him. Every nerve in her body warned her to be careful. But the problem was, like forbidden fruit she already craved another sample of his deep dark taste. The thought made her body quiver with a sense of anticipation.

And at that moment the air surrounding Rose Cottage stirred and trembled through the little house in a kind of awakening.

CHAPTER EIGHT

Summer was mending books when Ted and Marcus came to the store with the children in tow shortly before noon the next day. The boys took it upon themselves to show Sasha the children's section while Marcus asked to see the limited editions. It didn't take him long to announce his intention to buy the entire meager cache.

Paying for a couple of meals was one thing, but she didn't want him feigning an interest in her books trying to impress her. Or worse yet, thinking he was going to soften her up enough to thank him with sexual favors. Good books were like fascinating people to her and she wasn't about to let him use them as bargaining chips in their relationship.

"I'd rather you didn't bother. I prefer unique books like these to go to serious collectors. I don't need your charity," she added ignoring Ted's sharp intake of breath.

Marcus's brow lifted. "What do you think I plan to do with them, start a fire?"

She blushed. "No, of course not." Why was it she always seemed to be saying the wrong thing to this man? "Maybe I was a little hasty," she amended, "but you have to understand that certain books are special to me and I'd like to know that they'll be sincerely appreciated when they leave my store."

Ted sniffed. "For Pete's sake, Summer, I like books as much as the next guy, but you're acting as though you're getting ready to offer them up as a human sacrifice."

Marcus broke in before she had a chance to respond. "Books can become as invaluable as good friends. You needn't worry, Summer, I know how to take care of what's important and if it'll make you feel any better, I am a serious collector." He pushed the stack of books forward and took out his money clip.

Swamped with regret over her sudden outburst, she began to ring up the sale while carefully avoiding eye contact. Ted cut through her discomfort by declaring that since it was lunchtime she should join them for the noon meal. She was about to refuse, but the children were endearingly eager to have her go with them.

"All right, but I can't stay too long. You know Saturday is my busiest day."

They walked next door to the bakery that served lunch along with a variety of desserts. Ted tugged Summer aside while Marcus looked over the menu on a wall.

"What was that all about back there?" he demanded under his breath. "Since when do you turn down someone who wants to buy your books? You weren't just being a snob about it, you were rude and that's not like you."

"I thought he was..." Marcus looked their way and she stopped. "Never mind."

As soon as she'd eaten, Summer excused herself to return to work, but not before Marcus insisted he was taking them out to dinner that evening. She was about to beg off until she felt Ted's eyes on her and accepted, hoping to downplay her earlier bad manners.

But the simple invitation had upset the normal balance of her day. It caused her to be so distracted she made mistakes ringing up sales and forgot the name of one of her favorite authors when a customer asked. It wasn't until she reminded herself that it was only a dinner with her family and a friend that she stopped being so jittery.

She rushed home after work to get ready and, after standing in front of her closet surveying its scanty contents, she decided she definitely needed to go clothes shopping. Everything she owned was worn and dated. Sighing, she pulled out a navy blue crepe skirt, a creamy silk camisole, and her only blazer, which she saw was missing a button.

She was slipping into a pair of low heeled navy shoes when she heard a knock at the door. She hurried to open it expecting to see Ted, but found herself face to face with Marcus. Dressed in black slacks, a maroon open collared shirt, and his black leather jacket, he filled the doorway with the force of his masculinity. He handed her a large bouquet of daisies. "Ted said they were your favorite."

Summer could feel the instant fluttering of her heart when she took the flowers from him. "How lovely. Thank you."

"I was going to buy a box of chocolates, but I didn't want to overdo it."

"A woman can never have too much chocolate. Is Ted in the car with the kids?"

He rubbed a fingertip down the side of his nose. "He's not coming. He thought it would be easier if he stayed home with them and ordered pizza. Do you mind?"

She buried her nose in the snowy white petals with their cheery yellow centers trying to hide her surprise at the unexpected development. Thanks to her scheming brother this was turning out to be a date after all. "No, I don't mind. Come in for a minute while I put the flowers in water."

He stepped across the threshold and the small living room instantly seemed to shrink in size. "Take your time."

Summer hurried to the kitchen and was stepping onto a chair to reach a tall cupboard when Marcus came up behind her. She hadn't heard him come in and almost lost her balance. He steadied her by putting both hands around her slender waist giving rise to a whole new round of nerves.

"Let me help you with that." He reached over her head and plucked out the vase before lifting her down.

His nearness made her heart zip up into her throat. "Thanks."

His eyes scanned the area. "I like your décor. It suits you."

She looked up from arranging the flowers. "You mean I've managed to make a rabbit hutch look like a real home?"

"No. I mean I like your taste."

"Oh." She blushed at the compliment and her hands shook as she continued working with the flowers. "Most of the stuff is from secondhand stores and yard sales."

He ran a hand over the back of one of the mismatched wooden kitchen chairs. "Is that so? I've heard that kind of thing is quite a hobby with some people."

"Yard sales? They can be. They're delightfully addictive and endlessly fascinating. I get a lot of my books that way. You should try going to one sometime."

"Maybe I should."

She set the vase in the center of the kitchen table. "How's that?"

"Perfect," he said, but he was looking at her when he said it.

His nearness was driving her temperature up several degrees. "I'm sorry, but I'm afraid I don't have anything to offer you to drink."

"We'll get something at the restaurant. Ted told me about a place. Shall we go?"

By the time they walked out to the car the sky had gone pink coating, everything with a soft rosy hue. He drove out of town to a country inn where they were led to a cozy table in a dark corner. The isolation suggested an intimacy that added to Summer's heightened sensitivity to Marcus. She managed a smile when he pulled out her chair. She had to admit he had nice old-fashioned manners mixed in with all that hot male charisma.

She turned down his offer of a cocktail before dinner and ordered mineral water. She felt giddy enough, but he insisted she have wine with their food. She let him order for them both; tomato bisque soup, a salad of mixed greens, lamb chops with new potatoes, and baby peas. Their waiter brought a basket of freshly baked bread still warm from the oven along with a little China dish filled with curls of creamy butter.

By the time they'd had coffee, Summer felt more relaxed. She didn't care that it was probably due to the bottle of wine they'd polished off. It was a relief to be free from anxiety, but all that changed when he stood up and held out his hand to her.

She looked at him and frowned. "What?"

"I'd like to dance with you."

She thought about the way she'd reacted in Ted's kitchen and wondered if she'd be able to contain her emotions being in his arms again. She decided not to chance it. "I'm not much of a dancer. I'll ruin your shoeshine," she added hoping to deter him.

He merely smiled and tugged her gently from the chair. "Then we won't do anything too complicated."

The moment his arms went around her she knew she was in trouble. They were sharing the small dance floor with other couples, which left little room for maneuvering. Marcus held her close, fitting the contours of their bodies together, as he guided her to the tempo of the music.

She closed her eyes, breathed him in, and gave herself up to the heady sensations swirling around inside her. The song was a slow dreamy ballad made for lovers and romance. She was helplessly trapped by her emotions, as he stroked the side of her neck with his thumb in slow easy movements that made her shiver. Summer knew she had never wanted a man as much as she craved Marcus at this moment and the desire she saw in his eyes was unmistakable. She was in danger of losing control of the situation and the idea was both exciting and unnerving. She couldn't prevent the next shiver of awareness that coursed through her.

"You're trembling."

"I know. I can't help it." She drew in a shaky breath. "I don't understand what's happening."

"Yes you do," he murmured in a low growl.

Her heart tripped over itself. "Okay. I'll admit you're causing a definite glitch in my nervous system, but . . ." It was difficult remembering what she wanted to say while he continued to stroke, looking at her with those intense smoky gray eyes.

"But?" he prompted.

"I may not be the right person for you," she said recalling her feelings of inadequacy after reading his business card.

"I disagree. I think you're exactly right for me."

"How can you say that? We barely know each other. I think we need to be better acquainted before we rush into anything."

He pressed their lower bodies closer making it quite clear that he wanted to do more than dance with her. "That's exactly what I'm trying to do."

"I don't want to make a mistake."

"So you think making love with me will turn out to be a disappointment? What a blow to my ego."

"I . . .I didn't mean it like that," she stammered. "You're making me say all the wrong things. I just need more time to think about us, that's all."

"I can be patient when I know something is worth waiting for," he replied before leading her back to their table.

Summer barely remembered the drive home. He escorted her to her apartment, took the key from her, and unlocked the door. But when he leaned down to kiss her she put a hand on his chest and stepped back. "No don't, please. I might not be able to stop."

"Well now, that's encouraging." He smiled and touched her hair.

"I mean it, Marcus. Every time you touch me I feel as though I'll go up in flames."

Dark brows instantly lifted. "Good God woman, you expect me to leave after saying something like that? Why not let me come in and we'll do a slow burn together?"

She shook her head. "Not tonight. Please humor me for a little while longer." His smoldering look made her heart bounce inside her chest.

"All right, have it your way, but it's going to make me want you all the more."

"I appreciate the warning," she said with a nervous little laugh.

"Will I get to see you before I leave tomorrow?"

"Yes. Ted invited me to the house for breakfast." She stepped back while she still had the strength to let him go. "Thank you for a lovely evening and the flowers."

He nodded. "You're welcome; though it makes me wonder what would have happened if I had brought that box of chocolates."

CHAPTER NINE

Summer slipped inside and closed the door before she could change her mind. She walked to her bedroom on wobbly legs and plopped down on the bed. She'd just turned away the sexiest, most handsome man she'd ever met. She closed her eyes remembering the feel of his body pressed against her on the dance floor. He could be here right now with her, rolling around in a tangle of arms and legs.

She just didn't want to jump his bones on their first date and have him thinking she was an easy lay, or worse yet, desperate. She frowned. But when would they have the opportunity to be alone again? He was going home tomorrow. Her eyes snapped open and her fingers dug into the soft quilt. Had she lost her chance to be with Marcus?

There was also the fact that his sister-in-law had access to him on a daily basis and Summer couldn't see her turning Marcus out of her bed. She sat up straight and slapped the flat of her hand against her forehead.

"Sometimes I can be so stupid," she groaned and flopped back onto the bed.

She rose early the next morning after a night of feverish dreams all having to do with Marcus's sexy body and making love with him. It left her feeling dizzy in the head and quivery in the belly. She spent extra time on her hair and makeup and chose a pair of slacks and a blouse instead of her usual jeans and tee shirt.

She drove to Ted's and let herself in through the front door. "Hello?" she called.

"I'm in the kitchen, come on back," he answered.

She walked into the room and inhaled. "Hmmm, something smells yummy."

"Cinnamon rolls. From a tube," he clarified when she raised

her eyebrows.

She looked at the skillet he was stirring, scrambled eggs with bits of ham. "I was going to offer to help, but it looks like you have everything under control."

"As controlled as I can be with my limited culinary skills, not counting my barbecuing." He nodded toward a coffee pot. "Help yourself. You look nice by the way."

"Thanks." She pulled a mug out of the cupboard and filled it before adding a spoon of sugar. "Where is everyone?" she asked as casually as she could.

"He's outside with the kids."

"What are you talking about?"

He laughed. "Don't try the coy act with me. I caught the vibes between you and Marcus even before I interrupted your sexy clench. That's why I stayed home with the kids last night, so you two could have some time alone."

"Speaking of which, that was pretty sneaky. What's with the matchmaking?"

"I like to follow through when I see that I'm right about a guy. How'd it go?"

The children came bursting through the door at that moment with Marcus close behind saving her having to answer. The children greeted her cheerfully, but her smile faded when Marcus stared at her with a stony expression.

Ted turned from the stove. "Okay troops, breakfast is almost ready. Go wash up and anyone who leaves a towel on the floor doesn't get a cinnamon roll."

"I need to wash my hands, too. I'll go police them," Marcus offered.

Ted turned to Summer as soon as Marcus left the room "Was it my imagination or did it get awfully chilly in here all of a sudden? Did you have a falling out last night?"

"Not that I'm aware of, but I know when I'm being given the cold shoulder."

She pulled plates and glasses from the cupboard. Marcus had acted as if he were angry with her. Surely he wasn't punishing her for not inviting him to share her bed. She gave herself a mental shake. No, he was too mature for such juvenile behavior.

She decided she must have imagined the cool stare, but as they sat eating later it was obvious that Marcus was definitely shutting her out. She kept up a flow of light chatter with the children, but shivered inside at his chilly indifference toward her.

As soon as the meal ended, Marcus took Sasha upstairs to get ready to leave.

Summer had assumed she'd be riding along to the airport with them, but she certainly wouldn't be going now in view of his behavior toward her. She apologized for not staying to help clean up and hurried to the door not wanting to encounter Marcus again.

"Sis, wait. I know you're upset, but don't leave like this. There's obviously been some kind of misunderstanding. Let me talk to Marcus before you go."

She shook her head. "I doubt if he'd listen considering the mood he's in."

"But Summer..."

"I'm not staying, Ted," she bit out, opening the door.

Summer rushed outside and climbed into her car, but no matter how many times she turned the ignition the old vehicle refused to start. She sat back in frustration and began to think about Marcus's reaction to her this morning. Whatever feelings he'd had from the Disneyland trip and the things he'd said last night were clearly no longer important to him. The idea that he had only been nice to her because he wanted to take her to bed made her temper come up to the boiling point.

She realized it had been a mistake to believe he was interested in a more meaningful relationship. At least she could be thankful she hadn't slept with him and saved herself from the humiliating position of being a one night stand. She reached over again to try to start the car when the passenger door suddenly swung open.

Summer stiffened when Marcus slid inside making her glare at him. "Go away."

"I can't let you leave here without an explanation. I owe you that much."

"You don't owe me a thing. Now get out of my car."

He shook his head. "Not until I say what I came out here to tell you."

"Oh, so now you want to talk." She sat back and folded her arms over her chest staring straight ahead. "Well, get on with it. I have more important things to do."

"I'm sorry for my rude behavior."

She treated his apology with a sniff of indignation, but he continued. "I realized after I left you last night that you were right and I was moving too fast. The last thing I want to do is frighten you away by coming on too strong. I stupidly thought if I ignored you it would make it easier for both of us today. I was wrong."

She turned to face him, eyes stormy with temper. "I haven't had a male play games like that since I was in junior high school. You not only hurt my feelings, but you embarrassed me in front of my brother."

His mouth tightened. "I know and I'm sorry. But if it's any consolation to you I hurt myself, too."

"Well, you deserve it for pulling such a lousy stunt."

"You're right, but I still want us to be friends...more than friends."

"You certainly have a strange way of going about it." She blew out a breath. "You know I'm attracted to you, but you have to understand that I don't come from your world. Life is a lot different around here."

"My world?" A brow winged up. "And that would be...?"

Summer shrugged. "You know, Las Vegas, big money, fancy cars, beautiful women, and high powered jobs. You're used to a level of sophistication that I couldn't begin to compete with. I'm just a simple, uncomplicated small town girl."

"That's not how I see you. You're the most refreshing woman I've met in a long time. There are so many things about you that I enjoy and I know I've only scratched the surface."

Her eyebrows pinched together in a deep frown. "Are you feeding me a line?"

His mouth twitched into a half smile. "No, I'm trying to tell you that I want you to come to Las Vegas with Ted and the boys when they visit me next month."

"Ted's already set up a date?" she asked, surprised.

He nodded. "Yes. Will you come? If not for me, then for Sasha?"

She wrinkled her nose at him. "Don't play dirty." She tapped her fingers on the steering wheel. "I'm not sure I can get away. It hasn't been that long since I left the store for the Disneyland trip. I can't keep asking my friend to cover for me."

"I understand, but I still hope you'll try to work something out."

"I'll see what I can do." She thought he'd get out of the car then, but he put his hands on her shoulders instead and pulled her across the seat toward him.

"I think we both want this."

His kiss was slow and sweet. He drank from her mouth as though he were savoring fine wine. She slid into the kiss and parted her lips letting his tongue dip inside. He shifted his upper body pressing her back against the seat until she couldn't tell if it were her heart pounding or his.

Her earlier anger completely vanished leaving her feeling greedy for him. Heat unleashed, rose and flashed in quickening spikes of power. Her fingers dove into the thickness of his hair urging him on until her heart was literally smashing against her ribs. He nipped the tip of her chin and scraped his teeth along her jaw line before returning to her willing mouth.

Desire snapped in the air around them and when his fingers closed over the swollen tip of her breast, Summer felt hungry passion slap at her in a swift wave of desperate yearning. She was lost and drifting in a turbulent sea of emotion. She felt his hardening body and rubbed against him in silent invitation while he moaned in response.

He muttered her name and continued to ravish her mouth with an urgency that should have sent warning bells off in her head, but only had her begging for more. It didn't matter that it was broad daylight or that they were sitting in her car parked in her brother's driveway. She was beyond coherent thought.

She couldn't breathe, but she didn't care. She'd die happy if she could just touch him. But when she began to work her hands under his shirt, Marcus clamped his fingers around her wrists.

"Summer, wait." Her name came out in a strangled wheeze. "We can't; not here."

Dazed and trembling, she looked around her. My God, what

was it about this man that made her want to rip his clothes off and grab hold? Every nerve, every muscle in her body wanted him with an intensity that made her quiver with longing. "Marcus?"

He held up a hand. "Give me a moment," his voice was ragged.

His head leaned back against the seat, his eyes closed, as he took in slow, deep breaths. Summer looked down at her tangled clothing and almost groaned out loud. This definitely was not taking things at a slower pace. Lucky for them he'd had enough self-control to stop when he did. If it had been left up to her they'd probably be in the backseat naked and horizontal.

He opened his eyes and stared at her. "Was that an example of an uncomplicated small town girl's foreplay?"

She burned with embarrassment. "That was supposed to be a metaphor. What just happened isn't all my fault," she said, defending herself. "I can't help it if you get my hormones revved up every time you come near me."

"What the hell do you think you do to me? Not that I'm complaining mind you," he was quick to add.

She hid a smile when she saw him wince as he adjusted the front of his jeans over his aroused body. "I guess that makes us even now."

"Minx," he growled, yanking gently on a lock of her hair. "Does this mean you'll come to visit with Ted and the boys?"

"How many guestrooms do you have?" she asked, tilting her head to one side.

He sat up and rubbed his thumb lightly over her bottom lip. "Enough."

She sighed. "Better break out another set of clean sheets, then."

CHAPTER TEN

Summer realized she finally had the reason she'd needed to prod herself into buying some new clothes. She decided to drive to the next town, which was larger and had a better selection of stores. A warm flush of embarrassment crept up her neck when she remembered the old bathing suit and short outfits she'd taken to Disneyland. If she were going to go around exposing her fanny she may as well do it in style.

She had tried without success to find out if Marcus's sister-in-law would be hanging around during their visit. If the woman was going to be included, Summer wanted to give extra attention to the clothes she took with her. She doubted if she could compete with the kind of wardrobe Ms. Fancy Dancy Las Vegas probably had. But she certainly didn't want to go there dressed in clothes that looked like they came from a secondhand store's reject pile.

She pulled into a parking space at the mall and sat drumming her fingers on the steering wheel wondering where to begin. Thinking Marcus may have given Ted some kind of an itinerary, she dug into her big tote bag and pulled out her new cell phone.

When she'd mentioned having to borrow Marcus's phone Ted had insisted that it was time she had one of her own. She'd been about to refuse when he reminded her he'd feel a lot better knowing she had the phone when she was out and about in the event he needed to get hold of her during an emergency.

She pressed his number. "Hi, it's me. I'm about to spring for some new clothes for Vegas and I haven't a clue what to buy."

He laughed. "You're asking me, the guy who has trouble wearing matching socks? You really must be desperate."

"Come on, I need some help here. I thought maybe Marcus might have said something to you about any plans he has for what we'll be doing."

"Wouldn't it be easier to just call and ask him what you'll need?"

Her sigh was loud and impatient. "A lot you know. Women are supposed to know those kinds of things and I don't want him to think I'm a hayseed because I lack that particular talent. Did he say anything to you besides bring shorts and swimsuits?"

"There was no mention of me needing a tux, so I assume you can leave your tiara and ball gown at home."

She snorted into the phone. "Oh you're hilarious."

He laughed again. "I couldn't resist. He did say I might want to throw in a pair of slacks and sport shirt in case we go out to dinner or a show. Does that help?"

"It's not much, but it'll have to do."

"You needn't worry, you know. You'll look great no matter what you wear."

"You make me want to cry when you say sweet things like that. I love you."

"And I love you back. Now go and make the retailers happy."

She arrived on his doorstep five hours later with a blister on each little toe, her hair disheveled, and her clothes a wrinkled mess. His eyes got big when he stared at the several shopping bags clutched in her hands. "For the love of Mike, Summer, we're only going to be in Las Vegas for a weekend. It looks like you've bought enough stuff for a couple of months."

"I wasn't sure what to get," she said and giving him a sullen look, dumped the bags in the middle of the living room floor before kicking off her shoes to flop down on the sofa. "I can't for the life of me understand why some women actually enjoy clothes shopping. It's boring, time consuming, and expensive. My credit cards are still smoking."

"Rough day, huh?"

"You have no idea. It was the most tedious five hours I've spent in ages."

"I've seen you take an entire day going around to yard sales."

"That's different. Yard sale stuff is useful. Clothes are..." She made a face.

"Necessary unless you plan on living in a nudist colony. At

least it looks like you were successful if that lot is anything to go by," he said pointing to the bags.

"You can judge for yourself after you see what I bought."

Ted's mouth gaped open and he stared at her with real alarm in his eyes. "Wait a minute. You mean I'm going to have to sit here and watch you model all this stuff?"

She nodded. "Everything, except for the underwear, of course."

"Ah, have a heart, Sis. You know how much I hate that kind of thing."

"Did anyone ever tell you that whining is very unbecoming in a grown man? You were the one who said I could get even for making me pick up Marcus at the airport."

"There was no mention of torture."

"So sue me. Go get the boys. I bought something for them and don't try sneaking out the back," she called after him and couldn't hide a smile when she heard him swear.

Teddy and Buster came running into the room and threw their arms around her while eyeing the sacks spread out on the floor. Summer got down on her knees, grabbed a couple of bags and handed one to each of them. Buster's eager little fingers pulled out a dump truck while Teddy's hands latched onto a Spiderman action figure.

"What do you say to Aunt Summer?" Ted prodded.

"Thank you," their voices sang out along with a couple more enthusiastic hugs.

She smiled. "You're welcome."

"You didn't have to do that, Sis."

"Oh yes I did. That toy store was the highlight of my shopping excursion."

Ted turned back to the boys. "Aunt Summer is going to show us her new clothes. Won't that be cool?" They took one look at the array of bags and clutching their new toys to their chests, scurried out of the room as fast as they could go.

"Cowards!" Ted yelled.

"This is going to take a while. Shopping is thirsty work. How about an iced tea?"

"I'd rather have a shot of booze." He watched, as she began

taking clothes out of the bags. "Make that a double," he grumbled and headed for the kitchen.

Marcus and Sasha were waiting for them when they got off the plane. As soon as they'd gotten their greetings out of the way, he led them outside to a sleek white limousine waiting at the curb. The boys shouted and jumped up and down. Ted let out a low whistle. Summer was too surprised to do anything but stare.

"I thought the boys would get a kick out of it," Marcus said and held the door open while the driver loaded their luggage into the trunk.

The boys started to scramble inside, but Ted held them back. "Where are your manners? Ladies first."

Summer took Sasha by the hand. "Come on sweetheart, let's get in before those two roughnecks run over the top of us." Sasha giggled and climbed inside.

The air-conditioning made the interior blessedly cool. Summer sat back on one of the cushy almond colored leather seats and stared at the tiny lights in the ceiling. She'd never ridden in a limousine before and assumed they were there to emulate stars. The heavily tinted windows kept the glare of sunlight from intruding and the thick floor carpet muffled outside noise.

It had been uncomfortably hot standing outside on the curb and Summer was so thirsty her lips felt welded together. She saw that Ted's face was covered with a fine sheen of sweat, but Marcus looked almost cool. He leaned forward and flipped open a faux wood panel revealing a mini bar, complete with a built-in ice chest.

"Here you go, kids," he said and twisting off the caps handed them each a bottle of water. He looked at Summer and Ted. "What can I get for you?"

She asked for water while Ted opted for a beer. He took a long swallow and let out a sigh of pleasure. "Bless you, son. I was about to perish from thirst."

Marcus smiled and lifted a beer out for himself. "The heat can be a little hard to take if you're not used to it."

"It doesn't seem to bother you," Summer noted.

"I've lived here a long time."

The children played while easy conversation flowed back and forth between the adults. Summer was enjoying the amiable camaraderie, but the comfort zone ended for her when they arrived at Marcus's home and his sister-in-law met them in the entry of the sprawling Spanish style house. She looked flawlessly chic in her pale green linen dress making Summer feel like a waif in her simple cotton skirt and blouse.

"It's about time you got back." She brushed her lips over Marcus's mouth. "I'm at loose ends and thought you could take me to lunch," she said, ignoring the others.

He put down the suitcase he'd been carrying. "You should have called first. As you can see I already have plans, but you're welcome to join us for lunch here."

Summer was sure the woman remembered her from the pool episode, but when Marcus made the introductions, a cold stare was her only acknowledgement.

Her name was Patrice. The last name didn't register with Summer. She thought it sounded vaguely Italian, but didn't care enough to have it repeated.

Although she showed no sign of affection toward Sasha, the same thing couldn't be said for the way she acted with Marcus. She slipped her arm through his and acted like the lady of the manor making Summer frown at the obvious possessiveness. Marcus eased himself away and indicated he needed to show his guests to their rooms.

"They're staying here?" Patrice demanded in a razor-sharp voice.

"Of course they're staying here. I invited them."

"Surely they'd rather be on the Strip with the other tourists."

"They're friends, not tourists."

Summer chewed on her lip and Ted shifted uneasily. "We can book into a hotel if there's a problem with us staying here, Marcus."

"There's no problem. My housekeeper has your rooms ready."

They turned to follow him, but not before Summer caught the malicious look in Patrice's eyes and felt a chill crawl up her spine when she realized it was aimed at her.

CHAPTER ELEVEN

By the time they'd finished putting their luggage in their rooms and touring the house Summer felt totally intimidated by the size and elegance of the place. It was what she'd tried to tell Marcus about his world being different from hers. She thought of her cozy little apartment with its secondhand furnishings and knew she could never be comfortable living in a house that screamed wealth at every turn.

They settled in what Marcus referred to as the family room where she joined Ted and the children on a huge buff colored sectional. Chairs and small tables were grouped around the large room. The dark hardwood floor gleamed with polish while several brightly hued oil paintings relieved the monotony of the cream colored walls.

A gray-haired, dour-faced woman came in wheeling a cart laden with pitchers of iced tea and lemonade along with an assortment of sandwiches cut into small triangles, slices of fresh fruit and peanut butter cookies. Marcus introduced her as his housekeeper, Mrs. Gwen. Patrice didn't waste any time continuing in her self-proclaimed role of mistress of the house, insisting she'd rather have hot tea.

"Be sure you use my special blend and a proper teacup, not one of those awful mugs. Don't forget the fresh lemon slices," she demanded.

Although Ted and Summer tried to take part in the conversation, it wasn't easy with Patrice shutting them out at every opportunity by talking about people and events that pertained only to her and Marcus. To his credit he interjected general topics that they could comment on, but Patrice never let him stray for long.

As soon as the children finished eating Sasha wanted the boys to go to her room to play. Marcus and Ted gave their permission and Summer wished she could go with them. Patrice's haughty demeanor had begun to wear on her nerves.

She breathed an inward sigh of relief when Patrice finally announced she had to leave. She stood up and looked at Marcus. "I need to talk to you—privately. You can walk me out to my car after I freshen up."

"Are you sure you wouldn't rather have us stay at a hotel?" Ted asked as soon as she left the room. "I don't think your sister-in-law approves of our being here."

"You mustn't mind Patrice. This is my house and I want you to stay with me."

Despite his reassurance, the woman had looked at them as though they were something to be scraped off the bottom of her very expensive looking high heeled shoes. When Patrice returned she sneered at Summer, as Marcus excused himself to follow her to her car.

Ted frowned. "What was with the look she gave you?"

"Who knows? But she certainly acts as though we're trespassing on her turf."

"Yeah, I got that feeling, too. There were a couple of times she made me feel like I needed fumigating. Makes you wonder how much time she spends here."

Summer didn't want to think about that. "Maybe we should have gotten rabies shots."

He laughed. "I'll go check on the kids and unpack a few things. How about you?"

"Go ahead. I'll wait until Marcus gets back."

Mrs. Gwen came in the room a few minutes later. "May I give you a hand?" Summer offered, as the woman began cleaning up from their lunch.

"Guests do not help with the household duties," she answered in a frosty tone.

Summer bit her lip. She'd obviously committed a breach in etiquette. In her own way the woman was turning out to be as much of a snob as Patrice. Summer pointed toward a wall of paintings hoping to redeem herself. "Those are quite beautiful. Were they done by a local artist?"

"They're Mrs. Brennan's. She also did all the sculptures you see around the house. She was very gifted. Her work was often commissioned by wealthy clients, some quite famous." Her voice had softened and Summer didn't miss the underlying pride in her tone. But who could blame her? The paintings were breathtaking and the statues she'd taken the time to study were exquisite. "She signed her work with her maiden name, Van Burton. Perhaps you've heard of her?"

"Diana Van Burton?" Summer shook her head. "Sorry, no." She didn't miss the instant look of disdain reflected in the woman's expression and knew she'd earned more disapproval from the woman.

"I didn't think so. You'd have to have a healthy income to afford her art."

Summer didn't miss the implied insult to her financial status, but forced herself to smile. "Yes, I suppose so," she muttered. "Thank you for the lunch. It was very good."

She shrugged her bony shoulders. "Hardly cordon bleu, but Mr. Brennan thought it best to keep things simple for the children."

"I suppose you're used to preparing a more gourmet menu."

"It wouldn't take much of a menu to outdo what I served here today, but Mr. Brennan prefers that I don't fuss unless he's entertaining someone important."

Convinced that the woman was letting her know she definitely wasn't on the Brennan's social level, Summer did her best to swallow her growing irritation. "Does he entertain often?"

She realized it probably wasn't accepted protocol to question the help about their employer, but she'd already messed up any chance of winning a popularity contest with the women around here.

"Not since Mrs. Brennan's death. But when she was alive they gave the most wonderful dinner parties." Her expression took on a dreamy quality. "Her invitations were always in demand. I used to enjoy watching her prepare for the evening. She always arranged the flowers and set the table herself. It was all so elegant. Everything she did was a work of art."

Summer suddenly wished she hadn't been so nosy. "It must

have been beautiful."

"Oh it was; just as Mrs. Brennan was beautiful. She simply took your breath away. It's as though a lovely light has gone out in this house since her death." She gripped the cart handle and turned away. "I'll take these things to the kitchen now."

Summer thought she saw tears gathering in the woman's eyes, as she left. It would seem Mrs. Gwen had forged a tight bond with Marcus's wife. Summer let out a long sigh and began to roam around the room. Everything was obviously expensive. Even some of the smaller pieces of bric-a-brac looked as though they cost more than her store made in several months and this was just one room.

She'd suspected Marcus had money, but this house and his extravagant lifestyle were proving to be even more than she'd imagined. It had obviously suited his late wife and appeared to be the right setting for Patrice with her supercilious attitude and her contempt for the less wealthy.

Her eyes followed the high arched ceiling with the heavy dark wood beams and continued tracking until she was staring at a wall of paintings again. She thought about the things Mrs. Gwen had said about Diana Brennan. The woman had been blessed with extraordinary talent and apparently great beauty as well. She wouldn't be an easy person to outshine. Summer looked around the room and sighed again. Despite Marcus saying he wanted them to be more than friends, she had a feeling this would be her only visit.

As soon as Marcus returned she told him where everyone had gone. Looking at him and knowing she was so unsuited for him made her spirits sink. "I think I'll go hang up a few things if you don't mind."

He nodded. "Be sure and let Mrs. Gwen know if you need anything. All you have to do is press the intercom button on the wall next to the light switch."

Summer wanted to cringe, but made herself smile. "Thanks," she said, anxious to be alone for awhile.

But she was greeted by a nasty surprise when she went to the room she'd been given. Her suitcase wasn't where she'd left it. She wondered if Mrs. Gwen might have unpacked for her.

Puzzled, she checked the closet and dresser, but found them empty. She wandered into the adjoining bathroom and found her bag lying empty on the floor. Her clothes had been dumped in the shower and someone had run the water over everything. It wasn't too difficult to pinpoint the person responsible. Patrice had obviously taken a detour during her freshening up trip. Her fury wanted to build, but Summer forced it back. Let the woman play her immature pranks. She'd be damned if she would give her the satisfaction of tattling to Marcus.

CHAPTER TWELVE

They stayed in that night, but Marcus took them on a tour of the city and surrounding area the next day. He parked and they walked until the children grew bored and he suggested they go back to the house for a dip in his pool.

The cloudless sky was a brilliant blue, the sun a bright yellow ball of heat bouncing off the beige stucco walls of the house in shimmering waves, as they pulled into Marcus's driveway. Driven by the need to cool off, they all quickly changed into their bathing suits and hurried out to the backyard.

Summer could practically feel the heat sucking the moisture out of her skin, as she sat on a lounger in her new bikini slathering on sunscreen. She'd already taken a quick swim and had decided to do a little sunbathing before hitting the pool again.

She studied the artfully landscaped cactus garden with its rocks of various sizes and colors scattered among the succulents. She spotted a trio of water nymph figurines crouched in one corner by the pool and wondered if Diana had designed the area. The exquisite statues had to be hers.

Summer was straining to reach her back with sunscreen when Marcus came up behind her and took the tube out of her hand.

"Let me do that for you."

The first contact was a shock of sensation that caused her to tingle all over. The longer he continued stroking her skin the more it became a sweet torture. Heat and desire pumped through her veins. It was all she could do to keep from panting.

"Turn over."

Summer didn't miss the way his voice had gone all husky and so deeply male she felt the timbre of it vibrate within her body. She flipped onto her back and set her teeth, as he smoothed lotion down her legs taking special care to include her feet.

There was something erotic in the way he massaged each individual toe and arch. Then his long fingers glided slowly up her arms and across her shoulders before skimming just above her throbbing breasts. By the time his fingers brushed across her midsection she was almost whimpering.

He set the tube aside. "I think that's enough for both of us right now."

She watched him walk over to the edge of the pool and dive into its aqua depths.

Summer knew she wasn't the only one who had been affected by their contact. He wasn't immune to her. She knew she hadn't mistaken the need in his voice or the evidence in the hardening of his body. Summer felt the potency in his hands and knew she'd be lying if she pretended she didn't want more.

Marcus took them to dinner and a show that night, making Summer glad she'd been able to salvage her clothes. It had required the help of Mrs. Gwen and the dryer in the laundry room, but her little black dress hugged her slender body in all the right places. The dip in the neckline allowed a glimpse of cleavage and narrow straps showed off her creamy shoulders. The hem stopped just above her knees and featured a deep slit in the back.

They returned late in the evening and whisked the children off to bed. Ted pleaded fatigue and went to his room leaving Summer alone with Marcus. She had little doubt it was another one of Ted's not so subtle ploys to encourage a romance between them and she had mixed emotions about his efforts.

"Would you like to see my collection of first editions?" Marcus asked.

It may have been a new twist on the come and see my etchings line, but she felt she owed him after the snide remark she'd made in her store about him pretending to like books.

She smiled at him. "I'd love to."

The collection was so impressive, she regretted she'd ever doubted his motives. "Here are the ones I bought from you," he said pointing to a shelf. "They make a rather nice addition, don't you think?"

She had the grace to blush remembering her rudeness. "I

don't enjoy eating crow, but after seeing all this, I deserve to have every glossy feather shoved down my throat."

He laughed and pulled her gently into his arms. "A kiss and all will be forgiven."

Her heart instantly increased its rhythm. "I don't think we'll stop with a kiss."

"I certainly hope not." His eyes were deep pools of intent. "I'm sure you realized when you came in here with me that I intended to share more than books with you."

"Yes, I suppose I did, but I'm not sure about this," she said remembering how Ted had come upon them. "What about the children?"

"They're all tucked snuggly in their beds," he said outlining her mouth with a fingertip.

A little shudder rippled through her. "But what if...?"

"Summer," he sighed patiently. "I locked the door. If anyone tries to come in here, we'll know." He nibbled on her lips rubbing his mouth across hers taunting and teasing until a low moan escaped her. "Do you want me to stop?"

"Doesn't look like it." Her breath came out in a long quivering sigh, as she cupped his face and brought his mouth back to hers with a necessity born of desperation.

Their tongues touched, flitted back and forth making her sigh while pressing herself against him in silent invitation. He laid his lips against the pulse throbbing in the soft hollow at her throat and touched the quivering spot with his tongue.

Summer hated the idea of his clothes keeping her from touching his bare flesh. She wanted to feel his skin beneath her hands and tugged the shirt away from his slacks while he pushed a strap of her dress off one shoulder replacing it with his mouth. They continued to strain against each other, hands probing and searching each other's body.

When he brushed his thumbs over the tips of her breasts, Summer's gasp of pleasure seemed to echo inside her head like a clap of thunder. His hands twisted her hair and he deepened the kiss until she thought she would shatter into a thousand tiny pieces.

Heart hammering, dazed with a hunger she couldn't control,

Summer reached for the zipper on his pants only to have him close a hand over her fingers.

"Not here. I want you in bed, naked."

Hot desire blazed from his eyes.

She nodded her head in acquiescence.

A scream suddenly tore through the air. Summer jerked back. Marcus flinched and let out a heavy sigh. "Sasha must be having a nightmare. I have to go to her."

"Of course." She pulled up the straps of her dress. "I'll go with you."

Sasha was sitting up in bed sobbing when they rushed into her room. Marcus instantly crossed over and sat on the edge of her bed gathering her to him. "It's all right, honey, we're here." He looked at Summer. "I'll have to stay with her for a while."

She nodded. "I understand. I hope she'll be all right. I'll see you in the morning."

She turned to leave and caught a glimpse of a photo in a heavy silver frame sitting on the dresser. A breathtakingly beautiful woman smiled out of the picture—Sasha's mother. Unnerved by those dark almond eyes staring at her, Summer slipped quietly from the room and found Ted standing in the hallway.

"What's going on? I thought I heard a scream."

"Sasha had a nightmare. Marcus is with her now."

"Poor kid." Ted frowned. "Are you okay? You look a little shell shocked."

"I guess her scream shook me up."

His eyes traveled over her body. "You're still dressed. You must have been up."

"Yes. Marcus was showing me his collection of first editions."

Both brows winged up. "Showing you his books, was he?"

"That's right and for your information nothing happened like you're obviously imagining, so you can wipe that silly grin off your face. I'm off to bed now—alone."

"I'm sorry to hear that," he said barely smothering a laugh.

"Oh shut up," she grumbled and stomped off to her room, undressed and crawled into bed. But sleep simply would not come. After the passionate episode with Marcus she felt like an athlete who'd been given a great pep talk by the coach and, filled with raging hormones, rushed to the gym door only to find that it had been locked. Her nerves felt brittle with so much conflict swirling around inside her.

She couldn't stop thinking about how much she wanted to make love with Marcus, but every time she thought about it, an image of his wife intruded. Oh how she wished she'd never seen that photograph. She couldn't imagine him ever being able to forget such a lovely creature or to allow anyone else to take her place. He may need a woman physically, but she doubted if he'd ever truly love again.

She wondered if he were asleep now. Probably. He'd already proved more than once that he had better control over his emotions than she did over her own. She'd still been in a sexual haze when they'd gone to Sasha, but Marcus had returned to his father role as soon as they entered the room. She couldn't fault him for that. She knew if it had been her child, comforting her would be all that mattered.

Summer continued to squirm trying to settle into a position that would hopefully bring sleep, but finally gave up and kicked the covers off. Despite the room's air-conditioning, her body was flushed with an inner heat, which only added to her agitation. She needed to cool down. She first thought of a shower, but the idea of a quick dip in the pool was more appealing. She rolled out of bed and peeled off her nightgown. Not bothering with a swimsuit, she grabbed a large fluffy bath towel and wrapped it around herself.

She'd barely stepped outside when she heard a splash. She peered closer into the dim glow left by the pool lights and saw that it was Marcus. She stood for several moments watching his nude body slice through the water with powerful strokes. The urge to join him was strong, but a vision of Diana popped inside her head making her ease back into the shadows with a sigh of regret.

Back in her room, Summer tossed the towel aside and sat on the edge of the bed feeling more unsettled than ever. A few minutes later she heard a light tap on her door. Her first thought was of Ted. Maybe one of the boys didn't feel well. She hoped not, but if that were the case at least it would be a way to channel some of her restlessness.

She pulled her nightgown back on and hurried to open the door to reveal Marcus standing there with a towel slung low on his lean hips. Tiny drops of water dripped from his hair and beaded across his shoulders. She watched mesmerized as a trail ran down his chest and over his stomach following the arrow of dark hair that disappeared beneath the towel. She had the strongest urge to lean over and lick the drops away.

"May I come in?" She swallowed down a lump in her throat and stepped back with a silent nod. "I was hoping you would join me in the pool," he said, closing the door.

The breath backed up in her lungs. "You saw me?" she asked, surprised.

"Yes."

The look he gave her was so seductive her heart skipped a couple of beats and the heat from his eyes almost seared her flesh wherever his gaze fell. He reached out and ran a finger down her cheek continuing along the sensitive cord at the side of her neck.

"Marcus," his name slipped out in a quivery whisper. He stepped back and she watched, mesmerized, as the towel slowly slid from his naked body revealing how much he wanted her. Her eyes widened and her mouth gaped open. "Oh my God," she gasped.

He stepped up to her and leisurely drew the nightgown over her head and tossed it aside. "This time we go for the fireworks," he muttered thickly and snatched her into his arms.

CHAPTER THIRTEEN

She went without resistance and moaned when he crushed his mouth down on hers. There was no gentleness in the kiss. It didn't matter. She was ready to explode and his roughness fit her mood. They fell onto the bed together locked in an embrace.

Summer reached for him and pulled his face down to her willing mouth greeting him with a kiss as solid as his own. Desire rocketed through her and heat rose with such intense passion she thought her body would burst into flames.

Marcus trailed his mouth along her jaw, down her neck, and over to her breasts where he devoted considerable time showing his appreciation to their budded tips. She gasped with pleasure and arched her body straining toward him, as he dragged his tongue down her belly and dipped into the tiny well surrounding her navel.

He moved his taut body against her. The blood raced through her veins when she saw the smoldering lust mirrored in his eyes. Nerves raw, screaming with need, she opened herself to him. He raised himself above her, gripped her hips, and thrust forward in one powerful surge. They strained against each other riding waves of pleasure together until the room spun around and erupted into a million tiny points of light.

At the exact moment several hundred miles away a sound akin to a happy sigh echoed throughout the abandoned rooms of Rose Cottage.

Summer floated out of sleep still wrapped in a sexual haze. It took her a few moments to realize she was alone. Disappointed, she buried her face in the pillow Marcus had used, breathing in the scent that lingered there. He'd made love to her again during the night. It had been slower, sweeter, but every bit as powerful leaving her yearning for more. She'd been right in thinking he'd be a skilled lover, but even her wild imaginings hadn't prepared her for the incredible satisfaction such expertise could bring.

It wasn't until she was standing in the shower that she remembered Diana and was once again filled with misgivings. What was going through Marcus's mind? Was he having regrets? Did he feel he'd betrayed his wife's memory? Would he snub her as he'd done that day at Ted's? She didn't think she'd be able to stand that now.

There wasn't time to be alone with him again before they had to leave. But his goodbye at the airport was filled with a wealth of promise and the warmth in his eyes melted the cold lump of doubt she'd been nursing all morning.

She'd barely walked into her apartment when he called.

"Miss me already?" she boldly teased.

"Most definitely and I'm not the only one."

"Oh?"

"It's Sasha. I thought she understood that you were here only to visit, but apparently she'd convinced herself you were going to stay permanently."

"Oh my. Is she terribly upset?"

"I'm afraid so. She doesn't really remember her mother, but she knows that she was someone who went away. Then she became very close with my mother, but she was killed in an automobile accident last year. Sasha seems to think any woman she cares for is automatically going to disappear from her life."

"Poor little darling. Who can blame her? I had no idea about your mother. I'm so sad for both of you losing those two special women in your lives." Innate compassion made Summer want to help. "Why don't you put Sasha on the phone? Maybe hearing my voice will help." Her heart did a slow crumble when the sobbing child came on the line. "Please don't cry, Sasha. You're going to see me again. I promise."

"But...but why did you go? Didn't you like my house?" she asked between sobs.

"Yes I did, but I had to come back to my own house and my store. You remember my bookstore, don't you?" she asked softly trying to soothe the child's distress.

"Yes. Can I go…go there again some time?" she stammered between hiccups.

"Of course you can, but I'm not sure when that will be, so until then will you try not to upset yourself? It makes me sad to know you're unhappy."

"I want to come see you tomorrow."

Realizing she didn't understand the concept of time, Summer searched for a way to pacify her until she could talk to Marcus again. "That's probably a little too soon. But would you like me to call you tonight and read you a bedtime story?" she quickly added hoping to prevent any fresh tears.

"Uh-huh."

"That's a good girl. Now is it all right if I talk to your daddy again?'

"Okay."

Marcus came on the line. "I don't know what you said, but it definitely helped."

"I told her I'd call and read her a bedtime story tonight. I hope that's all right."

"That's very generous of you, but I should warn you that you may have set yourself up for a nightly ritual for a while."

"I don't mind."

"Thank you, Summer. I appreciate this. Will seven-thirty be all right? I usually try to have Sasha in bed by eight."

"That's fine. I'm happy to help in any way that I can."

"Sasha's not the only one who needs help. You and I have only begun. I meant it when I said I wanted to set up another visit as soon as possible."

She grinned into the receiver. "I'd like that."

"I'll talk to you more tonight after Sasha's story," he promised and hung up.

Summer barely managed to control her heart's somersaulting when the phone rang again. "You're wasting your time, you know. He'll never want to be with you."

She gripped the phone at the sound of Patrice's voice. "What did you say?"

"You heard me. Marcus is only being nice to you because he's hoping he can talk you into being Sasha's nanny. He's not in the least bit attracted to you."

Scalded by hot humiliation, Summer lashed out in a blaze of temper. "No? Well, maybe I should remind him of that the next time he sticks his tongue in my mouth."

She had the satisfaction of hearing Patrice's sharp hiss of breath. She almost added that wasn't all he was doing, but slammed the receiver down instead.

Shaking with anger, Summer marched to the bedroom to unpack, but she was too agitated for that mundane task. Grabbing her purse, she ran out to her car hoping a drive would ease her temper. She had no idea where she was going and was genuinely surprised when she found herself bumping along the rutted track toward Rose Cottage.

Parking in the weed choked driveway, Summer walked around to the garden in back to sit on a stone bench. The sun glinted off her hair striking flashes of gold among the honey curls. The cloudless sky touched the surrounding landscape with a delicate blue veil and a gentle breeze ruffled the leaves of a nearby maple tree. A bee buzzed close to her ear while birds chirped busily back and forth among themselves. Summer let out a contented sigh and closed her eyes letting her mind drift.

"I've met someone, Rose. He's nice. I think you'd like him. I know I sure do. He has a little girl; a sweetheart of a child. I'm feeling like something special could come of our relationship. But maybe you already know all this." The words had come out of her so unexpectedly it made her eyes pop open. She blinked. "Well, that was interesting. Anyone would think I've got a few loose bolts up here," she muttered tapping her head.

Pesky little knots of tension twisted in her stomach, as she sniffed the air half expecting to catch the scent of roses. But when she couldn't detect a trace of their perfume after several seconds, her body relaxed. Maybe Rose had heard her and maybe she hadn't, but Summer felt as though she'd shared a precious secret with a trusted friend.

She continued to sit there enjoying herself, but in her contentment Summer didn't notice the sudden stillness in the air. Nor did she sense a dark presence that lurked in the shadows watching her with eyes that burned with malevolence.

CHAPTER FOURTEEN

Ted knocked on her door a few days later as Summer was heading out. "I came by to see if you wanted to go for coffee while the kids are at soccer practice, but it looks like you've got plans."

"Sandy told me about an estate sale that supposedly has a fine private library. It's a few miles out of town. I thought I'd check it out. Want to ride along? We can grab a coffee after."

"Okay, but I'll drive," he said glaring at her car. "I don't trust that old rust bucket of yours. I wish you'd let me loan you the money to buy something more reliable."

"We've been over this before. I don't know when I could pay you back and you already have enough expenses to worry about. Besides, my car's not unreliable. It's just a little temperamental."

Ted rolled his eyes when she patted the hood, as they skirted around her vehicle.

Summer bought all the books in the sale and Ted helped her carry them outside.

"No wonder you never have any extra cash," he said, hoisting the boxes into the trunk.

"I have to keep my store stocked and I got a better deal by taking all of these. There are some real gems here. Don't worry, I'll make a nice profit when I sell them."

After the boxes had been transferred to her store they walked next door for coffee. Holly, the owner's daughter greeted them with her usual friendly smile. They'd known each other all their lives. The slender brunette had been in the class between Summer and Ted. After her graduation, she'd gone away to college, met a man, married, and had a son. But the marriage had gone sour and after her divorce she'd returned and now taught at the local elementary school.

Summer scanned the room. "I haven't seen you working here

76

very often. Is your mom okay?"

"Yes. I talked her into taking a much needed day off." She said. "And how are things with you, Ted?"

"Okay. The boys still seem to think I know what I'm doing most of the time."

"That counts for a lot. I see Teddy on the playground. He's getting tall."

"Yeah, he almost outgrows his jeans before I get him out of the store."

Holly gave a knowing nod. "Tell me about it. So what can I get for you two?"

"Coffee and a couple of your mom's blueberry muffins," he said.

"Coming right up."

Summer didn't miss Ted watching Holly. She wondered if it was her imagination or had she sensed a spark there. She secretly hoped so because they were both too young to live their lives only for their children, however noble the intent. Since Ted had plotted to get her into a romance with Marcus, she decided it was her turn to play cupid for him.

"Did your mom get those crates moved from the alley in back?" she asked when Holly brought their order.

"No, and Dad keeps putting it off. I plan to do it for her today."

"They look heavy. Maybe Ted could lend a hand?" Summer looked at him.

"I'd be glad to help. I still have time before I have to pick up the kids."

"Thanks Ted, I'd really appreciate it."

Satisfied that her plan had worked, Summer finished her food and got up. "I've got to get back. See you later, Holly. Thanks for the ride this morning, brother dear."

He nodded. "You might want to reconsider checking the yellow pages for wrecking yards. Your clunker would be a prime candidate."

"Hey, is that any way to talk about my child?"

He snorted out a laugh. "You're comparing your car to a child?"

"Why not? It leaks fluids, refuses to move when I need to get someplace in a hurry, and puts out enough noise to have the neighbors giving me dirty looks."

Holly laughed, creating tiny dimples in each cheek. "She's got you there, Ted."

Back in her store Summer attacked the boxes of books with the eagerness of a hungry person going after a juicy steak. She loved books, especially old ones and couldn't wait to examine this latest assortment. She set the nicer ones with their gold binding and beautiful lettering aside to be savored in more detail later.

When it was time to close up for the day she went into the storage room in the back and lifted a thick volume from a shelf. Her fingers moved fondly over the ornate front with its burst of bright colors and collage of fairytale creatures scattered across the cover. It had been a gift from Rose and was her favorite of all her fairytales books.

Taking the book with her, Summer locked up the store and drove home, opened a can of soup for dinner, and sipped slowly while she lovingly turned the pages carefully choosing stories to read to Sasha over the next several days. The child's pale face with those large dark eyes that had known too much sorrow flashed inside her mind along with the sound of her piteous weeping.

She hoped to banish that aura of sadness and replace it with the simple wonder and happiness all children deserved. She wanted Sasha to see some beauty in life even if it meant she had to coax her into the realm of an imaginary world to accomplish it.

Thinking of Sasha brought Marcus to her mind, as Summer continued to thumb her way through the book slipping in little pieces of paper to mark pages. Besides being handsome enough to make her breath stop in her throat, he was a complex mixture of emotions including his gentleness toward Sasha, the sadness when he spoke of his late wife, the humor when he was in a playful mood, and the raw passion when he'd made love to her.

Her body burned with heat remembering how he'd made her feel. She closed the book and sat there trying to imagine what it would be like to spend her life with a man like Marcus, but quickly shook her head to chase that premature thought away. She reminded herself that one night in a man's bed did not constitute a marriage proposal. She had risen from the table to rinse out her bowl when the phone rang.

"I know I'm early," Marcus said. "Am I catching you in the middle of something important?"

"No, not at all." She looked at her book lying on the table. "I'm all set for Sasha."

"I need to discuss something with you before you start reading to her. I've got to say this quickly while she's out of the room. I've encountered a bigger problem since we last talked. I have to go to Europe next week for five days on business. I've been putting it off for months, but it can't be delayed any longer."

It wasn't difficult to see why he was concerned. "You're worried about how Sasha will react to your absence."

"Yes. She gets upset when I'm gone even for a day. That's the main reason I try to do most of my work from my home office. God knows what she'll do when she finds out she won't be able to see me for almost a week."

"Can't you take her with you?" she suggested.

"I'm going to be stuck in meetings and doing presentations every day as well as some evenings. How can I justify leaving her with strangers in a hotel room when she can't handle being in her own home with a woman she knows? She couldn't take it."

"You don't think Sasha would be all right with Mrs. Gwen for that long?"

"Mrs. Gwen tolerates Sasha well enough, but she's really not very good with children. I could probably get her to do it mainly because of Diana, but I hate to ask."

Summer remembered the things the woman had said about his wife. "I gather Mrs. Gwen was very fond of Diana."

"That's putting it mildly. The woman practically worshipped her."

So she'd been right in thinking there had been more than mere admiration on the woman's part for her late employer.

"There has to be something you can do."

"I've thought of what I hope will be a solution, but I'm reluctant to mention it."

"Really? Why?"

"Because it hinges on you. I realize I have no right to ask you and the last thing I want to do is put any kind of burden on our relationship. But would it be possible for Sasha to stay with you?" He pressed on before she could answer. "I know this is a huge imposition, but Sasha's comfortable with you. You've probably noticed that my sister-in-law isn't exactly the maternal type."

Having the opportunity to show Patrice and Mrs. Gwen she could be useful was appealing, and the fact that Marcus was willing to trust her with Sasha's care gave her a sense of personal triumph. Then too a part of her felt sorry for him not having anyone else he could rely on.

"I'd love to have her, but you'd better talk to Sasha before we go any further."

"Thank you, Summer. I'm more grateful than I can possibly say."

"You're welcome, but Sasha hasn't said yes, yet," she reminded him.

"Somehow I have a feeling she will. You've touched a cord with her."

"I'm glad. She has with me, too."

Marcus stayed in the doorway leaving Sasha to look around Summer's bedroom. Her eyes strayed to the twin beds. "Am I going to sleep in here with you?"

"Yes, but it'll be fun. We can pretend we're having a slumber party every night."

"What's a slumber party?"

"It's when you have a friend sleep at your house and you pop popcorn and stay up past your bedtime. You have pillow fights and giggle a lot."

"Daddy doesn't like me to stay up late."

"Oh, I don't think he'll mind this time."

Marcus came fully into the room then and got down on his haunches. "What do you think, Sasha? Could you stay here with Summer while I go away for a few days?"

The little girl looked at Summer. "Could we have ice cream sometimes?"

"You bet and I'll be sure to let you pick your favorite kind."

Sasha looked at Marcus. "Okay Daddy, I'll wait for you here." She framed his face in her tiny hands. "But you have to promise to come back," she said in a grave voice.

Marcus gathered her close. "I promise," he assured her in an equally serious tone.

Three days into her visit and much to Summer's relief Sasha was doing better than she had expected. She took her to work with her every day and gave her little jobs to do. Back at the apartment she let Sasha play in her makeup tray and try on her costume jewelry. They grocery shopped together and Summer let her help prepare their meals. A special highlight was baking chocolate chip cookies for Ted and the boys.

Ted made sure the boys were available to play with Sasha after school and made arrangements for her to visit Teddy's classroom. Not to be outdone, Buster insisted he should get to share her with his preschool classmates, too.

Marcus called every day and sometimes twice confessing that he felt a bit of separation anxiety of his own. "How's everything going today?"

"Still no complaints. I'm afraid you've missed talking to your daughter, though. She's visiting Buster's classroom right now."

"First Teddy's and now Buster's. I can't believe Sasha's let you out of her sight like this. You've done more for her in these few days than all the months of counseling."

"I'm enjoying her. It's been fun teaching her girlie things."

"I've tried to fill in the blanks, but I guess I haven't quite covered everything."

"Don't beat yourself up over it." She glanced at a wall clock. "Listen, I've got to run, Marcus. I don't want to be late picking Sasha up. You can call her back tonight. I'm sure she'll want to tell you about her day."

Summer hung up and hurried to her car and arrived with a few minutes to spare, which she knew was important. Being where she said she'd be and on time had been a crucial factor in building Sasha's trust. Buster ran over and hugged her.

She hugged him back and smiled at the teacher. "Hi. Everything go okay?"

"Yes. Sasha was a little shy at first, but eventually joined in with some of the activities and seemed to enjoy herself."

"I'm glad. Thank you for having her."

"It wasn't a hardship. She's a sweet child and well behaved. I had the feeling that she would have enjoyed staying longer."

"Maybe I'll have her visit me again sometime and she can come back." Summer looked around the large cheerful room with its little tables and chairs and shelves filled with toys and books. "I don't see her. Is she in the restroom?"

The teacher gave her a puzzled look. "Why no, she's gone."

CHAPTER FIFTEEN

Flashing lights, wailing sirens, and blaring horns couldn't have caused any more panic than Summer felt at the woman's words. "What do you mean, she's gone?"

"Her aunt picked her up a couple hours after you left. She said she called you and you knew she was coming. I wouldn't have let her go, but both Sasha and Buster identified her. Apparently her father had returned from his trip earlier than expected and was waiting for them at home. Sasha was very excited at the prospect of seeing him." She frowned at Summer. "You seem upset. Is something wrong, Ms. Gabriel?"

Summer's first reaction was to yell at the woman for not calling her to verify Patrice's claims, but knew she wasn't the person who deserved to be rebuked. "I'm not sure yet, but I realize you did what you thought was right. Excuse me while I make a phone call."

She dragged her cell phone out of her purse, as she ran to her car and called Marcus at his hotel. But there was no answer and no response when she tried his cell next. She left him messages and sat in her car for several minutes drumming her fingers on the steering wheel. Feeling the need to share her concerns, she called Ted on her way home and blurted out everything in a frantic voice.

"Take it easy. Have you called him?"

"Yes, both his room and cell, but I had to leave messages. Oh God Ted, Marcus is going to be so angry with me. He trusted me to keep Sasha safe and I failed miserably."

"Stop right there. You had no idea Patrice was going to pull something like this. Better call his house and tell the housekeeper what's going on. Ask her to let you know if Patrice shows up there. You might also get Patrice's home phone while you're at it in case she decides to take Sasha to her house. Hopefully she'll let you talk to her."

"Good idea. I should have thought of it, but I'm just so furious with that woman I'm not thinking straight. She doesn't even like Sasha. Why would she do something like this? Do you think she's trying to impress Marcus with some latent maternal thing?"

"If that's her plan she's certainly going about it the wrong way. My guess would be she's trying to make you look bad. But I have a feeling Marcus isn't going to be impressed with her tactics. In the meantime, call Vegas and let me know what happens."

Summer thanked him and had barely pulled into her apartment complex when her cell phone rang. She almost wept with relief when she realized it was Marcus. She told him what had happened stumbling over the words in an effort to get them out as quickly as possible. He swore with such violence she instantly began to stammer out an apology.

"I'm not angry with you, Summer. Patrice has a lot of explaining to do. I'm just frustrated that I can't deal with her right now the way I'd like to. Stay close to your phone while I try to find out what's going on. I'll call you back as soon as I have information."

Summer would have apologized again, but he had already cut the connection. She climbed the stairs to her apartment with frustration and nerves battling inside. Her hand shook as she unlocked her door. Seeing Sasha's personal belongings in the bedroom made the band of tension tighten around her chest. She was placing clothes into the little suitcase with the picture of Cinderella on the front when Marcus called.

"Patrice took Sasha to her house, originally," he told her, "but Sasha became distraught as soon as she saw I wasn't there. Patrice drove her home and insisted Mrs. Gwen deal with her after she was unable to stop the child's hysterical crying."

Summer's stomach muscles twisted into knots. "Oh Marcus, I can't bear to think of Sasha being so upset."

"How do you think I feel?" he asked, his tone sharp edged with frustration. "I did what I could to calm her down, but she's worked herself up to the point that I'm afraid I didn't do any good. She nearly tore my heart out when she kept begging me to come home. I've a flight out tonight, but it's going to be morning before I can get to her. Summer, I hate to ask, but is there any way you could go and stay the night with Sasha?"

"Of course I will, but I'd rather you clear things with Mrs. Gwen first."

"I can do that, but don't worry she's not handling the situation well and will be more than happy to have you there. I'll make arrangements for a ticket to be waiting for you at the airport and a car to take you to my house. Once again I'm in your debt."

"It's the least I can do. I would never have left her at Buster's classroom if I'd thought something like this could happen. I'm so sorry to put you both through this."

"I lay no blame on you for any of it. I don't know what Patrice hoped to achieve by this stunt, but I have every intention of finding out."

Summer hung up and threw a few things into a small carryon bag before calling Ted. He insisted on driving her to the airport. .Ted arranged for the boys to stay with Holly's parents and invited her to ride along.

Summer thought the two of them looked so right together she couldn't help thinking that sometimes out of chaos good things could still happen.

As Marcus had promised, she was met and driven to his house where a panicky Mrs. Gwen waited at the door. "I've done all I can, but the child won't settle down. I put her on the sofa in the family room."

Seeing that the woman was willing to accept help, Summer nodded and followed her. As soon as Sasha saw her, she threw herself into Summer's arms, sobbing. "Maa . . . Maa . . . Mommy."

Surprise shot through Summer and Mrs. Gwen gasped, clearly shocked. Summer scooped Sasha up into her arms. "Come on little one, let's get you to bed."

She carried the trembling child to the bathroom talking to her all the while in a soothing voice. She bathed her before carrying her to the bedroom where she helped her into a pair of pajamas. They sat in a rocking chair and Summer sang every song she could remember from her childhood until Sasha drifted into an exhausted sleep. But when she tried to lay her in bed Sasha's eyes flew open wide and wild and, making a desperate grab for Summer, clung to her whimpering with fresh sobs. Summer kicked off her shoes and crawled into the bed. "Is this better?" Sasha nodded and burrowed against her. "Shall I tell you a story?"

"A happy one."

"Oh yes, I know lots of those." Summer began rubbing Sasha's back. She had barely launched into the beginning of her tale when she felt Sasha's body slowly relax. But she continued on, talking in soft tones always stroking letting the child know she was there and even when she was sure Sasha had fallen asleep Summer waited. She didn't want her to wake up and panic again.

It had been a stressful day for both of them and Summer realized she'd been running on pure nerves the last several hours. The longer she lay there the more relaxed she herself became. She closed her eyes until her breathing slowly began to mingle with Sasha's.

When Summer awoke Marcus was standing looking down at her. She blinked a couple of times and gave him a sleepy smile.

"You're here," she whispered.

"And so are you I'm happy to see," he said in an equally quiet voice.

Beams of sunlight streamed in through the curtain panels laying a delicate lacy pattern across the dark wood floor while dust motes danced freely in the air before drifting downward in merry abandonment. Keeping an eye on the sleeping child, Summer eased herself off the bed.

Marcus motioned for her to follow him into the hallway. He looked so weary she wished she could cradle him against her body the way she had Sasha.

"How is she?"

"Better. She was exhausted, but I couldn't get her to settle down until I crawled in bed with her. That's why I'm still in my clothes. How are you? You look pretty beat."

He dragged a hand over the dark stubble on his cheeks. "It's been a long night."

"I won't argue with that," she said "Didn't you get any sleep on the plane?"

"Not much. The only thing that kept me sane was knowing you were here with Sasha. I can't thank you enough for coming on such short notice."

"You trusted me to take care of her. I couldn't have anticipated that Patrice would have done something like this, but I wanted to do what I could to fulfill my promise. Have you talked to Patrice yet?" She knew she probably should wait until he had a chance to rest, but she couldn't stand not knowing.

His mouth pressed into a hard line. "Yes."

"Why in God's name did she do this to Sasha?"

"She claims she would have watched her if I had asked and decided it was her family duty to bring Sasha back home."

"Family duty? Patrice?" She sniffed. "Oh, please. I'm sorry, but she doesn't strike me as the mommy of the year type."

"No, as I've said before it isn't exactly her forte."

"How did she know Sasha was with me?"

"She came by the house and Mrs. Gwen told her."

"How thoughtful." She shook her head. "Sorry, that was sarcastic, but Mrs...."

She was interrupted by Sasha's urgent cry, "Mommy! Mommy!"

Marcus's brows shot up. "Mommy? What in the world?"

Summer held up her hands, palms out. She certainly didn't want him thinking she'd put the idea in his daughter's head. "Not my doing. I'm just as surprised as you are." They hurried back into the bedroom and Summer smiled at her. "Look who's here."

"Daddy!" she shrieked and reached her arms out to him, her eyes bright with excitement. "You came home."

He lifted her into his arms and hugged her close. "Hello my little love," he said, kissing her on the forehead. "Did you have a nice sleep?"

She nuzzled his neck. "Uh-huh. Summer came and she slept in my bed with me."

She leaned back and gave him a noisy kiss on his cheek. "Your face is scratchy."

"I know. I need a shave, but I wanted to see you and Summer first."

"She's going to be my mommy."

Summer felt herself burn with embarrassment when Marcus looked at her. "Is she now? Who told you that?" he asked in a gentle voice.

"I told me."

"Oh, I see."

Sasha looked at Summer. "You want to be my mommy, don't you?"

It was one of those times when the innocence of a child can cause an awkward situation for adults. "I don't think..." She stopped, swallowed, and started over. "How about I just be your very good friend like I've been doing?"

Sasha's bottom lip immediately began to wobble and her face scrunched up ready for fresh tears. "Don't you want to be my mommy, Summer?"

She wished Marcus would help her out. The last thing Summer wanted to do was hurt such a sensitive child and she'd obviously already said the wrong thing. "A woman should be married before she's someone's mommy."

She gave an inward groan knowing it sounded as though she was angling for a marriage proposal. How much deeper was this hole going to get before it swallowed her?

CHAPTER SIXTEEN

Sasha's face lit up. "You can marry Summer today, Daddy. Okay?"

Now that the pressure had been put on him, Summer wondered how he was going to squirm his way out of it, but he merely smiled and kissed her on both cheeks. "We'll talk about it at breakfast. Right now I have to take a shower and you need to get dressed."

Summer watched him leave wondering how he could act so blasé while her insides were literally buzzing with tension.

"My clothes are in here," Sasha said, leading her to a dresser.

It was a wonder she didn't put the child in plaid shorts and polka dot shirt the way her mind was in turmoil. Sasha wanted to wait until Summer could go with her to breakfast, so Summer hurried with her shower and the one change of clothes she'd brought.

She couldn't imagine what Marcus was going to say without doing any further damage to his daughter's fragile self-confidence. She'd certainly fumbled in trying to give an explanation to the child. The awkwardness of the situation made her blush with embarrassment, as she walked to the dining room hand-in-hand with Sasha.

Children can't remember to pick up their toys, feed their pets, or say please and thank you half the time, but when you'd like them to forget something they suddenly have the best memories in the world. Summer didn't get a chance to dissuade Sasha before she immediately jumped into the heart of what was on her mind.

"When are we going to marry Summer, Daddy?"

Summer stared down at her coffee cup and held her breath.

Marcus pushed his chair away from the table and patted his knee. "Come sit here a minute, honey."

She went to him and he lifted her onto his lap. "I want you to listen carefully because what I have to say is very important."

Sasha nodded.

"People like to get to know each other well before they marry and we haven't had a chance to be with Summer long enough to do that. I'm happy you like her and I know she likes you too. We're going to just be friends for now. So you'll have to be patient and wait to see how things turn out."

Sasha frowned at him. "What's patient?"

"It means we aren't going to talk about marrying Summer until I say so."

"But Daddy..."

He held up his hand. "You heard me, Sasha. I need you to do as I ask. We can't always have what we want when we want it."

His voice wasn't unkind, but it held just enough authority for her to stick out her bottom lip in a mutinous pout.

Marcus put her off his lap and told her to go back and eat her breakfast, but it didn't take long to realize she wasn't touching her food. She continued to sit there mutely glowering at him. Mrs. Gwen came in with fresh coffee and offered to fix something else for Sasha, but Marcus shook his head.

"That won't be necessary. She already has a plate of perfectly good food in front of her. It's her decision if she chooses not to eat it."

As soon as he and Summer finished eating he offered to show her some of the casinos she'd missed before.

"I thought you were tired. Maybe you should rest first," she said.

"The shower revived me. I'm too keyed up to go sleep right now."

"You could always take a sleeping pill," she suggested.

He shook his head. "When I'm ready to sleep, I'll sleep."

Her eyes drifted to Sasha and back to him with an imploring look. "I don't know."

He let out a sigh. "You may go with us, Sasha, but only if you find your smile."

"I want Summer to stay with me," she said in a stubborn little voice.

"Well, I'm afraid you aren't going to get your way on this because I'm taking her with me," he said in a firm voice. "You can either start acting like my sweet little girl and go with us, or stay here with Mrs. Gwen and sulk in your room."

"I would like to have you come along, Sasha," Summer said trying to ease the tension between father and daughter. "How about you come and help me get ready?"

The child hesitated for a few seconds before sliding off her chair and taking hold of the hand Summer offered.

In Summer's room, Sasha sat watching while Summer brushed her teeth, combed her hair, and put on fresh lipstick.

"People can move to new places can't they?"

"Yes sometimes," Summer agreed, smiling at the child's obvious tenacity.

"Are you always going to live in your 'partment?"

"I don't know, but I like living near my brother and the boys."

"Would they be sad if you moved away?"

"I think so. I know I would be. I might even cry if I had to leave them."

Sasha wrinkled her stubby nose. "Big people aren't supposed to cry."

"Who told you that?"

"Nobody. I just think they don't."

"Oh, but they do, especially when they're very sad and sometimes even when they're very happy."

"That's silly. Why would people cry if they're happy?"

"I guess it's because they don't know what else to do when they feel so good and it just kind of spills out of them."

Sasha gave an indignant sniff. "You're supposed to laugh when you feel happy."

Marcus knocked on her door just then. "Are you two ready?"

"Hang on a second." Summer gave Sasha a quick squirt of her cologne. "There, now your daddy won't be able to tell one of us from the other."

"Yes he will 'cuz you're bigger and you're going to be my mommy."

Summer's mouth dropped open. "You mustn't..." Sasha had

opened the door to Marcus, cutting off her protest.

Because Sasha was with them, Marcus didn't linger at the first two casinos, but stopped at one that featured activities for children. He won a stuffed bear for her in a ring toss game before they went back to the house for a leisurely swim in the pool. He insisted Sasha take a nap and despite her protests, she quickly fell asleep.

"Why don't you go to bed now?" Summer suggested.

"I thought you'd never ask," he grinned and scooping her into his arms, headed toward his bedroom.

She gasped in surprise. "Marcus! What on earth are you doing? Put me down before Mrs. Gwen sees us."

He nudged the door open with his shoulder and kicked it closed with his foot. He carried her to the bed and immediately joined her. "There, now you're down."

"You need rest," she protested and started to scramble off the bed, but he lowered himself and held her there with his body.

"I need this more," he said covering her mouth in a kiss filled with a hunger that instantly stirred her senses and left her breathless.

He may have been tired, but it took nothing away from his lovemaking. His hands moved over her arousing them both to new heights of passion. In between kisses, he pulled off her clothes while she busily yanked at his garments wanting to devour him and be devoured. When the last barrier had vanished, her body rose to meet his in a sizzling embrace.

Her name came out in a rumble and consumed by desire, they melted together in a fierce union groaning into each other's mouths. Giving and taking, they shared their hunger with greedy eagerness. Higher and higher pleasure rose, slammed into them, swirled around and through them until at last they fell trembling in a shuddering heap.

Summer lay with her eyes closed taking in gulping breaths, as she felt Marcus's heart hammering where he lay sprawled on top of her. Her own heart was beating a mad rhythm while her head felt as thought it were spinning around inside.

"I feel wonderfully wrecked," he groaned and rolled away to flop onto his back.

She smiled and kissed him lightly on the chest. "Bet you'll sleep now."

He smiled sleepily. "Bet I will," he muttered, closing his eyes.

She kissed him again and slid off the bed. "Better than a sleeping pill any day," she whispered and grabbing her clothes, went into his bathroom.

Summer smiled hearing his soft snoring when she returned. She stepped into the hallway where she literally bumped into the housekeeper. "Oh, Mrs. Gwen, I'm sorry I didn't see you there."

"Obviously."

Flushed with embarrassment, Summer quickly improvised. "I was just...um, talking to Marcus about Sasha."

Mrs. Gwen's mouth thinned to a taut line. "Is that so?"

The woman's eyes raked over Summer, her tousled hair, wrinkled clothes, and face bare of makeup.

"Yes, but he decided to take a nap. He's very tired from his long flight."

"Apparently not that tired."

Knowing about the woman's loyalty to Diana, Summer supposed she had to expect a certain amount of hostility. But that didn't mean she couldn't defend herself.

"Look Mrs. Gwen, it's immaterial to me whether or not you approve of my relationship with Marcus," she said abandoning any pretense. "But perhaps you should remember that this is his house and you're his housekeeper, not the custodian of his personal life."

Pale eyes glared at Summer. "You could never replace Mrs. Brennan."

"I'm not trying to replace anyone. I understand how much you miss her and I'm sure she was a wonderful person, but you have to let her go," she said, softening her tone.

"No, Ms. Gabriel, it's you who should let Mr. Brennan alone, so he can mourn in peace. You being here luring him into sinning with you is a sacrilege to his lovely wife."

Summer stiffened. "His wife is dead. Do you expect Marcus to bury himself too?"

Her look was openly contemptuous. "No, but Mrs. Brennan would want him to be with someone more suitable than you."

CHAPTER SEVENTEEN

Summer had been at home a little over a week. She called Sasha nightly to tell her a story. She hadn't told Marcus about her disturbing conversation with his housekeeper and, although she did her best not to dwell on it, she still felt the sting of the woman's insults.

She may not have the proper credentials to be the ideal wife for Marcus, but at least she had a sense of satisfaction knowing she had connected well with Sasha.

Marcus seemed to think so too and never failed to compliment her after each night's story session. As his admiration grew, he asked if he could tape her as she read a story. At first the idea made Summer feel inhibited, but she often forgot he was there once she became caught up in the tales. When she mentioned the taping to Ted, he asked her to make one for the boys. She did as he asked, but still read to them in person whenever possible.

She wondered if Marcus ever read to Sasha himself. She felt it might be a good way for him to add some extra nurturing to his parenting. God knew the little girl needed all she could get. Summer was never more aware of this than when Sasha kept asking when they were going to see each other again.

Ted assured her they were always welcome and Marcus had made it clear the door to his home was open to them as well. But Summer wasn't anxious to return to Las Vegas after her clashes with Patrice and Mrs. Gwen and she supposed they shouldn't allow Sasha to think they could keep running back and forth. She talked to Ted about her concern, but he felt Marcus wanted an excuse to keep Summer on his radar.

She hoped he was right because she realized her feelings had gone beyond mere physical attraction. She was half in love with the man. That came as a surprise, but it wasn't an unpleasant one.

It was like having a shimmering little ball of pleasure swirling around inside of her.

Summer allowed herself a few days to get used to the idea before taking Ted up on his statement that they were always welcome. She "iced the cake" with a promise to clean his house and organize the meals. She was so certain Marcus would be anxious to come that it was a blow to her ego when he turned her down.

"I'm sorry Summer, but we're going to Maui for a few days. Patrice has a condo there. She's been trying to make up for her fiasco with Sasha and I feel I should give her the benefit of the doubt."

"I'm sure she appreciates that," Summer hoped her voice didn't betray how she really felt. The thought of him and Patrice in a cozy condo with Sasha as their only chaperone dug at her like tiny sharp claws. "When are you leaving?"

"In a couple of days."

"So soon?"

"I would have told you before, but I hadn't made up my mind until today."

"I see. Well, I'm sure you'll have a wonderful time surrounded by all that sun and ocean. Be sure to use plenty of sunscreen on Sasha, but I guess you'd know that from living in Las Vegas. Send me a postcard if you think of it." She was babbling and knew it was a poor way to hide her disappointment, but it was the best she could do considering she had been so ill prepared for his unexpected announcement.

"Summer, I think you know I would rather be with you," he said. "But Patrice is Sasha's aunt and I feel I should maintain some kind of bond. It's what Diana would have wanted."

"I understand, really I do. "

"I promise we'll make plans to fly up your way as soon as I get back."

"There's no need to rush." She wanted to groan out loud at the lie.

"Speak for yourself. I have this insatiable desire to be with you again. I keep having this fantasy that one of these days you and I are going to have a chance to spend more time alone. Do you know any spells that might whisk us off to some lonely mountaintop?"

His comments helped to smooth out the earlier nicks in her pride and she laughed. "None that come to mind. I'll have to read up and see what I can find."

"You do that."

Patrice seemed adept at finagling ways to spend time with Marcus and she had the added advantage of living close by him. She couldn't prevent the Maui trip, but Summer knew she'd have to come up with her own plan to compete with the manipulative woman. She thought fast.

"Since I don't know any spells, how about we do this the old-fashioned way? If I get Sandy to watch the store what would you say to going off alone with me for a few days when you return?"

"That fantasies sometimes do come true?"

Summer called Ted as soon as she hung up to let him know Marcus wouldn't be coming.

"How come? I had my money on his jumping at the chance to see you again."

"I appreciate your confidence in me, but he and Sasha are going to Maui...with Patrice," she added. Saying the words brought back her uneasiness.

"What! After what she did with Sasha?" He gave a snort of disgust. "Well, crap."

"My sentiments exactly."

She gnawed on her bottom lip for a moment. "Ted, I invited myself to go away with Marcus when he gets back. I'm talking just the two of us, if he can work something out for Sasha, of course. Do you think that makes me sound too desperate or over the top brazen?"

"Giving Patrice some competition, huh? Good for you. This is the twenty-first century, kiddo. Men sometimes like to have the woman do a little chasing. It's good for the old male ego."

"That may be, but I don't want to overdo it and end up driving him away. When does the chasing become too much?"

"Depends on the guy. Don't worry you'll know if you're coming on too strong if he starts to back off. But I don't think you have to be too careful with Marcus."

"Why do you say that?'

"Because the guy's nuts about you. Whatever Patrice is trying to accomplish with this trip won't work. You're the one he wants."

Ted couldn't have chosen a better time to say such a thing and the idea of Marcus going to Maui with Patrice suddenly didn't seem so daunting. "Consider yourself kissed."

Summer was anxiously waiting for Marcus to return when one by one, Ted and the boys came down with stubborn cases of the flu. She hired temporary help in the store, so she could spend as much time as possible nursing them. When it became obvious they weren't going to recover soon, she realized she'd have to cancel her plans with Marcus.

The problem was how to let him know. Summer didn't want to call him while he was in Maui. He'd vowed to keep in touch, but she assured him it wasn't necessary. She thought the fact that he'd sounded disappointed was a good sign. She didn't want to emulate Patrice and push too hard. She wanted him to be eager to see her and she did have his promise that he wanted to spend time with her when he returned.

She felt some consolation in that. Summer looked at the telephone and sighed. Although she wasn't looking forward to it, she'd have to leave a message with Mrs. Gwen. She hated the idea of telling the woman that she'd made personal plans with Marcus, but it was only fair that he know ahead of time. She gritted her teeth knowing the woman would be only too happy to know their rendezvous would have to be canceled.

Summer had just settled Ted and the boys in bed and had run by the store to give Sandy a break. She checked the mail and her heart fluttered when she picked up a manila envelope postmarked Hawaii. She smiled as she slit open the envelope and pulled out an 8 x 10 colored photo. But the grin on her face changed to a frown when what she saw was a picture of Patrice and Marcus standing with her arm tucked into his. She wore a long cream colored dress with bright yellow hibiscus flowers scattered over the material. Marcus had on a pair of black slacks and a white formal Hawaiian shirt. They were both wearing lush flowered leis.

Summer's immediate thought was that the photo had all the appearance of a tropical wedding. An invisible fist gripped her by the throat. Her fingers trembled when she reached into the envelope to see if there was any message. When she slid out a copy of a marriage license she didn't have to look to know whose names she'd find there.

CHAPTER EIGHTEEN

The knowledge hit her like a painful blow to her body. Her stomach churned and for a moment, she thought she was going to be physically ill.

And to think she'd told Ted she was worried about hurting Marcus! No doubt she had Patrice to thank for informing her of the wedding. The woman had made no secret that she wanted Marcus. And she hadn't been above using deceit to get him, but Summer hadn't wanted to believe that Marcus had insinuated himself into her life because of Sasha as Patrice had insisted.

Now, with this indisputable evidence what else could she think? Photos and documents didn't lie.

He had heartlessly toyed with her and used her affection as a tool to gain his objective. Her stomach continued to twist into writhing, sickening knots remembering how easily she'd been taken in by his veneer of respectability.

Her body trembled when she thought of the times they'd made love. She had believed it was as special to him as it had been to her. The feeling that something beautiful had been building between them suddenly shriveled up and died and was replaced with a terrible sense of loss.

She tried to shove the offending pieces back into the envelope, but her shaking hands refused to perform the simple task. Crumbling the paper into tight balls, she tossed them into the trash and slumped down on the stool behind the counter cradling her head in her hands.

Shock slowly seeped through her. Blood pounded at her temples, while her heart beat with a painful answering throb of its own. Shattered. She felt utterly shattered. She couldn't think of anything but the photo and Patrice with her arm clinging possessively to a smiling Marcus. She closed her eyes, squeezing them tightly willing the image to go away. Thankfully no customers entered the shop. She knew she wouldn't be able to wait on them.

When Sandy returned she looked at Summer and frowned.

"Are you all right?"

"No, I'm..." She wiped a hand over her forehead. "Just a headache."

Sandy made a sympathetic sound and shoved her purse beneath the counter. "You're probably worried about Ted and the boys."

"Yes; yes I am."

"Well, you go on now and take care of them. You're looking a little pale. It might not be a bad idea if you made yourself a nice cup of tea and took a nap. You don't want to get sick yourself. Don't worry about coming back tonight. I'll close for you."

Summer gave her a grateful look. "Thank you Sandy I really appreciate it."

She drove straight to Ted's and let herself in with her key. The house smelled of stale air and sickness. Summer wrinkled her nose and opened a couple of windows. She peeked in on the boys and saw that they were asleep. But Ted raised his head off the pillow when she stuck her head around his bedroom door.

"You don't look so hot. Are you feeling sick, too?" he asked in a croaky voice.

Summer realized she wanted to cave in and actually felt her body sag and her legs threaten to give out beneath her. She pressed one hand to her head and the other to her stomach. "Yes, I guess I am." She walked over to the king size bed and kicked off her shoes. "Move over," she said in a voice thick with unshed tears and climbed on the bed.

She was at the shop working several days later when Marcus called. "I was beginning to think you'd dropped off the face of the earth. Why haven't you returned any of my calls?"

Bile rose up in her throat. How did he have the nerve to act as though nothing was wrong?

"Didn't you get the message I left with Mrs. Gwen?" Summer managed to ask.

"About Ted and the boys being ill and postponing our getaway? Yes. I was tempted to fly up there and see if I could help, but she assured me that I wasn't needed."

That didn't surprise Summer. The woman would do anything to keep her from Marcus, but it didn't matter now. In fact, it was helpful. "She's right. We can take care of ourselves." She kept her tone devoid of emotion, not wanting to give him the satisfaction of letting him know how much he'd wounded her.

"You don't sound as though you feel well yourself. Are you ill?"

She hesitated. "I suppose you could say that."

"Shouldn't you be home in bed?"

"Some of us females don't have rich husbands. I have to work to pay my bills."

"You're in a mood."

She gritted her teeth and looked around the empty store. "I've customers waiting."

"I can see I've caught you at a bad time, but before you hang up, do you think you'll feel well enough to call Sasha tonight? She's missed hearing from you. She wanted to call you from Maui, but I thought it only fair that I give Patrice that time with her."

She gripped the edge of the counter, her nails digging into the wood. My God, did the man not have a conscience? Anger pumped out of her in hot waves. Bitterness reared its ugly head and her patience snapped. "Oh yes, you mustn't disappoint Patrice," she said with heavy sarcasm. "And just so there won't be any further misunderstanding, I won't be calling Sasha tonight or any other night."

"Summer, for heaven's sake I didn't mean that I expected you to stop calling her permanently. It was just while we were on Maui. Even if Sasha wasn't so fond of you it goes without saying I can't have a relationship with anyone that would exclude her."

"I'm well aware of that, but are you?"

"I've just said so haven't I? What are you implying?"

"I told you that you do things differently in Las Vegas than we do here. But you seemed to have conveniently forgotten that conversation, so let me spell it out for you. I'm not interested in having a relationship with a man who's carrying excess baggage."

She wanted to hang up, but waited thinking he'd at least offer her an apology. "Are you referring to Sasha as excess baggage?"

She heard the instant anger in his voice, but wasn't about to let him make her the villain. "This has nothing to do with Sasha. That child has more compassion in her little finger than you have in your entire body. She deserves so much better, but you obviously didn't take that into consideration before you ran off to Maui."

She heard him quickly inhale. "I'm feeling at a definite disadvantage here. I don't know what's made you so angry, but it's obvious I've done something to upset you."

She gave a loud snort. "You think?"

"Summer, you're not making any sense. You know why I went to Maui. Tell me what the problem is and we'll work it out."

This time she did slam the receiver down. It should have made her feel better, but it didn't. Instead, she felt cold and brittle inside followed by a dreadful emptiness.

She thought that would be the end to it, but she had underestimated Marcus. He showed up at the store the next afternoon. He stormed inside, quickly scanned the empty room, and flipped the closed sign over before snapping the door's lock. Summer shot from behind the counter glaring and spitting fire. "What do you think you're doing?" she demanded. "It's not closing time yet."

"It is now." His voice was as hard as his expression and his eyes had the look of a storm brewing within their gray depths.

She stomped toward the door. "Get out of the way."

"Not until I find out what the hell is going on with you." He stood with his arms folded across his chest blocking her way.

She slapped her hands on her hips and stared at him with enough hostility to make a lesser person back down, but he merely returned her scowl with a fierce one of his own. "You could have called and saved me the annoyance of this unwelcome visit."

"I tried that several times, remember? And quite frankly I've had enough of your hanging up on me. You left me no alternative but to come here and see you in person."

She faced him, her body going rigid. "What do you want from me, Marcus?" she asked, struggling to control her fury.

"How about a little enlightenment? You obviously have a fire burning in your belly and I want to know why." He dropped his arms to his sides and moved toward her.

Suddenly feeling like David facing Goliath, Summer spun around and stepped behind the counter. "Maybe I'll send you one of your precious e-mails."

"Tell me what's happened to make you act like this. I think I deserve that much."

Anger burning at the edges of her brain was making her head throb. "Why are you doing this? What do you hope to gain by this charade? Haven't you humiliated me enough already?" It came out sounding like a plea making her clamp her mouth shut.

He frowned. "What charade? Summer, I honest to God do not understand what you're talking about. How is it that I'm supposed to have humiliated you?"

"Does Patrice know you're here?" she demanded, exasperated at his pretense.

His frowned deepened. "Patrice? No, why should she?"

"Well, as your wife I would think she'd want to know when you go out of town." If she didn't know better, she would have sworn his look of shock was genuine.

"My wife! What the hell are you talking about? Patrice and I aren't married."

Eyes blazing with temper, she glared at him. She wanted to hit him; knew that she couldn't. "Oh stop lying, can't you? It demeans us both. She sent me copies of your wedding photo and the marriage license. You'll have to pardon me if I don't send a gift."

A nerve jumped in his cheek. "I don't care what she sent. We are not married. How could you think I'd do something like that to you? You know me better than that."

"No, as it turns out I don't know you at all. Documents don't lie, Marcus."

"They do if they're fake. Let me see them."

"Do you honestly think I'd keep those odious things? I threw them away."

Eyes narrowing ominously, his gaze raked over her. "You threw them away? How careless of you, but then on the other hand how convenient wouldn't you say?"

His sarcasm hit her like a slap in the face. "Are you accusing me of lying? Oh, that's choice coming from a hypocrite like you. What's the matter, have I spoiled your plans to keep me on the sidelines when you feel like a change from your shrew wife?"

His nostrils flared. "If you wanted to end our relationship you could have done it without this elaborate sham. You think because I took you to bed I can't live without you? Well, think again," he said in an icy tone. "I've never had to beg for female company and if I did you'd be at the bottom of my list after this."

She gasped at his insult. A stab of pain, sharp and cruel dug deep and she felt herself wilt under his blistering glare. But she tipped her chin up in a brave attempt to ignore the hurt. "Get out of here you egotistical ass."

He arched a brow. "So the little country mouse has some teeth after all."

"Enough to protect my cheese from a big city rat." She pointed to the door.

"Oh, don't worry, I'm going. Some people aren't worth my time, present company included," he snarled in brutal rejection and unlatched the lock. "I was about to say you're all flash and no class, but looking around here, you don't even have the flash. I could have given you so much more, but this hole in the wall business and pathetic town are obviously all you need," he sneered with a ruthlessness that sliced her to ribbons.

A surge of hot fury scorched her throat. "Leave, damn you!" she yelled.

But he was already outside, the sound of the slamming door echoing around the room with a terrible finality. She watched the sign sway in a wild swishing rhythm. It took her several seconds before she could make herself move to lock the door again. Her hands were unsteady and her legs shaking, as she slowly slid to the floor where she huddled with her face pressed against her drawn up knees.

CHAPTER NINETEEN

Misery continued to squeeze her insides in a tightening clamp, as she sat fighting the invasive despair that engulfed her. The last rays of the sun had dipped below the horizon by the time she took her purse from beneath the counter and walked out to her car. She drove mindlessly before she realized she was headed to the cottage.

As soon as she arrived she stumbled around to the back, sank down onto the bench and hugged her arms close to her body in an effort to shield herself against the crisp night air. Shafts of moonlight silvered the ground. An owl hooted softly in the distance followed by frantic rustling sounds from a nearby clump of weeds.

"It's over, Rose. I've lost him." Her voice wobbled. "He didn't want me." She buried her face in her hands and began to cry in earnest. "He didn't want me," she repeated, as fresh sobs shuddered through her body.

She rocked herself while the air close to her gradually filled with a distinctive rose scent followed by a soft keening wail. Eyes wide, Summer jumped to her feet and looked frantically around her, "Rose? Is that you?" she asked through trembling lips.

Before she had a chance to wonder if she'd imagined it, the weeping abruptly stopped followed quickly by harsh laughter. The new sound grew until it became a maniacal screech that sent chills through Summer's body. The floral aroma faded, replaced by the putrid stench of death. Heart bouncing inside her chest, Summer covered her ears with her hands and stumbled away praying she wasn't having a breakdown.

A week later Summer was still trying to put the bizarre incident behind her while dealing with Marcus's rejection when she received another envelope in the mail. This one had a Las Vegas postmark. Her first impulse was to toss it, but her innate curiosity wouldn't allow that luxury. It was a newspaper article with a photo of Marcus and Patrice at a high priced charity auction to which he had donated one of Diana's paintings.

Marcus looked exceptionally handsome in his tuxedo and Patrice unquestionably glamorous in her long gown. They fit in naturally with the list of famous people in attendance, something Summer knew she would never have been able to do. Hadn't she tried to tell Marcus in the beginning that she may not be the right person for him?

She looked down at her jeans and tee shirt and once again realized how different her lifestyle was compared to theirs. It was little wonder Marcus had chosen Patrice over her. As much as she hated to admit it the woman was definitely more suited to him.

She looked at the picture in her hand. This was factual. What she thought she'd had with Marcus had been based on an illusion and illusions could be dangerous things; especially if someone was foolish enough to mistake one for reality.

Summer struggled to put Marcus out of her mind in the weeks that followed his hostile departure, but it wasn't easy. She kept remembering more than she wanted to and had to fight to protect herself against the painful slices of memory. But those little slivers of time often intruded despite her best efforts to block them out.

It wasn't as though they'd had a long term relationship. But there had been the promise of one, at least in her mind. Perhaps it was that disillusionment that was making it so hard to forget Marcus. How could she have known meeting him would turn out to be such a disastrous detour in her life?

Sasha was on her mind almost as much as Marcus. Summer knew she'd be lying if she said she didn't worry about the child. The women who'd been important in her life had died and she'd bonded with Summer. Some days Summer was so swamped with worry it was all she could do not to pick up the phone and call the little girl. But she'd think of Marcus's deceitful manipulation and become angry all over again.

He had seen that she was good with his daughter and how

quickly Sasha had absorbed the affection. It still infuriated Summer to think that he'd gone so far as to take her to bed to entice her into staying. It was beyond humiliating that Patrice had been right about him pretending a personal interest. No one enjoyed being made to feel like a fool. Her anger rose even more when she thought about Patrice's coldness toward Sasha. How could Marcus who professed to be so concerned about his child's welfare marry a woman like that?

These were the kinds of things that disturbed her and the only way she could escape them was to keep as busy as possible. She spent some of her time helping Ted paint his kitchen and the boys' bedroom, which put her in the mood to redecorate her store.

She gave special attention to the children's section. It was her favorite part of the store and she'd done everything she could to give it the feel of a miniature fairyland.

She was just getting ready to read to a group of children one afternoon when a man she didn't recognize came into the store. He was tall and solidly built with a thick mane of snowy white hair. His clothes were casual, but expensive looking, and he had a distinguished air about him that made Summer think he'd be more at home in a boardroom than her humble store.

She greeted him with a friendly smile. "Hello."

"Good afternoon." He looked around him. "Nice store. Excellent ambience."

Her smile widened at his compliment. "Thank you. I do my best."

"Are you the proprietress?"

"I am. May I help you find anything in particular or would you like to browse?"

He returned her smile, showing large white teeth. "Perhaps a little of both. The woman in the bakery next door mentioned that you sometimes carry old limited editions."

"Yes I do, but I'm afraid my selection is rather small. You're welcome to look at what I have, though. They're over here." She led him to the corner where she kept the treasured items inside a cupboard.

She unlocked the glass paneled door. "Please feel free to take your time. I've a group of children waiting for me to read to them, but if you have any questions let me know. I'll need about twenty minutes with the kiddies."

"Ah yes. I saw the sign on the door that said it was story time. It's set me to wondering. Are you a princess, or perhaps a good witch or a bad witch?"

She saw the laughter in his eyes and treated him to a mischievous wink. "Oh, I'm definitely good with just a little touch of wickedness to keep me from being too boring." He chuckled and she pointed to the books. "I hope you'll find something you like."

Turning away, she slipped into a long royal blue silk robe covered with bright gold stars; a happy find at a yard sale. She settled herself on the tall stool with legs painted like animal feet while the children gathered in a semicircle on the floor. She never tired of seeing their eager faces staring at her with expressions of anticipation.

Summer put a finger to her lips. "Now be very still and listen carefully and if we're lucky the fairyland creatures may peek in to hear the story today."

She smiled at the sound of their muffled giggles and opened the book she'd chosen. It was filled with old fairy tales. A quick flash of sadness raced across her thoughts when she recalled it was one of the books she'd read to Sasha.

Summer wasn't sure when she became aware of the stranger standing silently by, listening to her. But she didn't allow her attention to waver. That would spoil the fascination, which had woven itself around the enthralled children entwining them within its enchanted web.

When she finished, the children begged for more and she indulged them with a silly poem about a clumsy pink bug with a blue nose and eight toes on each of his feet. Some left with mothers or caregivers, while others stayed and purchased books. Once everyone had cleared out and Summer was slipping out of her robe, the stranger approached her.

"The robe lends a nice touch. I hope you didn't mind my shameless eavesdropping. It's not every day a grown man imagines himself chasing after fairies."

She laughed. "We should all do that now and then. I'm glad

you enjoyed it."

"Quite a bit, actually. I sometimes think it's a shame we have to grow up at all. You were magnificent. Have you had any kind of formal training?"

She blushed at the generous compliment. "No, but when I was a child my mother used to take me to visit an old woman who was a fabulous storyteller. I suppose I picked up some tips from her without realizing it."

"The teacher imparts the knowledge, but it is the student who chooses how to apply it. Your friend would be proud to know what you do here. Are any your tales?"

"Some." She stepped behind the counter. "The poem was mine."

"You have a delightful talent." He set a couple of books down. "I'll take these."

"I'm glad you found something."

"Yes, so am I. Have you ever taped your stories?"

His persistence surprised Summer. "You mean to sell? No, I only do it for fun and to amuse the children."

She rang up the sale and slipped the books into a bag. "It's also a good way to promote business, as I usually pick up a few sales after I finish reading."

"Yes I noticed that. Please allow me to introduce myself. My name is Jonathan Gray." He reached into his inside jacket pocket and handed her a business card. A quick glance and she saw that he was an attorney from southern California. "I wish you'd think about marketing your stories. There are a lot of children besides those who are lucky enough to come into your store who would benefit from your gift. I'm especially interested because I have an eight year old grandson who has been blind since birth."

"Oh, I'm so sorry, Mr. Gray. You know there are some good tapes on the market. I can give you the names if you'd like."

"I'd appreciate that, although I am aware of quite a few and I've already bought several for him. But there's something different about your style. You have a certain rhythm and a special flare you bring to a story that I've not heard before. It's utterly captivating. I could see here today that the children sensed it, too."

"That's nice of you to say, but I enjoy myself as much or more than they do."

"That's obvious and it comes through, which is why you're so good. Your natural vivacity has the ability to capture the imagination in the most pleasant way. It's as if you become a part of the story yourself."

"I suppose I do in a way." She was beginning to think his glowing compliments deserved something in return. "I'd be happy to make a tape for your grandson if you think he'd enjoy it," she offered.

"That's kind of you, but why would you do that when you've not met him?"

"Why do people wave at trains and smile at babies? Because it feels good."

"This is most generous of you, Ms..."

"Gabriel. Summer Gabriel."

"Summer," he repeated. "It suits you. I'll be in town for a few days or you can mail the tape to the address on my card if that would be more convenient for you."

"I'll start right away. It shouldn't take me long." She pushed a tablet toward him. "Jot down the stories you think he'd like and I'll go from there. Write down where you're staying here in town and a phone number where I can reach you. I should be able to get the tape to you while you're here."

"All right, I'll list a few stories, but please be sure to include some of your own work." He withdrew a gold pen from his blazer and began writing in a bold hand.

When he was ready to leave, she walked to the door with him. "There's one thing I feel I must say before I do the tape. The children here today were four and five year olds. A lot of eight year olds aren't interested in fairytales, so your grandson may not be that receptive to my stories. They usually care more about the action hero of the moment."

"Yes, I know. Jimmy, my grandson, has discovered those, but I want him to know there's something else available and certainly much more worthwhile in my opinion. You do your stories, Ms. Gabriel and I'll see to the rest."

She nodded. "Fair enough."

Summer watched him climb into his silver Jaguar and wave as he drove away. She looked at his card and sighed. Too bad he wasn't a few years younger.

She went back inside and began tidying up while her mind wandered. Talking to the man about Rose now made Summer smile remembering how she'd sat listening to Rose's stories. She had easily imagined herself as a princess living in a castle, a fairy perched on top of a flower, or a mermaid swimming in a cobalt colored ocean. She recalled the excitement and wonderment she'd felt as her child's brain absorbed each word.

She hadn't been out to the old place since her last disturbing encounter. Fear had kept her away. She tried to rationalize that what she'd thought she'd heard had been nothing more than her imagination. Or was it? There was only one way to find out.

A short time later Summer was in her car heading for the cottage. It wasn't an easy drive. Nature had steadily been reclaiming the land over the years, clogging the road leading up to the house with weeds and fallen tree branches. Summer maneuvered around them while trying to avoid several large furrows carved in the dirt track by winter rains.

She parked and stood listening to nature's poetry of sound with its birdsong, insects, and trees swishing like gentle surf. Her eyes scanned the house. Some of the protected plywood boards had rotted away from the windows. Vandals had thrown rocks breaking several panes that left gaping holes staring back at her like lifeless eye sockets.

She peeked inside. Sheets cloaked in dust covered the few pieces of furniture giving each one a ghostly shape. Rodent droppings were scattered across the grimy floor and spider webs hung like fragile gossamer vines. The white walls inside and out had faded to a dingy gray. Several shingles had blown off the roof allowing rain to leave stains trailing down the walls.

She made her way to the back garden as the late afternoon sunlight cast elongated shadows that plucked at the ground. She stared at the rose bushes Rose had cared for so lovingly all the years she'd live here. Huge and badly in need of pruning, their thick thorny stems reached out in every direction like grotesque arms.

She sat on the stone bench and listened. When she could detect no sound that nature didn't intend, Summer breathed a sigh of relief. She stared at the house. A layer of gloom had settled over the cottage and now, that sadness cut into her. If the cottage were hers, Summer would have given it all the love and attention it needed to make it a home again.

She thought about how much the house had meant to Rose and the way she'd kept it and the gardens tidy even in her later years. It had been a memorial to her late husband's memory. Summer remembered her mother talking about the love Rose had nurtured in her heart for him right up until the day she'd died. There had been such sadness in her mother's voice when she'd said it that, even as a child, Summer understood her mother had never known that depth of feeling with her father.

Love could sometimes be elusive, but not for Rose. She had loved her husband so deeply it had endured even beyond his death. Summer realized she had begun to think she might be able to have that kind of bond with Marcus, but she'd obviously expected too much from too little and missed his true character hidden behind the deceptive façade.

She continued staring at the house. It had been a monument to love, but now it stood in shambles. In the past, she'd always been able to look beyond the ruin, but today it filled her with a sense of loss. Perhaps she felt the neglect so keenly now because she knew what it was like to lose love.

Feeling a nagging restlessness, Summer slid off the bench, sank to her knees, and began tugging at the weeds with a sudden burst of energy. She knelt there furiously jerking at the unwanted growth, but the more she worked the more miserable she felt until tears filled her eyes and spilled over to run down her cheeks in thin translucent streams.

Who was she crying for? Herself or Rose? Both, perhaps. Summer knew she was shedding too many tears here. She'd lost the sense of peace when she needed it most. Before she realized what she was doing, she began to give voice to her troubled thoughts.

"I wanted what you had, Rose. That love and trust. Why did Marcus deceive me?"

She yanked away at the unwanted growth until a good size plot had been cleared. She may not be able to repair the house, but she could try to make the grounds look more presentable. Whoever owned the cottage now obviously wasn't concerned about what happened to it. That hurt too, but her tears weren't going to change that or push back time and have things be the way they were before.

She stood and was brushing the dirt off her hands and away from her jeans when a light breeze stirred the air. It seemed as though it were whispering something. Her eyes darted around the area in a fearful glance, as she remembered the strange sensations she'd felt here before.

Nothing like this used to happen when she came here as a child. Why now? Summer wondered if, perhaps, her emotions became more sensitive when they were clouded by sadness or was it her imagination playing tricks on her.

The wind blew again bringing the scent of roses so strong it clogged her throat and this time there was no mistaking the plea it carried, "Help me...please!"

CHAPTER TWENTY

Summer knew she had to talk to someone about what she'd been experiencing. Either she was having a serious mental problem or there was something going on at the cottage. She drove straight to Sandy's house. Her family had lived here for generations and if anyone could shed light on the cottage's history, she'd be the one.

Summer told her briefly what had happened and was relieved when Sandy didn't tell her to go check herself into a mental ward. "So you're heard ghosts? I've often wondered if the stories my relatives have told over the years carried any merit."

"What do you mean 'ghosts'? Wouldn't it just be Rose?"

"My family always maintained there were two; Rose and her twin sister, Rena."

Summer was stunned. "Rose had a twin sister? I had no idea."

"Not surprising. Rena died in a car accident before you were born. She lived the fast life in Hollywood. Fancied herself an actress. She made Rose's life miserable."

"God, why?"

"Because she was insanely jealous of Rose and would take away anything she could that might bring her a bit of happiness. When Rose became engaged, Rena tried to seduce her fiancé, but he was too much in love with Rose and brushed her off. This made Rena so furious she vowed to spend the rest of her life making Rose pay."

"What a terrible person she was and now she's pestering Rose even in death."

"Yes. Some say it was no accident Rose's husband drowned."

"Dear God," Summer gasped. "It's the old story of a good twin and an evil one."

"One of my great aunts theorized it was a love/hate relationship for Rena, but being a twin, a bond of sorts was still there. It might be a good idea if you let things be."

Summer exhaled a long weary sigh. "I can't. I have a feeling whatever is happening won't stop until I do something to help. I have to figure out what's going on."

"Better be careful. Rena would be a dangerous ghost to have riled with you."

A clammy film snaked over her body. "I'm starting to realize that."

Shocked by the things Sandy had revealed, Summer wanted to concentrate on something else for a while. Focusing on the tape she'd promised Jonathan, proved to be the perfect distraction. He was so pleased with the results that he insisted on taking her out to dinner before he left town.

She smiled at him across the table. "Are you enjoying your trip, Mr. Gray?"

"Jonathan, please. Yes I am. I've wanted to drive up this way and now that I'm semi retired I finally have the time. I realize I've been in a rut going to the same places."

"I suppose we're all guilty of that to some extent."

"Well, don't wait until you're my age to fulfill any dreams you may have of seeing this wonderful country of ours."

"Your wife didn't accompany you?"

"We're divorced."

"Oh, I'm sorry," she apologized and looked down at her plate.

He waved away her apology with a flick of his hand. "It's ancient history. We're actually quite good friends now. We just made an awful team as husband and wife."

"It's nice you're on friendly terms. How many children do you have?"

"Just the one son, Robert, and besides Jimmy, he also has a daughter, Sarah."

"Both the apples of your eye, I'll bet," she said smiling.

"Indeed. Beneath this jacket beats the heart of a very proud grandfather. Tell me, do you have a young man wondering what you're doing with an old coot like me?"

"I seriously doubt anyone would use that term to describe you. No, there's no one special in my life at the moment," she told him, keeping her smile carefully in place.

He shook his head. "I find it difficult to believe that you haven't been scooped up and carried over someone's threshold with a wedding ring on your finger."

Her cheeks grew warm. "You're very good for my ego."

They continued talking in a comfortable way and when it was time to leave Jonathan walked with her to the parking lot. Although he'd offered to pick her up, Ted insisted she take his car because he didn't trust what he called a slick big city lawyer.

"Thank you, Jonathan. I enjoyed myself." Summer held out her hand and to her surprise and delight instead of shaking it, he brushed his lips across her smooth knuckles. She laughed. "I've always wanted to have a man do that."

"I'm glad I'm the first. The men in this town must be blind. If I were younger I'd be tempted to give them a few lessons in how to court a lovely lady."

She laughed again, a happy little chuckle of sound. "I have a feeling they're lucky you don't live around here. You'd have a lot of the ladies buzzing around you."

He answered with a quiet laugh of his own. "Now who's doing the ego boosting?"

He held the car door, as she slid inside. "I have a feeling your special knight will come for you, Summer."

She shook her head. "I doubt if there's any out there looking for me."

"Don't be too sure of that."

A couple of months had gone by since Summer made the tape for Jonathan's grandson, but they'd talked on the phone a few times. She found herself liking him more and more. He'd assured her Jimmy enjoyed her stories and had played the tape several times. She possessed enough vanity to hope he wasn't embellishing the truth.

She was in the store dusting one afternoon when Ted came bursting through the door waving a popular magazine in his hand.

"Have you seen this?"

She glanced over her shoulder. "I don't know. What is it?"

"There's an article in here about the tape you made for Gray's grandson."

"What? No way!" She tossed the feather duster onto the counter and snatched the book out of his hand. "Let me see that."

"Did you know you were going to get this write-up?"

"No." She poked her finger at the page. "This makes me sound pretty good."

"You're more than good," he insisted with obvious pride. "Haven't I been telling you that for years? It's about time other people realize it. I wonder if Marcus has seen this. He thought you were great, remember?"

"Don't go there, Ted," she warned.

He held up his hand. "Chill out for a minute. I'm going to pull big brother rank because I have something I need to say. It's time you start taking your own advice."

"What advice?" she snapped. Mentioning Marcus had spoiled her mood.

"Don't jump down my throat. I'm only trying to help. You keep telling me to get on with my life. Don't you think it's time for you to start doing the same:"

She waved the magazine under his nose. "I thought I was."

"I meant with men. You haven't dated anyone since Marcus. I know you don't want to talk about him and I don't blame you. I hate that he hurt you and I still can't believe I was so wrong about him. Marrying his conceited sister-in-law doesn't fit."

"Well there's no accounting for taste, but he obviously married his own kind. He decided I was good enough to be his child's nanny, but not classy enough to be his wife. I know you mean well Ted and I appreciate what you're trying to do, but you know how I feel. Now as far as I'm concerned this part of the conversation is over."

"Fine. I've had my say." He pointed to the magazine. "According to this you'll likely start making commercial tapes. I assume Gray is behind that idea."

She frowned at him. "Stop calling him by his last name like that."

"Like what?"

"Like you don't trust him. Like you think he's taking advantage of me."

"How do you know he isn't? Did he tell you he wanted to market your tapes?"

"He mentioned it, but nothing was ever set."

"Well, don't sign anything until you're sure it's legit."

"I'll be careful, but I doubt Jonathan is out to take advantage of me. Where are the boys?" she asked, wanting to change the subject.

"Holly took them to the park with Miles."

"That's sweet. I know you like her, Ted." She didn't miss the dull red color that crept into his face. "She's a lovely person. Why don't you let me stay with the boys some night, so you can take her out on a proper date without having the kids tag along?"

He rubbed a hand around the back of his neck. "Do you think they'd mind?"

She laid a hand on his shoulder. "We're not going to let them forget Rebecca if that's what's bothering you. Please don't sacrifice a chance to be with someone because you think you'd be betraying her. Bec would hate that. You'd have to go a long way to find anyone as nice as Holly and the boys like her," she added hoping to convince him.

"I know, but I haven't wanted to rush her. She's already been burned once."

"So it's up to you to restore her faith in the male species. I guarantee you Holly will be thrilled to accept a one-on-one date with you. If you're too chicken, I'll set up something for you."

He gave her a horrified look. "The hell you will. I can get my own dates. There should be a law against a younger sister bullying her older brother," he grumbled. "There's something undignified about it." He called her a pest, but she heard him start to whistle as he stepped outside.

Summer called Jonathan that night. "I assume I have you to thank for the article."

"Good, you saw it. I know one of the editors and asked him to listen to Jimmy's tape. He was impressed and volunteered to run the piece. I hope you don't mind."

"How could I? It's very flattering."

"It's genuine praise for a talented artist. When I hinted you might be interested in making commercial tapes he was quite enthusiastic. How do you feel about that?"

"The tapes? Kind of scared, but I'm willing to listen to your ideas."

"I hoped you'd say that. I've taken the liberty of talking to the head of the children's division of a company that produces these kinds of tapes. He'll offer you a contract, but he wants to be guaranteed three tapes up front."

"That wouldn't be a problem, but I feel as though you're moving too fast."

"I don't think so."

She thought of Ted's warning. "I don't know much about contracts."

"I'll take care of that for you."

She let out a nervous laugh. "I can't afford you, Jonathan."

"Summer, I'm not doing this to make any money off of you. I thought you understood that. Once I saw how much Jimmy enjoyed your tape I knew there were a lot of other children who would benefit from your gift. I especially want to make sure the tapes get into hospitals and care facilities for youngsters with special needs."

"I'd want to donate to those places. It would be worth it to me if I thought I could give those kids some relief from their suffering."

"I'll check back with you in a couple of weeks." He paused. "You're a good, sweet woman, Summer, and I'm not the only man that thinks so."

He hung up leaving her to wonder about that cryptic statement.

Some of Summer's happiness was tarnished a couple of days later, when she received a copy of the magazine article with the words: DEVIL'S WORK written in black marking pen across the paragraphs. The envelope came from Las Vegas.

Just a little reminder of what you think of me and how I 'sinned' with your precious Marcus, Mrs. Gwen? Well you can go straight to hell for all I care and take him with you. She dropped the envelope and its contents in the wastebasket.

Summer wished she could dispose of the emotions that churned inside of her as easily. She didn't want it to matter that a housekeeper thought she wasn't good enough for her employer. She especially didn't want to surrender to her own feelings of inadequacy when she compared herself to Diana and Patrice. But she couldn't deny the grip of envy that pulled at her when she thought of how they seemed to have what Marcus wanted. All she had was herself and who she was. Maybe it wasn't much in their eyes, but she wanted to believe her storytelling ability was the one thing she had over those two women. It hadn't been enough to hold Marcus, but hopefully it would be something meaningful to others.

The next time Jonathan called he'd made the arrangements for Summer to fly to Los Angeles and go into a bona fide studio to make a professional tape. Nerves jangled through her, but she tried to think this could have the potential to help sick children.

Her tension shifted into high gear when she walked into the studio, but once she started reading and noticed the rapt expression on the young technician's face, she began to relax. Before long the stories had transported her into another world. By the time the session ended Jonathan expressed his admiration so glowingly that Summer felt herself blushing to the roots of her hair. "I want you to consider a video."

Alarm, instant and disturbing rushed to the surface. "Oh no, I couldn't."

"Of course you can."

She shook her head and pressed her palms against her flaming cheeks. "The words will jam up in my throat."

"I seriously doubt that. You must give yourself more credit, Summer."

"Can't we wait? What's wrong with just the audio tape? I've barely got used to that. We can add some background information on me and a picture if anyone needs to have more," she added on a sudden inspiration hoping to sway him.

"I've already made arrangements to do that, but you need to

take the next step. You saw how that grown man looked watching you and I know how you affect me. I want everyone to have the opportunity to see you in action. Your voice isn't the only thing that is fascinating. The way you move and your expressions are priceless."

"That's because I knew I wouldn't end up having a bunch of strangers seeing me. Just thinking about it makes my head hurt. I'll be terrible, Jonathan."

"You'll be wonderful," he countered.

"I'm not sure I could carry it off," she pleaded desperate for him to understand.

He patted her hand. "I have every confidence that you can. Would two weeks be enough time to gather the material you'd need for the first tape?"

"Yes. No, I mean no!" She put her hands on either side of her head. "Please stop."

"I'm sure they'll want to start taping early, but we'll work out a time and I'll let you know as soon as everything is settled," he continued ignoring her plea.

"Don't make it too early in the day. My voice needs a chance to wake up."

He nodded. "Good point. We'll want you to include some of your original material besides the stories you choose from books. Will you agree to do that?"

"Sure. I have reams of stuff." She blinked. "Wait a minute, what just happened?"

He smiled. "You just made a very wise decision. One that will not only benefit your future, but will also bring a great deal of enjoyment to children and adults alike."

She gave him a suspicious look. "Did you intend to have me do this all along?"

"Not at all. I was only thinking of Jimmy in the beginning. When I gave the tape to my friend at the magazine I made it quite clear he was under no obligation. I merely wanted his opinion, but once he came on board things moved on from there."

Renewed panic stirred inside her, took hold, and squeezed like a vise. "I appreciate what you're trying to do and your confidence in me, but I really, really don't think I can do this."

"I understand your apprehension, but think what it will mean to bedridden children to see you on a television screen telling your stories. You'll be giving them the opportunity to forget for awhile that they can't run and play like other healthier kids."

"Well, when you put it that way how can I refuse? But if I turn out to be a flop don't say I didn't warn you."

"You have talent, my dear and talent gives its own reward." He smiled. "You're going to do fine. I have very good instincts. You must trust me on this."

"You had me agreeing before I knew what I was doing." She cocked her head to one side. "Do you honestly believe you're steering me on the correct path?"

He studied her for a moment. "Let's just say I'm doing everything I can to be sure that I do," he said in a voice suddenly devoid of any playfulness.

CHAPTER TWENTY-ONE

Summer rolled her shoulders and moved her head from side to side trying to relieve some of the stiffness that had settled around her neck. The movement made the elaborate tiara she wore shift a bit to the side. She reached up and adjusted it back into place. The crown was part of the costume she'd been given to wear, which included a silver and pale blue flowing gown with matching satin slippers.

She assumed the idea was to make her look like some kind of fairy godmother or a princess, which had her feeling a little ridiculous. She reached over to a small side table and took several long swallows from a water bottle. The taping was more complicated than she'd anticipated, but she had to admit it was an interesting process.

She looked up as the technician gave her the sign that her break was over and they were ready to start again. She nodded and picked up the large volume she'd been reading from, cleared her throat, and waited for his signal to begin the next story.

It was late in the day by the time the taping was completed. Jonathan insisted on taking her out for a meal and Summer was hungry enough to agree. She knew the company wanted her to record a second tape right away and was genuinely surprised when Jonathan advised her to hold off.

She frowned at him. "I don't get it. I thought you were all gung-ho for me to do this. Why put the brakes on all of a sudden?'

"It'll give us a chance to get some feedback. Let the public have this first taste and chew on it for awhile. We want to make them hungry for more."

"What if they end up not having an appetite for this kind of thing?"

"They will." He patted her hand. "You worry too much."

"I'm trying to be realistic, Jonathan. I don't want to get too excited about the outcome in case I flop. I've told you before, the stuff kids watch is out of my league."

"That's the main course. Your stories are the dessert."

She couldn't help laughing. "You must be hungry, you keep referring to food."

"Starving." He winked at her. "Chasing after dragons will do that."

Although he offered to put her up in a hotel for the night and book a flight for her in the morning, Summer was anxious to get home. Ted picked her up at the airport and she spent most of the drive home answering his questions about the taping. She invited him in for coffee, but he declined saying Holly was with the boys.

She took a shower and wrapped herself in her old pink terrycloth bathrobe before shuffling into the kitchen for her coffee. She smiled thinking how eager Ted had been to get back to Holly. Summer knew he didn't need her in his life quite as much as he had in the months right after Rebecca's death since he'd started seeing Holly on a regular basis.

She missed her time with him, but she wasn't jealous of Holly. It had been a long time since she'd seen him so happy and she was actually hoping he and Holly would get married some day. She knew they were being cautious when it came to that serious a commitment. They'd both lost spouses, one through death and one through divorce.

It brought thoughts of Marcus to her mind and what they could have had together. It annoyed her that she still missed him when she should be experiencing nothing but anger at his deception and be grateful he was out of her life. She couldn't understand why she was finding it so difficult to forget him.

Even more disturbing was how Sasha was never far from her thoughts. Summer wondered if the child missed having her in her life. It still bothered her that Marcus had been so careless with his daughter's feelings. She tried to believe that Patrice was making more of an effort to be closer to the child, but had a hard time imagining it. She could only hope Sasha hadn't suffered any negative backlash from her father's decision.

Marcus looked across the desk at Sasha's pediatrician, as he read the folder in front of him. It had become an all too familiar scene. "What's wrong this time?"

"The same thing we've talked about before. It's pretty much psychosomatic. Sasha is making herself ill because she continues to heap stress on herself."

Marcus kneaded his temples trying to ease the headache he felt coming on. "It's this thing she has about wanting a mother. I've tried to reason with her and I've had her to the best counselors, but she rarely deviates from the subject."

"Obviously, but she's definitely conflicted. I've noticed she always talks about the same woman." He consulted his notes. "Summer."

A sharp twist in his gut joined the throbbing inside Marcus's head. "Yes, I know."

"Tell me about her," the doctor invited sitting back in his chair.

"We met by chance on a trip to Disneyland. Summer was there with her widowed brother and his two sons. We stayed at the same hotel and spent time together."

"I take it the friendship continued beyond the vacation."

"Yes. I spent a weekend at her brother's and they all came here once. Summer also helped me out with Sasha on a couple of occasions. Sasha connected with her and now she keeps insisting Summer's going to come back and be her mother. Neither Summer nor I put the notion in her head in case you're wondering. I can't believe she's still hanging onto the idea. I thought it'd be an out of sight out of mind kind of thing."

"How long has it been since you've seen this Summer?"

Marcus let out a ragged sigh and slumped back against the seat. "A lifetime."

"I see. So you connected with the woman, too and are suffering with Sasha."

"I've been very careful not to show my feelings to her."

"I'm sure you have, but children are more perceptive than we give them credit for. I won't take advantage of our friendship and ask what happened with the woman. But is there any chance you could work some kind of visitation schedule with her for Sasha?"

"I doubt it. Summer doesn't live close and even if she did it wouldn't work because we didn't exactly part on amiable terms."

"I gathered that. Does she know how Sasha's been affected by her absence?"

"I haven't been in touch with her, but she knew Sasha was having problems before, so she probably wouldn't be too surprised that things haven't improved. But the way I acted the last time I saw Summer rules out any chance of her wanting to willingly come back into my life." His bleak voice reflected the hopelessness he felt.

The doctor sat forward and folded his hands on the desk. "I'm sorry to hear that, but as difficult as it obviously will be for you, I'd advise you to get in touch with her for your child's sake. If she has any empathy at all hopefully she'll come and help Sasha."

Marcus didn't tell him he'd been working on a plan to ease his way back into Summer's life and he was closing in on the final stages. All he needed now was luck.

That night Marcus lay in the dark until he finally kicked off the covers and went into the bathroom. The lights over the mirror showed every line in his face and the crescents that darkened the skin beneath his eyes bringing his fatigue into sharp focus.

He needed sleep, but couldn't remember the last time he'd had a full night of rest. Worrying about Sasha and the desperate need to make things right with Summer filled him with an impatient frustration that never seemed to give him a moment's peace.

His heart ached for Sasha. She was so fragile. As her father he was supposed to protect and provide for her, but he hadn't been doing a very good job of it lately. He'd brought Summer into Sasha's life and it was up to him to try and get her involved again.

He turned off the light and went to check on her. She was curled in a fetal ball sleeping with her arms wrapped around her stuffed teddy bear. But he knew she could wake at any moment crying out, desperately unhappy. He did his best to comfort her, but it was never enough. He stood there fighting the guilt that ripped through him.

When he glanced over at the bedside table and saw the CD player his stomach muscles tightened. It had become a permanent fixture. She insisted he play Summer's tapes every night before she went to sleep. How could Sasha stop thinking about Summer as long they played them? He supposed he should have told the doctor about this.

He worried that keeping this connection was doing more harm than good, but when he suggested they stop listening to the stories Sasha burst into tears. He had tried reading to her himself and, although she listened politely, she still asked to hear Summer. Perhaps if they had had a friendlier closure the last time he'd seen her it would be easier for him to contact Summer now. But there had been too much anger between them for any hope of that. He was as bad as Sasha wishing she'd come to see them again. It wasn't pleasant to realize he'd become a restless dreamer with nothing else to hope for.

He left Sasha sleeping and went to his office rather than back to bed knowing he'd only toss and turn. He opened his desk drawer and lifted out some photos he'd taken at Disneyland and when Summer had visited them here. He touched a fingertip to one of the pictures. She looked so fresh and pretty standing there holding Sasha by the hand.

Aware of Summer's rising success with her storytelling tapes, he was genuinely happy for her. He'd listened to them several times and always felt a mixture of pain and longing hearing her voice. How could he expect his daughter to stop thinking about Summer when he couldn't get her out of his own head?

He never stopped being amazed at the way she made every story come to life. The old woman at Rose Cottage had certainly planted a creative seed when she'd told her tales to Summer. But he had a feeling she'd seen the natural potential waiting for an outlet. He'd started to wonder several weeks ago if people ever sent their own original stories to her and if so, what she did with them?

He put the photos away and booted up his computer. It wasn't easy to organize his thoughts, but this was a vital part of his overall plan. If he didn't do it just right it'd probably be the death knell to any hope of a future with Summer. He thought of Sasha and squared his shoulders with a fierce determination, but his hands weren't quite steady when he placed them on the keyboard.

TWENTY-TWO

It had been several weeks since she'd made her debut video and Summer hadn't stopped writing down ideas while Jonathan was gearing her up for the next taping. He suggested the photo show her in a field of wild flowers surrounded by several children. Summer liked the idea so much that she'd already chosen the spot and talked to some parents, including Ted and Holly for permission to use their kids. She couldn't stop the quick image that flashed in her mind of Sasha sitting between Teddy and Buster, but made herself shake it away knowing it could never be.

She was in the store waiting on customers when the mailman arrived and set the mail on the counter. She thanked him and shoved it aside. It wasn't until later in the afternoon that she had a chance to give it her attention. A plain brown envelope caught her eye. It had a Los Angeles postmark, but no return address.

She slit it open and dumped out a disc and a short typewritten note. Whoever it was hadn't bothered to add a signature. The person wanted her to listen to a fairytale they'd written. She sighed and jammed everything back into the envelope. She wasn't a literary critic and she was too busy to get involved in critiquing someone else's work.

That night while she was trying to develop an idea for a story Summer took a break and made a cup of tea. She started thumbing through the mail she'd brought home from the store and came across the envelope with the disc. She'd forgotten she'd brought it home and was about to toss it into the trash when she hesitated.

Where would she be in her storytelling career if Jonathan hadn't encouraged her to make her first tape and release it to the public? Everybody needed a helping hand now and then. This person might actually have a good story and what right did she have to discourage someone from realizing their dream?

She dug out the note again and read the instructions at its end on how to get in contact with the sender. She went into the living room and sat on the sofa, took a couple sips of tea and fought back a yawn before settling herself more comfortably. She could only hope the tape wouldn't run too long and that she wouldn't fall asleep in the middle of it. Her first impression wasn't favorable when she realized the person hadn't included a title or an introduction.

She picked up her cup with one hand and pushed the play button with the other. With the cup halfway to her mouth, she heard the voice of a man coming from the tape and almost dropped the hot liquid in her lap. She hastily set the cup aside and, struggling with the sudden unexpected rush of emotion, her pulse began to vibrate with painful recognition.

Her hearing must be playing tricks on her or there was something wrong with the machine. She reached over, stopped it, and pushed rewind. The man's voice continued in the same manner. She leaned forward and forced herself to focus on the words.

"Once upon a time there was a lovely little princess who lived in a grand castle with her father. Although the man loved his daughter with all his heart and would gladly get her anything money could buy, she was very sad because she didn't have a mommy. You see, her mother had become ill and one day the fairies came and took her away."

Summer swallowed a lump in her throat and reached for her tea. Her hand shook as she sipped, listening to the somber voice.

"Even though the child could barely remember what it was like to have a mother she wished very much to have one again. Then one day the father and his daughter met a wonderful young woman. They were both quickly attracted to her and soon became friends. The little princess asked her daddy if their new friend could be her mommy, and although the man had fallen in love with the woman he was afraid if he asked her to marry him too soon he might frighten her away. So he decided he should be patient and wait in the hope that the young woman would come to love him, too."

Tears filled Summer's eyes and dribbled down her cheeks.

"But while he was waiting a wicked witch cast a spell on the young woman turning her against him. The man did not believe there was a spell. He became very angry because he thought the young woman had made up a lie to get him out of her life. His pride had been sorely bruised and he said cruel things to the woman vowing he would never forgive her for rejecting her."

"Wicked witch?" Summer's hands gripped the sofa.

"But he found it impossible not to think about the woman and as time went on both he and his child missed her more and more. The little girl cried herself to sleep many nights and became frailer with each passing day. No one could ease her unhappiness. The father suffered his own personal sadness and soon their house was filled with sorrow."

Summer pressed fingertips to her trembling lips. "Oh, Marcus," she whispered.

"Then one day the man found out that the wicked witch truly had cast a spell. This so enraged him that he ordered her out of his life and banished her from his home. She tried to work her evil magic on him, but she failed because his love for the pretty young woman was too strong. The witch finally admitted defeat and went far away."

Summer's heart beat hard and fast. He'd sent Patrice away. There was joy mixed in with the other emotions tearing around inside her.

"The man didn't know how to tell his true love of these things and how much he needed her, so he and his child grew increasingly despondent. His loneliness continued to consume him and since there was no joy in his castle he took his child and moved to be near the woman they loved. He hoped that some day she would at least agree to be his friend even though what he really wanted was for her to love him, too. Or perhaps she might at least take pity and be kind to his little girl even if she couldn't forgive him."

Summer stopped the machine. She had to. Her breathing was coming in short sharp pants. She made herself take slow even breaths before she drained her cup of tea to ease the ache in her throat. She waited several more seconds before pushing the play button again and willed herself to bear what was to come next.

"The man is hoping and praying for a happy ending to this fairytale, but he knows it will only be possible if his beloved would agree to give him another chance. The man and his child are waiting for the young woman they both love in a place the local people call Rose Cottage."

Summer gasped and clutched a hand to her throat. How could that be? The cottage was no longer fit for human habitation. Had she misunderstood? She went back to listen again. *Rose Cottage. Dear God, Marcus was at the cottage!*

"He knows this is a special place for her and hopefully with the blessings of the fairies the cottage will be able to work its magic and bring love back into his life once again. The woman need only come and knock on the front door and the man will be waiting to welcome her with open arms."

The recorder shut off. Summer sat trying to absorb the details. It was close to midnight. Would she be making a fool of herself is she drove to Rose Cottage at this late hour? Could Marcus really be living there? She hadn't been to the cottage in some time.

She replayed the entire story to be sure she hadn't imagined any of it. He sounded sincere and she'd have to be totally insensitive not to realize how poor little Sasha had been suffering. She gnawed on her thumbnail trying to decide what to do. Summer knew she wouldn't get any sleep tonight if she didn't go and see what was going on. But would she be setting herself up to be hurt again?

She looked around the room and knew she wouldn't find any answers here. She hurried to her bedroom and dressed quickly before grabbing her purse and the first jacket at hand. She was almost at the door when she backtracked and rushed over to a bookcase.

Holly looked toward the parking lot of Summer's apartment building, as she and Ted drove by on their way back from a movie. "I didn't see Summer's car."

"She's probably parked further back now that she got rid of her old clunker."

"Could be or she may be working late collecting stories."

Ted's brow knitted into a quick frown. "She'd better not be. She knows how I feel about her being at the store alone at night. Would you mind if we swing by to check?'

"Not at all. I know you worry about her and I do, too. She seems so lonely. I think she misses Marcus more than she's letting on."

"Yeah, I know. The boys and I don't see nearly as much of her as we used to."

"Maybe that's my fault. I've been taking up a lot of your time."

He gave her hand a quick squeeze. "Don't take on that guilt. Summer knows she's welcome at the house anytime. But I think she's trying to find her own way and she won't be able to do that if she keeps feeling responsible for the boys and me. Besides, she was the one who encouraged me to ask you out. She threatened to call you herself and set up a date if I didn't make a move."

She looked at him and laughed. "You're kidding."

He shook his head. "I swear. Put the fear of God in me."

"Well, bless her heart. I owe her one." She touched his cheek. "Big time."

Smiling, he reached for her hand again and raised it to his lips for a quick kiss.

The store was dark, the colorful display of books in the two front windows hidden by the night. The gold lettering: SUMMER'S WORLD, was obscure enough that a person wouldn't be able to read it if they didn't already know what it said.

He'd thought the title fitted Summer's personality because storybooks had always transported her to worlds beyond reality. It wasn't that their childhood had been so bad. Their mother had managed to see that they had the basics. But in a world filled with color their's had pretty much existed mostly in shades of gray because of their selfish father. Summer had found her own unique way to change all that through her imagination.

Ted dropped Holly at her house and circled back to Summer's apartment building. He took his time driving through the parking lot scanning the vehicles in the glow of his headlights, but her car wasn't there, which meant she probably wasn't home. Unwilling to accept that, he pulled into an empty parking place, cut the engine, and headed for her apartment, taking the stairs two at a time.

When he didn't receive any response to his repeated knocking, he dug out the extra key she'd given him and let himself inside. He called her name, as he checked each room, but was greeted by silence. He stood staring at her bed. It hadn't been slept in.

Ted knew it wasn't like her to be out this late on a work night. He thought about Holly's comment that Summer seemed lonely. He knew loneliness sometimes led to depression and depression could turn into despair. A tiny spark of unease stirred in his gut along with feelings of guilt wondering if he'd been leaving her on her own too often.

"Whatever the hell you're up to I hope to God you know what you're doing, Sis," he muttered to the silent room.

TWENTY-THREE

Lost in thought, Summer missed the turnoff and had to turn around and backtrack. There weren't any streetlights in the country and the narrow lane leading to the cottage wasn't marked. She was thankful she at least had a more reliable car. She was in a strange unsettling mood and didn't want to add to it by breaking down so far from town.

The sky, gray all day with a muted sun had finally released the rain that trailed down her windshield in slender streams. The dark rainy night and her vivid imagination made for a potent combination, surrounding her with a lot more atmosphere than she'd bargained for. She tried not to think about what secrets may be hidden among the shadows that clung to the landscape.

Surprised relief filled her at seeing that the road was no longer cluttered with the debris she'd always had to avoid. But the good feeling instantly vanished when she rounded a curve and saw what she thought was a woman standing in the middle of the road. Summer stomped on the brake pedal bringing the car to a shuddering halt.

Could this be Rose revealing herself at last and coming to greet her? Summer leaned forward, studied the apparition, and realized the clothes weren't right and the woman's expression was anything but welcoming. Summer's lungs filled with a scream and burst forth echoing inside the car, startling her with its suddenness. She squeezed the wheel harder and forced herself to look at the sight before her.

"I know who you are, Rena, and that you want to stop me, but you won't."

Determined to get past her terror, Summer slid her foot over to the gas pedal and made the car go forward again eliciting an unearthly shrieking sound, as the vehicle tore through the ghostly figure. A quick glance in the rearview mirror revealed nothing but darkness and slashing rain, but fear slid over her skin like icy fingers.

Heart hammering, stomach jumping with nerves, Summer made herself drive on until she saw the hazy glow of lights up ahead. Her pulse continued to throb as she fought down the panic pressing against her chest. A porch light had been installed in front and more light filtered through the front windows offering a welcoming warmth that helped to take some of the edge off her nerves.

She eased the car up to the front gate and saw an unfamiliar pickup truck parked at the side of the house. She bit her lip. Despite Marcus's tape, she worried she might be barging in on a stranger. A steady stream of smoke poured from the chimney and spiraled upward swirling crazily in the wind. She stared at the house taking in more details.

The exterior had been given a new coat of whitewash. The rain made the walls shimmer with a glossy sheen in the beam of her car's headlights. Flowers in the front flowerboxes bowed their tiny heads under the weight of the raindrops. The rose bushes she could see had been neatly pruned and the old picket fence replaced with a new one.

Summer smiled, forgetting her earlier fears for a moment knowing how pleased Rose would be to see her little house looking so fresh and homey again. It brought back a flood of memories of enchantment and childish dreams, but she wasn't a child any longer, she reminded herself and it wasn't Rose waiting behind those windows.

The storm had become more intense. Huge trees emitted strange groaning sounds. Their branches whipped wildly through the air reminding her of an octopus ready to attack. Other noises came at her, ominous in their anonymity. Fear rolled inside her and curled like a fist. Summer knew sitting in the car wasn't going to do any good, but she had to take several deep breaths before she could make herself move. She opened the car door, keeping a wary eye out for ghostly figures.

The night air hit her with a shock of cold wet wind. She slammed the door and quickly made her way to the gate. She struggled to open the latch with numb fingers while needles of rain hit her in the face and pelted her hair. By the time she finally managed to gain entry she was drenched. She started to walk toward the house, but stopped when the door opened spilling a wide wedge of light onto the wet walkway.

A tall figure stood framed in the doorway. It was impossible to make out the person's face. A prickle of unease made her falter. She couldn't be sure if it was human or another specter ready to do harm. The figure gestured for her to come inside, but fresh anxiety streaked up her spine. Eyes glazed with fear, she stood riveted to the spot, until she told herself she'd come too far to give up now.

She started to walk forward on legs that wobbled, but the wind picked up and the force of it drove her back until she stumbled and almost fell. The storm howled and whipped around her. The sound reminded her of a voice screaming in fury and Summer had a sick feeling it was more than nature hurling the icy water that sliced across her body.

She braced herself and wiping water out of her eyes, peered into the curtain of rain. "If this is you trying to stop me Rena, it won't work. So you may as well slither back into whatever hole you crawled out of," she forced the words through clenched teeth.

Summer moved determinedly forward. When she stood in front of the doorway she could see that it was Marcus. The shock of defying an evil ghost faded, as instant joy encircled her heart. Focused on him, she wanted to throw herself against him and have his arms hold her close. But he merely gestured for her to cross the threshold.

Confused by his unexpected reserve, Summer stepped inside blinking in surprise at the room's transformation. Ignoring Marcus for the moment, she looked around her with a sense of rediscovery. The pure white walls, the quaint furnishings, and the homey little touches she remembered were all in place. It was so familiar and yet somehow different. Maybe it was having Marcus here instead of Rose that changed the tone.

She turned to study him. He appeared leaner than she remembered and there were new lines furrowing his forehead and bracketing either side of his mouth. She wanted to smooth them away and see those lips tip in a smile, but her rain soaked clothes and the encounter with Rena made it difficult for her to control her body's shaking.

She obeyed his gesture that she should go closer to the fire where she stood and held out her trembling hands toward the flames. Neither of them had uttered a word and Summer didn't want to be the one to break his puzzling silence.

She was beginning to feel like she'd entered some kind of surreal dream. First with Rena and now Marcus. God knows images of him had invaded her sleep often enough. He stared at her as though he were devouring her with his eyes. She saw how stiffly he held himself and felt gripped by her own uncertainty.

Because he continued to stand there without touching her, Summer decided to follow her instincts. She walked toward the bedroom, pushed the door open, and saw an iron bedstead. Rose's bed. It looked wonderfully inviting with its colorful patchwork quilt pulled back to reveal snowy white sheets. Marcus stood just inside the doorway watching her with that same wariness. Summer shivered with cold again and slowly began to peel off her wet clothes.

After a moment's hesitation, Marcus came fully into the room and began to undress. The small bedside lamp cast a soft golden light over him revealing whipcord muscles and the hard flesh she had so loved to explore when they'd made love. But she thought he looked drained. He reminded her of Ted after Rebecca's death. He bore the same deep stress that can cause a depletion of the heart, the mind, and the soul rendering the body so exhausted even the simple act of breathing becomes an effort.

They finished undressing and, because Marcus didn't move, she took him by the hand and led him to the bed. They crawled in together and Summer held him until she felt some of the tension ease out of his body. Although they were lying naked in each other's arms and they had been apart for months, strangely enough they did not make love.

Marcus finally broke his silence. "I wanted to drag you in here, but you stopped. I feel bad about this awful storm. It frightened you. I could see it in your eyes."

Her heart jerked remembering Rena's ghost. "It was...yes, the storm," she mumbled and wished she could tell him the real reason for her fear.

"I'm so sorry for the way I acted before and I..." He stopped, cleared his throat.

Hearing his uncertainty shook her to the core. He sounded so unlike the arrogant, angry man who'd slammed out of her store. "I know. Go to sleep now. We'll talk later."

She had little doubt he'd suffered from their separation and his torment had the added weight of having to bear the responsibility of Sasha's unhappiness.

Feeling an overwhelming need to comfort, she began to stroke his temple easing her fingertips in his hair. She realized he'd let it grow longer than she remembered it, as she wove her fingers through the heavy waves. Summer continued to stroke and soothe while enjoying the feel of his length stretched out so close to her.

The scent of him, the sweetness of all that bare flesh at her fingertips made a little shiver of happiness tremble through her. They would make love; she knew that. Just as she knew the waiting would make it all the more pleasurable for them both. The anticipation made her body flush with warmth.

She listened to the storm moaning around the cottage in a kind of frenzied weeping, clawing at the windows straining against the sturdy little house. Thunder rumbled across the sky and lightening lashed out streaking through the night with long jagged fingers. But warm air and the scent of roses filled the room. A voice echoed inside her head, "Be at peace, you are safe."

Summer caught her breath, feeling emotion slam into her. She knew instinctively that Rose had somehow made sure Rena wouldn't be bothering them for now. She let out a long shaky sigh and snuggled beneath the quilt locked in her lover's arms. She closed her eyes. She was home.

CHAPTER TWENTY-FOUR

Summer wasn't sure what woke her. It might have been the sudden calm. It wasn't daylight yet, but she listened and realized the worst of the storm had blown itself out. The raging rain of the night before made a soft pattering sound against the windows.

She was about to turn and see if Marcus was still asleep when she felt him shift. His body felt taut where it pressed against her. His fingertips moved in a slow lazy rub along her thigh, across her stomach, and up to cup one breast. She smiled in the darkness. No need to ask if he was well rested and awake. He nuzzled the side of her neck.

But she gave him a gentle push. "I bought you a present."

He ran a thumb over the tip of a breast. "I know."

The sensation sent a hot spark shooting through her. "Something besides myself. It's in my coat pocket. Wait." She pushed her way out of bed. "I'll be right back." She hurried from the room and returned a moment later with her hands behind her back.

Marcus propped himself up on one elbow. "What do you have there, candy?"

"Something better." She brought her hands in front and held up a slender volume. "Erotic love poems. I've been saving them for us. I want you to read them to me."

His eyes raked over her nakedness and desire flared within their smoky depths. "It would be my pleasure . . .later." He patted the bed. "Come here."

She set the book aside and climbed in beside him. He immediately pulled her against him in one fluid tug. His kiss made her gasp. She kissed him back and heard him moan. His mouth roamed over her face and blazed a searing trail down the side of her neck making her feel shivery inside.

139

His hands moved on her body with swift, hard caresses, touching, stroking with increasing eagerness. Summer was acutely aware of bare flesh against bare flesh and that first real bite of need coiling in her belly. She breathed in his maleness savoring the scent.

He rolled pinning her beneath him and began covering the satin smoothness of her breasts with quick ravenous kisses that made her blood pound. "I thought about us being together like this a hundred times," he rasped in a ragged groan.

She rubbed her hands over the swell of his firm buttocks and up the long line of his back tracing the hard muscles there. "Oh God, I know. Even when I thought you had betrayed me I still couldn't stop from wanting you."

He stared at her, his eyes piercing with intensity. "You have me, Summer. You've always had me," he murmured hoarsely before his tongue drove between her parted lips.

She felt the evidence of his desire pressing fiercely against her making her quiver with tiny tremors of pleasure. Waves of passion washed over her, as his hands and mouth continued to brand her body until she gasped and clung helplessly to him. He raised his head after several seconds and their eyes locked in a feverish stare.

She wanted his mouth on her again knowing she would never have enough and she'd hungered for the taste of him for too long to deny herself. Staggered by the crushing need, she dragged his face down to her while he captured her lips in a long drugging kiss that sent flashes of fire burning through her. Intensity built stirring the senses. She had to have more. She felt the unleashed power in him and heard his jagged breathing mingling with her own harsh panting and knew his need was as great as her own. He raised his head and stared down at her, engulfing her within his heated gaze. He pinned her hands to the bed teasing her with his mouth making her weak with need. She struggled to free herself. "I want to touch you, Marcus. Please let go of me."

Beads of sweat dotted his forehead. "I've been helpless for too damn long. Do you think I'd let go of you now? You belong to me. Say it!" he demanded fiercely.

She stared into his eyes, drowning in twin pools of dark desire. "I'm yours."

He waited a couple heartbeats and then plunged forward. She gasped and rose up to meet him, quickly matching his rhythm further inflaming the intense passion that consumed them. Steaming jolts of hot pleasure raced between them skyrocketing out of control. Need slammed into them, taking them higher and higher, as they rose to unknown peaks, soared to incredible heights, and let their passion take them over the edge until they cried out in their mutual climax to collapse and tumble down together.

Summer felt his heart thundering against her and the wild answering from within her own body. She lay catching her breath trying to make her eyes focus through the blur of sensations. In the past, Marcus's lovemaking had seared her with his possession. But now, as she lay beneath him she knew he had branded her forever his.

She heard a sound and felt her insides coil with tension. More sounds came; soft noises she wasn't sure she could identify. She frowned. Had she imagined what might have been a happy sigh?

"Marcus?"

"Recovering here," he mumbled with his face pressed against her shoulder.

She ran her hands over his sweat slicked back. "Did you hear anything?"

He stirred and opened slumberous eyes. "I heard you."

All thoughts of ghosts fled, as she blushed remembering her cry of release that had rolled through her like a fully loaded freight train. "I couldn't help it."

He shook his head. "Don't think you ever have to hold back." He pressed his lips on her forehead. "I'm sorry I rushed you. I had intended to make this a long, slow love in with plenty of innovative foreplay."

"We can always take it slower the next time."

"That's a promise." He smiled and dropped a quick kiss on the end of her nose before easing his body away to flip back the covers and move off the bed.

She sat up letting the sheet fall to her waist revealing her bare breasts rosy from their lovemaking. Her heart quickened at the sight of his body framed in the early morning light. She felt the urge to leap up and sink her teeth into him. "What are you doing?" He pulled open a dresser drawer and took out a pair of pajamas. "We need..."

She waited while he stood staring at her. "What were you going to say?"

He shook his head like a man trying to fight his way through thick fog. "I don't remember. My brain has drained down to my feet," he muttered, but managed after a few seconds to hold up the garment in his hands. "Pajamas."

Summer nodded. "I know what they are, but why do you want them?"

"What? Oh! In case Sasha comes in here."

For one quick embarrassed moment Summer wondered if it had been Sasha she'd sensed in the room. Now was not the time to mention the possibility of it having been Rose or Rena. "I thought I heard something earlier. Do you think we woke her?"

"It was probably just the wind. If Sasha were awake she'd be in bed with us right now." He pulled on the pajama pants while Summer slipped into the top.

She burrowed against him when he slid back into bed. "Is she doing better?"

"No, but she will be as soon as she discovers you're here. She's sat by the front windows every day watching for you to come. I was so grateful when I saw you standing on the walkway I damn near went down on my knees and kissed your feet."

"I wouldn't want you to do that. A man should be allowed to keep his dignity."

"Pride has already cost me too much. I've made too many mistakes because of it."

She couldn't allow him to shoulder all the responsibility in their breakup. "So have I. I should have known Patrice wasn't to be trusted. I played right into her hands."

"She messed with both of us." He framed her face between his palms. "I've never slept with her, never had the slightest desire to. I want you to know that, to believe it."

"I do now." She grinned. "But maybe you should convince

me some more."

He pushed her back onto the mattress and began working the buttons loose on the pajama top she'd just donned. "Maybe I should."

There were so many things she wanted to say to him, but the words vanished at his touch. She moaned in surrender while her heart pounded inside her chest. Marcus kept his vow and took his time even when she urged him to hurry. He lingered over every soft curve tormenting and arousing until Summer thought she would go mad with wanting him. By the time he gave into her pleas she was ready to erupt.

It was a long time before they stirred again. He shifted his body to lie on his side facing her. She gave his shoulder a halfhearted slap. "You nearly drove me insane."

"I said I wanted to take it slower this time."

"It's not fair that you have such control and I immediately fall apart."

"If you think it's easy for me to hold back you're very much mistaken. It takes every bit of willpower I have not to just jump on and take. Patience is not without pain."

They were quiet for the next several seconds. Summer heard his breathing begin to slow and deepen. "Are you asleep?"

"Working on it," his words came out sounding slightly slurred.

"Hold off a sec if you can. I've got to ask the one question that's been plaguing me. Why didn't you contact me as soon as you found out about Patrice's duplicity?"

He heaved out a long sigh. "How could I after the awful things I said to you?"

"I wasn't exactly Miss Manners, but I admit you left me feeling low enough to rub noses with a snake."

"You weren't the only one. My self-esteem had been sorely wounded that you believed I'd do something as callous as elope with her."

"Think how I felt when I saw that stuff she sent."

"They were obviously forgeries."

"Well, they certainly looked real enough at the time."

He looked at her. "You can't have any idea how hard it was

for me to walk away and leave you. I felt as though my insides had been ripped to shreds." He stroked her cheek. "I was already in love with you at that point, Summer."

Tears of emotion filled her eyes. "Oh, Marcus I was in love with you, too. That's why I was so hurt." She sniffed and rubbed a hand over her eyes. "How about we forget what happened before and start fresh?"

"It's got me stoked," he growled and pressed his hardened body to hers.

CHAPTER TWENTY-FIVE

They were in the kitchen the next morning having coffee when Sasha burst into the room, dove onto Summer's lap, and began to cover her face in wet kisses. "Summer, you found us! I knew you would," she gushed with childish excitement.

Summer hugged and kissed her back. "And it looks as though you found me, too."

Marcus smiled at his daughter. "Hey, don't I rate a kiss?"

She slid off Summer's lap and onto his giving him a loud smacking kiss on the mouth before turning back to Summer. "Do you like this house?"

"I've always liked this house. I used to come here when I was a little girl."

"Daddy told me. Now you can live here with us and still see Ted, Teddy and Buster while you're being my mommy." She beamed looking very pleased.

Marcus groaned beneath his breath. "Sasha, what did I say about giving Summer time before we talked about this?"

"But Daddy, we've waited so long already." She looked at Summer with a hint of uneasiness in her dark eyes. "You want to stay with us, don't you?"

Summer looked and saw the longing mirrored in both Marcus and Sasha's eyes. She would have walked over hot coals in her bare feet rather than disappoint them. "I'd like to be your mommy if it's all right with your daddy, but most people would think it'd be nice if he married me first." She kept the teasing tone in her voice and didn't look at Marcus.

"We're marrying Summer. Okay, Daddy? You said we would if she wanted to."

"I remember." He gave Summer a sheepish grin. "This isn't quite the setting I had planned on when I proposed to you. I don't even have a ring to give to you."

"I don't need candlelight and flowers if that's what you're worried about."

"Well, then will you marry us? Me?" He hooked an arm around Sasha and drew her to his side. "We both love you very much."

Summer could only nod because her throat was all but closed with the tears she was trying hard not to shed. Sasha threw her arms around her neck. "Goody! See Daddy, I told you Summer would be my mommy." She kissed her on the mouth and turned back to him. "Now you kiss her too, Daddy."

As soon as his mouth touched her lips Summer didn't want him to stop. It wasn't every day a woman received a proposal of marriage. But she knew they had to restrain themselves with Sasha sitting there watching. Summer eased herself away.

"I think this calls for a celebration. What would you like me to fix for breakfast?"

"I want to help make Mickey Mouse pancakes like I did when I stayed with you."

Summer kissed Sasha on the end of her pert little nose. "Mouse pancakes it is, then."

Later, as they sat eating Summer glanced around the kitchen. "You've done a wonderful job restoring the place. I hated coming here seeing the way it had fallen into disrepair. I pulled weeds one day, so I could feel I was doing something useful."

"I tried to keep the integrity of the house intact as much as possible."

"I see that. It's the same as it was when I came here as a child, except that the roses were blooming then."

"I'm not much of a gardener, but I'm hoping to have them bloom again eventually. I'll go to the local nursery and see what I'm supposed to do to help things along."

"I should warn you that it probably won't do any good. That's not a criticism aimed at you. Those bushes haven't produced a single leaf or flower since Rose's death."

His brows lifted. "You're kidding. Does anyone know why?"

"No. They just grew big and ugly and never bloomed again."

"Really? That's too bad considering the name of the cottage.

Maybe the soil needs rejuvenating with fertilizer. I think I'll still make that trip to the nursery."

"I wish you luck."

Sasha scooped up the last of her miniature pancakes and sucked on her fingers while syrup dribbled down her chin and onto her tee shirt. "Sasha, you need to go wash your face and hands and put on a clean top." Marcus watched her leave the room and turned back to Summer. "You don't sound very encouraging about us having the roses."

"I'm sorry. Maybe you're right about the fertilizer. I appreciate your wanting to try. It'd be lovely seeing them." She looked around the room again. "I love this place."

"I know. That's why I bought it when I knew I had to be near you."

She couldn't stop the swell of emotion that filled her. "That is so incredibly sweet of you. I always knew this cottage is what dreams are made of. Can you imagine what an inspirational place it'll be for me to write my stories?"

"The thought did cross my mind," he said in a dry tone.

"I'm glad I didn't come out here and spoil your surprise after I heard the rumors in town that someone was working on the place."

"I had to take the chance that you'd stay away."

"This house was filled with a lot of love at one time."

He leaned over and brushed a quick kiss over her mouth. "It will be again."

She smiled, touched his face. "Yes. We'll make it a cozy vacation spot."

He sat back and studied her. "Actually, I'd like to make it a permanent home."

She hadn't expected that. What would he say if he knew they might be sharing the house with a couple of ghosts? "How can you be sure you'll be happy here?"

"I know because you're here."

Tears of gratitude wanted to come, but she forced them back. "I don't know what to say, Marcus; you've overwhelmed me. You're giving up so much without asking me to compromise a thing. The cottage has been a kind of sanctuary for me, but what about you? What if you miss Las Vegas?"

He reached over and taking hold of her hand began to rub his thumb across the knuckles. "You are my sanctuary, Summer. The life I had in Las Vegas was over for me a long time ago. This is what I want now."

"But what about your work?" she persisted.

"I own the company. I can run it from here with an occasional side trip. I also have enough investments to never work again if I so choose. You won't starve with me."

"I don't doubt it, but I feel guilty about you leaving your beautiful house."

"Don't. It had become more like a prison cell trapping old memories best laid to rest. I sold everything with the exception of Diana's artwork. Some is still for sale in a gallery there, but I put several pieces in storage for Sasha when she gets older."

"It's good that you did. She should know how talented her mother was." She took a sip of coffee before looking at him again. "What did you do about Mrs. Gwen?"

"That turned out to be the hardest part in leaving."

Her fingers tightened on the cup. "What happened?"

"She really broke down. I knew how much she cared for Diana, but I hadn't realized how difficult it was going to be for her to leave the house. I tried to ease the hurt by giving her six months pay, one of Diana's paintings, and promised to keep in touch."

"That was generous of you." She toyed with her spoon. "But what did she say when you told her you were moving here to be with me?"

"I expected her to be happy if not for me, then for Sasha's sake, but she seemed agitated and even angry. I'm sure it's nothing personal against you. It's more likely she didn't want me to sell the house, period. I suppose in her mind she thought I should have kept it as a kind of monument to Diana."

She saw no point in contradicting him about how Mrs. Gwen felt about her. "Sounds like it. What do you think she'll do now?"

"As luck would have it she found a job as a housekeeper to Constance Lily. She's the woman who owns the gallery in Las Vegas where Diana's work is displayed. Hers had recently retired And, since she knew Mrs. Gwen, she hired her right away."

"I'm sure it was a relief to you both."

"It was. Mrs. G's husband died before she came to us. She didn't have children. We were all she had. I wanted to be sure she was taken care of. I didn't like the idea of feeling that I was tossing her out after she'd given my family so many years of service."

Although Mrs. Gwen had resented her, Summer couldn't prevent a tug of sympathy knowing how much the Brennans meant to the woman. "No, that would be hard."

Sasha returned at that moment. "I'm all clean now, Daddy."

He nodded his approval. "Good girl." He looked at Summer. "I was thinking, since we're going to stay here, we could add on to the cottage." He picked up his mug.

"For the babies," Sasha piped up in a cheery little voice causing Marcus to choke.

"What did you say?" Summer asked in a strangled voice.

"I want to have two brothers just like Teddy and Buster, and a baby sister. You want to have babies don't you, Summer?" she asked with the wide-eyed innocence only a young child is capable of.

Marcus gave her an exasperated look. "I'm beginning to think I'm going to have to gag you, Sasha."

Summer laughed and squeezed both their hands. "Yes, let's have lots of babies."

The three of them chatted happily, as they made plans for the future while they cleared away the breakfast dishes. Most of the morning was gone by the time Summer said her goodbyes and reluctantly left the cottage. She'd been so happy that she hadn't given another thought about ghosts or the fact that she'd gone missing for several hours.

Summer sang in the car on the drive back to her apartment and was still humming when she stepped inside to hear the phone ringing. She tossed her purse aside and hurried to answer it. "Yes? Hello."

"It's about time you picked up."

She flinched at the sound of the angry voice and gripped the receiver. "Ted?"

"Where the devil have you been all night?" he demanded.

Summer blew out a breath, preparing herself to let him know that Marcus had come back into her life. What would he say? He may not approve knowing how hurt she'd been when they'd parted. She wanted Marcus, but she needed her brother, too.

CHAPTER TWENTY-SIX

"Well, I..."

"I've been worried half out of my mind," he snapped, cutting her off. "Have you checked your answering machine?"

"No, I just walked in the door."

"Well, don't bother. All the messages are probably from me, each one more frantic than the last. Damn it Summer, you didn't even have your cell phone on. How is a person supposed to get hold of you?"

"I'm sorry I forgot. Is everything okay? Has something happened to the boys?"

"They're fine, which is more than I can say for myself."

"I should have called you. I was..."

He broke in again before she could finish. "It's your business what you do in your leisure time, but you can't blame me for worrying when you're usually home every night or let me know when you're going out. I went by the store and your apartment last night and again this morning."

"I'm sorry I worried you. I wasn't there because I..."

"It's not like I expect you to keep me informed of your every move, but I couldn't help but be concerned. I know you're a grown woman, but when I call in the middle of the night and you don't answer do you have any idea what that does to my nerves?"

She breathed deeply. "I spent the night at Rose Cottage."

"What are you talking about? The place is a wreck."

"Not anymore. Marcus bought it and had it restored."

"Do you want to run that by me again?"

"You heard right."

"So the rumors that the cottage was being worked on were true and now you and Marcus have kissed and made up."

Her lips curved into a mischievous smile. "Actually, we did more than kiss. We ended up going to bed together and..."

"Hey! You say one more word about that and I hang up," he warned.

She laughed. "You are such fun to tease. Anyway, we're back together."

"Yeah? How together are we talking here? I don't see Patrice sharing. It's your business what you do like I've already said, but I hate to see you get involved with a married man no matter how much I wanted you to be with Marcus."

"There wasn't any marriage. Patrice faked the whole thing. She had everything planned before they went to Maui. They were at a friend's wedding. She knew they'd be dressed up, so she had the photographer take their picture."

"What about the marriage license you said she sent?"

"She went to one of those places where you can get phony documents made."

"I'll be damned. She really must have been desperate. But why did Marcus wait so long to tell you? He could have saved you a whole lot of heartache."

"He didn't know anything about it and when he did find out he was afraid to approach me. I never told you, but he came to the store right after Patrice sent me all that stuff and we had a terrible argument. We said some pretty awful things to each other."

"I can imagine. So, where's Patrice now?"

"I don't know, except that Marcus kicked her out of his life."

"It's about time. So he bought Rose Cottage. That must have come as a shock."

"To put it mildly. But he's done a beautiful job of restoring it. It's just how I remembered it from when I was little."

"What happens now? What are his intentions where you're concerned?"

He sounded so protective she had to smile. "You can relax. His intentions are quite honorable. He's asked me to marry him and I've accepted." She had to choke back the swelling bubble of happiness that sprang up into her throat.

He let out a low whistle. "Well, well. When's the happy event taking place?"

"We haven't set a date yet, but I'm hoping it'll be soon."

"I can't blame you considering all the time that's been wasted. So I guess this means you'll be moving to Las Vegas and staying in the cottage in between times."

She didn't miss the disappointment in his tone. "No. He knew I wouldn't want to leave you and the boys. He sold his house. We're going to live at the cottage fulltime and eventually add on some rooms."

"Really? Hey, that's great. Sounds like he's been doing a lot of planning. Congratulations. I'm happy for you both. I knew Marcus was crazy in love with you."

"Oh you did, did you? And just how did you come to that conclusion?"

"Women aren't the only ones capable of being observant. We men do have our moments. Besides, the guy practically drooled every time he looked at you."

She laughed. "That's not exactly an attractive image, Ted."

"You know what I mean. I bet Sasha is thrilled."

"She is and quite pleased with herself for playing matchmaker. You two should go into the business."

It was his turn to laugh. "Hey, what can I say? It finally worked. Tell Marcus to come by the house one of these days, so I can share a congratulatory beer with him."

"I'll do that." She looked at her watch. "Listen Ted, I've got to get ready for work. I'll talk to you later. Give my love to the boys," she added and hung up.

She took a quick shower, dressed, and hurried out to her car sidestepping a couple of rain puddles on the way. Her cheeks were flushed rosy with the nip in the air and her eyes were bright from the joy that flowed through her.

The first thing she did was check her e-mails. There was one from Jonathan with information on how her tape was selling. He mentioned setting up visitations to hospitals and care facilities that specialized in juvenile patients. He also added a postscript about starting her next tape. She decided to call him before she got too busy.

"Summer, what a lovely surprise. Did you receive my latest e-mail?"

"Yes. That's why I'm calling."

"What did you think of my suggestions?"

"I definitely want to see those children and do another tape, but I'd like to delay it a bit if that's all right." She hurried to explain. "Please don't think I'm trying to slack off, but all that on top of making arrangements for someone to run the store will take some planning. I also need to devote some time to my personal life for the time being."

"Oh? Personal, as in do I detect a whiff of romance in the air?" he teased.

"You're very perceptive, counselor." She took a deep breath. "I never told you, but there was someone very special in my life. Something happened and we parted before I met you. But we've just gotten back together and he's asked me to marry him. He's a widower with an adorable little girl. We need to catch up on lost time."

He paused. "Well, this is quite a surprise, but obviously a wonderful one for you."

"Yes it is. You see, I never thought I'd ever be in contact with him again."

"Life can be funny that way. Just when you begin to think something is over it's actually only the beginning. When are the happy nuptials going to take place?"

"We haven't discussed a date, but I'd rather not delay too long."

"No, I wouldn't think so from what you've just told me. Let me know when you decide about the tour and we'll work things out according to what's best for you."

"Thank you for being so understanding. I hope I'm not upsetting your plans."

"I'll get over it if I'm invited to the wedding," he teased again.

She laughed. "Consider it done. I'll let you know my schedule as soon as I can."

"That'll be fine. You've become very special to me, Summer. You deserve to be happy and it sounds as though this man and his child are just what you need."

She felt moved by the sincerity in his voice. "They are."

"Summer, there's something I need to tell...oh, never mind, it'll keep," he said and hung up leaving Summer wondering what he had been about to say.

CHAPTER TWENTY-SEVEN

Besides choosing a wedding date, Summer needed to talk to Marcus about her idea of being married in the garden at the cottage. She wanted to keep it small with just Sasha, Ted, the boys, and probably Holly and Jonathan as the only guests. But she realized Marcus must have people he wanted to invite. She approached him as soon as he arrived at the store.

"Whatever you want is fine with me. Sure you don't want a big church wedding?"

She shook her head. "Not my thing. How about you?"

"Been there, done that, don't need to do it again. Just tell me when and where."

"I'm thinking two weeks. Will that give you enough time to be ready?"

"I'm ready right now."

"I may not want a fancy production, but I refuse to elope, Marcus."

He sighed. "Okay, I got it. Two weeks. I'll mark my calendar."

"Well, that was easy." She let out a slow breath. "I have something I think is quite special that I want to share with you about Rose Cottage. You already know that I used to visit the old woman who lived there when I was a little girl. She didn't have children of her own, so I think I kind of filled that void for her."

"Sounds like it."

"One day she told me a story about a young couple who heard about this cottage and as soon as they saw it they knew they not only wanted to buy it, but they also wanted to be married in the garden. She told me how beautiful their wedding day was and how much they loved each other. The man was in the Army and was supposed to report to duty soon after they were married. He decided to take one last walk into the woods before he went away, but he never made it back to the cottage."

"What happened to him?"

"He drowned in the stream," she said softly, her eyes never leaving his face.

He was quiet for a moment. "Rose was talking about her husband and herself."

"Yes. He's the one who planted all the rose bushes for her."

"Did she ever remarry?"

"No, and she wore her wedding band almost to the end of her life."

"Almost?" he asked, lifting a brow.

"One day while Mom and I were visiting, Rose asked me to go into the garden with her. She pointed to an area and said that was the spot where she'd taken her wedding vows. She asked me to get a trowel from the shed and dig a hole. She took a little tin box from her apron pocket. She always wore long white aprons with pockets over long dresses and high laced up black leather shoes. Anyway, she slipped off her ring and put it inside the box and asked me to bury it."

Surprise flickered in his eyes. "Why in the world did she want you to do that?"

"I think she knew she was going to die soon."

"I would have thought she'd want to be buried wearing her ring."

"She wanted me to dig it up to wear when I married and she hoped I'd take my vows in the garden at Rose Cottage as she had done."

"Wouldn't it have been easier if she just gave the ring to you then or made arrangements for you to have it when you married?"

"I think she wanted it to stay at Rose Cottage until then."

"That's quite a story, sad, but also beautiful at the same time. I'll be hugely disappointed if you've been making it up."

"Every word is true. You can see for yourself when we dig up the ring."

"When will that be?'

"I was thinking tomorrow morning if that's all right with you."

"Why wait? There's still plenty of time before dark. Can you close up early?"

She hadn't expected him to be so anxious. "I have a feeling you're not quite sure you believe me. Is that why you want to do this right away?"

"I want to believe you because it's a touching story, but there's still a part of me that needs to see the ring. I guess I'm one of those have to see to believe kind of guys."

He continued the discussion as they drove to the cottage. "Rose took a big gamble that you'd end up with her ring. What if I hadn't been the one to buy the cottage?"

"She told me no matter what I had to do I must find a way to dig it up and somehow make arrangements to be married in the garden."

"Did she have any family at all?"

Summer bit her lip, wondering if she should mention Rena, but decided against it. "Just some distant relatives, I think. When I was old enough to ask about them, the attorney who handled the will had passed away. I didn't pursue it after that because I didn't have anyone I wanted to marry at the time."

"She obviously thought a lot of you. Since she didn't have any children or other close relations, I wonder why she didn't leave the house to you"

"She wanted to, but my mother forbid it."

He shot her a quick glance. "Good lord, why?"

"Different reasons. She knew we couldn't afford to maintain two houses, and the cottage wasn't big enough for all of us. Rose made it clear she didn't want it rented out. Also, my mother knew my father would badger her into selling it."

"You've never talked about your father. Is he still alive?"

"No," she said in a tight voice.

"I'm sorry."

"Don't be. I can't grieve for what I never had."

He gave her a sharp look. "He must have known how much you loved the place."

"He knew, but that wouldn't have mattered because he was short on sentiment, but long on needing cold hard cash to support his gambling and his women."

Marcus' hands tightened on the wheel for a moment. "So that's how it was. I'm sorry Summer I didn't mean to open up old wounds."

"He taught me that not all men are princes." She couldn't hide the hint of bitterness.

"Do you think seeing the kind of man your father was may have made you overly cautious and a little afraid to trust men in general?" he asked in a gentle voice.

"I never thought about it, but I suppose you could have something there."

"Rose should have had a stipulation in her will that your father not be allowed to get his hands on the property."

"Even if she did there was still the fact that we couldn't afford the upkeep."

He continued to probe. "Did you worry you wouldn't be able to find the owners?"

"I just assumed things would work out. There was also the possibility I wouldn't have to get permission if the cottage remained deserted."

He nodded. "True."

"You also have to remember that I was a little girl when Rose died and I didn't understand the significance of what she was asking until I was older."

Marcus pulled into the driveway of the cottage a couple of minutes later. He helped Sasha out of the car and they all walked around to the back garden. "I'll get a spade."

Summer pointed to an area when he returned. "Between those two rose bushes."

But he hesitated. "I'd like you to sit down for a minute. I need to say something before we go any further with this. I should have told you as soon as you came to the cottage." He turned to Sasha. "I want you to go over there and play, sweetheart."

"But Daddy, you said we were going to dig up a treasure."

"We'll get to that in a few minutes."

"Is your talking going to take a long time?"

"I hope not." He pointed to a corner of the garden. "Be a good girl and scoot."

Summer watched the child go. "Can't what you have to tell

159

me wait for Sasha's sake?"

"It could, but I think it's better that I have my say first."

"Have I done something wrong?" she asked, frowning.

"No, I'm the culprit here."

A chill ran through her. "I don't like the sound of that. You're scaring me."

"I'm sorry, but I'm afraid I haven't been completely open about some things."

Her heart skipped inside her chest and her mouth went dry. "What things?"

"Things that you have a right to know."

Summer closed her eyes unable to bear seeing the troubled look on his face.

He paced in front of her for a few seconds. When he finally stopped he shoved both hands into his pants pockets before he spoke. "I think you should probably look at me while I have my say." Summer slowly opened her eyes and stared at him. He took one hand out of a pocket and ran it around the back of his neck. "It was no accident that Jonathan came into your store and heard you read that day."

Her brow furrowed into a deep frown. "I'm not sure I understand."

"I sent him."

"What do you mean? Are you saying you know Jonathan?"

He gave her a wary look from beneath his lashes. "Yes. He's my attorney and a good friend."

"I don't think I'm going to like hearing this because it smacks of deception."

"I suppose it does involve a certain amount of dishonesty, but what I did wasn't only to help me. I had your best interests at heart, too. That you must believe, Summer."

She clasped her hands tightly together in her lap. "I'll have to see about that, won't I? Just exactly what have you done and does it involve anything illegal?"

"Of course not. I was talking to Jonathan one day and he happened to say he was planning on driving up this way to check on some property his family owned. He mentioned your town and I told him what a great place it was and..."

"You didn't seem to think it was so great that day in my store," she reminded him.

He winced. "It's not going to help if we go back over that fiasco. People say a lot of things they don't mean in a fit of temper, most of which they usually regret. You know I don't feel that way. I wouldn't be here if I did, Summer."

She shrugged. "I suppose not. So what were you going to say about Jonathan?"

"I asked if he would mind going to your store. I gave him a time that I hoped was the same schedule you had for reading to the children when I was there."

Her eyes narrowed. "Why did you want him to see me?"

"Apart from the fact that I was desperate to know how you were, I also wanted to do something to make up for the terrible things I said to you. I thought I might be able to do that by drawing attention to your storytelling. I was so certain he'd be impressed with your ability I played him one of Sasha's tapes to entice him to pay you a visit when he came here."

She jolted off the bench and glared at him as anger quickly solidified like a ball of lead inside her stomach. "You've been making a fool of me."

He pulled his hand out of his pocket and reached for her, but she backed away. "It wasn't like that. There was never any intention to cause you harm. You're a fabulous storyteller, but without an extra push I knew only the people in this town would ever know that. I wanted Jonathan to hear you firsthand and hopefully help you go further."

He grabbed her arm when she started to walk away. "Let go of me."

He shook his head. His mouth was set in a line as stubborn as her own. "Not until you agree to hear the rest of what I have to say. Please Summer, I'm trying to do the right thing here. I know I've upset you, but it's important that you know everything."

She pulled her arm free and plopped down on the bench. Marcus joined her, but was careful not to touch her.

"The two of you have certainly been busy orchestrating your scheme. Which one of you came up with the blind grandson idea?

161

Was that to play on my sympathy?" She made no attempt to disguise her disgust at such tactics.

He shook his head. "Sadly Jimmy really is blind."

"Oh." She looked down at the ground while irritation rolled over into pity. "I'm truly sorry," she said, "but that doesn't mean I'm happy with Jonathan's part in this. I like him. I trusted him. He should have told me what was going on."

"He wanted to, but I asked him to wait. He got a kick out of helping me in the beginning, especially when I told him I was trying to win you back. I think he felt like he was playing cupid. But he became increasingly unhappy with all the subterfuge and threatened to tell you the truth if I didn't do it myself. I had a devil of a time holding him back until the cottage was ready and I could personally reveal everything to you."

"I suppose it is some small comfort knowing he was in my corner, but he certainly played his part well when I told him about you and Sasha."

"Don't be too hard on him. He was thrilled when I told him you'd agreed to marry me." He watched her for a few seconds. "Are we square on this now?"

She shrugged, struggling to control her lingering pout. "I guess so," she mumbled.

"Good, because I have something else to tell you."

"Oh God, now what? You're making me crazy here, Marcus."

"I know and I'm sorry, but don't worry you'll like this part. Remember I told you Jonathan was coming here to look at some property?"

"Yes, so?"

"Well, it just so happens that the property was Rose Cottage."

"No way! You're making that up."

He shook her head. "It's true. Those distant relatives of Rose's happened to be Jonathan's family on his mother's side. He knew about the cottage, but had never been here. He was planning on coming to look it over because he'd pretty much decided to sell it since it had been empty all these years. I told him how special it was to you and asked him to let me buy it."

"Just like that?" She snapped her fingers. "Sight unseen?"

"Why not? I was willing to do anything to get you back. But once he'd met you and found out about your friendship with Rose he wanted you to have it, too."

She pushed herself off the bench, too unnerved to sit any longer. "I can't believe this. If what you're telling me is really true, it's almost like a fairytale."

"It's real enough all right and there's more to the story."

Her eyes got very big. "I think I'd better sit down again."

He smiled and tugged at her until she gave in and sat on his lap. "Rose wanted you to have the cottage so much that she put a stipulation in her will that if the family tried to sell it they had to give you first crack at it and if you didn't buy it she insisted you have the chance to at least give your approval to any prospective buyers. She also mentioned that you should be allowed to be married in the garden when the time came."

She punched him on the shoulder. "You beast! You let me go on about that when all the time you already knew."

His mouth twitched in amusement before he kissed her on the end of her nose. "It was more enjoyable hearing you tell the story than reading it in a dry legal document."

"But if what you just told me about the will is true, then Jonathan went against Rose's wishes because no one ever asked me if I wanted the cottage or if I would give my blessing to whoever bought it."

"He didn't know about the provision when he promised it to me, but as soon as he realized what we were up against, we devised a plan. I haven't signed any papers yet."

"But what about all the money you've invested in fixing up the place?"

"Jonathan said he'd reimburse me if you and I didn't end up living here, but I wouldn't allow myself to think about that kind of failure."

She felt a quick shudder go through him. "There wasn't a chance of me refusing once I saw you again," she confessed. "But you did take a costly gamble, Marcus."

"I didn't care about the money. I did it for you, hoping it would bring us together again. Now I'm asking, will you allow me to purchase Rose Cottage? Jonathan is waiting for your approval. I told him I'd let him know as soon as you made your decision."

All thoughts of being angry with him dissolved at his pleading look. She leaned over and gave him a noisy kiss on the mouth. "How could a girl refuse such an offer?"

He leaned his forehead against her brow. "Thank God that's over."

"Did I tell you how much I love you, Marcus Brennan?"

"Not in the last few minutes." He pulled her more fully into his arms and covered her mouth in a possessive kiss before she had a chance to say another word.

Summer's face was flushed a pretty pink when she finally wiggled off his lap. She picked up the shovel and handed it to him. "Time to start digging, pal. I've got a wedding to plan and I need that ring."

Marcus laid the shovel aside. "I think it would be better to use a trowel. Considering how small the box must be, I might damage it with a shovel. I'll be right back."

Summer watched him lope off to the garden shed and dropping to her knees, began to tug at the weeds. He returned with a couple of trowels and a pair of garden gloves for her. Once they had cleared the unwanted plants away, they dug deeper into the patch of earth.

Marcus was the first to stop. "I think I have something here." He tossed the trowel aside and began to feel around with his fingers. Seconds later he withdrew the box and immediately handed it to her.

She brushed the dirt off. "It's just as I remembered it." Heart pounding, she lifted the lid with trembling hands and stared at her prize.

CHAPTER TWENTY-EIGHT

Sasha had grown tired of chasing butterflies, following a beetle's progress, and picking flowers. Seeing that the adults were still deep in conversation, she decided it would be all right if she went exploring. The surrounding forest had been beckoning her since the day she arrived. She'd asked to be taken into the woods, but it never seemed to be the right time and her daddy said she was too young to go on her own.

Well, she didn't think she was too little. She could do lots of things all by herself.

She knew there was a gate at the back of the garden hidden in a corner behind some bushes. She could be back before they even noticed she was gone. Taking one last look over her shoulder and seeing that no one was paying any attention to her, Sasha found the gate and nimbly slipped through.

She stood on the other side of the fence looking around with eyes brimming over with anticipation. The sense of freedom she felt made her heart thump rapidly inside her narrow chest. With so much to see, she wondered which direction she should take. A shiver of excitement made her feel bold and taking one last look over her shoulder she moved forward.

She heard the chirping of a bird overhead and then spied a perky little gray squirrel sitting on a nearby log staring at her with its big brown eyes. Sasha smiled and took a few cautious steps toward the tiny rodent. But much to her disappointment it scurried off its perch and ran toward the trees with a flick of its bushy tail.

"Wouldn't it be fun to see where he lives and maybe even find a whole family of squirrels living in their own special tree?"

Sasha spun to find a woman standing behind her. "Who are you?"

"A friend." She smiled and held out her hand. "Come , let's

find that squirrel before he gets away."

"Daddy says I shouldn't talk to strangers."

"Oh, but I'm not a stranger. I know your daddy and I know these woods. I can have you back before he even knows you're gone. Isn't that what you wanted to do?"

Sasha hadn't liked the way the trees looked in the nighttime, especially when it had stormed and they moved back and forth like giant monsters. But today the sun was shining and they didn't look scary at all and she did so want to explore.

She thought it must be wonderful to live in a tree that reached up really high. She leaned back and looked up wishing she could climb to the very top of the tallest one. Maybe she would be able to touch the sky or bounce on a cloud. Everyone said Heaven was up there. Maybe she would be able to see her mommy or her granny.

She was so intent on finding the squirrel that she forgot about staying close to the cottage and let the woman lead her deeper into the woods.

"There he is!" Sasha cried. She had spotted him rummaging among twigs on the ground. She crept closer to have a better look only to have him dash up a tree where he sat on a high limb.

"Please don't keep running away, Mr. Squirrel. I want to be your friend." She touched the gnarled bark of the old tree and craned her neck up. "Is this where you live?"

He darted over to another tree almost disappearing into the thick foliage. The woman squeezed her hand. "Hurry, we don't want to lose him," she said and tugged Sasha along forcing her to go further into the forest to keep the animal in their sight. But a few minutes later he ran up an especially tall tree and vanished from view completely.

Sasha sighed in disappointment, but quickly perked up when she thought she heard a new sound. "What's that noise?" she asked cocking her head to the side.

The woman frowned at her. "Noise? Oh, you mean the water."

"My daddy told me there's a stream here in the woods. I wish I could see it, but I'm not supposed to go there by myself."

A malicious gleam came into the woman's eyes. "It's lucky

you've got me to take you, then, isn't it? Come, let me show you."

Filled with a renewed sense of adventure, Sasha followed the woman. Her heart tapped more rapidly against her rib cage at the thought of seeing fish and frogs and maybe even some ducks. The sound of rushing water was definitely getting louder now. Her breath came quickly in her anxiousness to reach her goal. She was soon rewarded when they broke through the last barrier mere yards from the water's edge.

Swollen from the recent rains, the familiar gentle flow of the stream had been transformed into a swiftly rushing current harboring a dangerous power a young child wouldn't understand.

"You have to get closer, so you can have a better look." the woman urged.

Remembering her father's warning made Sasha hang back. "Daddy says I can't."

The woman's eyes flashed with angry impatience. "Your father isn't here to see what you do and you did say you wanted to see it." She pulled Sasha to the very edge.

"No, I don't want to," she cried and tried to pull her hand away, but the woman held on squeezing tightly. "Let me go. I want to go home. I want my daddy."

"Don't be such a big baby." She forced Sasha to squat down and lean precariously close to the water. The woman pointed to a flash of silver rushing by. "Did you see that? It was a fish. Wouldn't you like to touch one?" She stretched Sasha's thin body forward straining her ever closer to the swiftly moving water.

"No, no I can't reach them." Fear had taken the place of any desire for adventure now and Sasha began to cry. "You're hurting me."

"Just a little closer," the woman urged pushing Sasha toward the water.

The voice was silky smooth with an evilness that even a child could recognize.

Sasha stared at her with eyes gone wide with terror while she struggled to break away, as the woman began to shove her toward the edge.

"Sasha."

The child turned at the sound of the quiet voice and would

have fallen into the water if a firm hand hadn't eased her away from the edge. The second woman held Sasha by the hand while the first woman glared at them both and made a hissing sound.

Sasha's lips trembled. "That...that mean lady is scaring me."

"I know, but she's gone now."

Sasha turned and frowned at the empty space. "She said I could touch the fishes."

"Yes, but now isn't a good time."

"Why not?"

"I'll tell you." The woman guided her to a log and sat down patting a place next to her. "They can't let you touch them because the water is making them move too quickly to stop. You'll have to wait until the stream isn't so deep and fast."

"When will that be?"

"When the last of the rains have stopped and the water isn't so high. Then you can climb down the embankment, take off your shoes, and step into the water. The fish will be able to swim much slower then and will even come around your bare toes."

"Really? Have the fishes ever gone around your toes?"

"Many times."

"Do they bite?" Sasha crunched up her nose. "I wouldn't like that."

"No little one, they don't bite. You might feel them nibble, but it tickles."

Sasha giggled. "I think that might be very funny."

"It is. Why don't we go tell your daddy and Summer all about it? They can bring you back here when the water is just right." She stood up offering her hand.

Sasha clasped the woman's slender fingers. "You know my daddy and Summer?"

"Oh yes."

"I think I'm supposed to go that way," she pointed. "Wait." She looked around. "I'm not sure. I think I'm lost." Tears quickly welled in her eyes. "I want my daddy."

The lady gave the little hand a reassuring squeeze. "It's all right I know the way. Come, let us go before it gets dark and your daddy begins to worry about you."

Sasha sniffed away her tears. "I live in Rose Cottage."

"I know."

"But we don't have any roses. Summer says they've been gone for a long time."

"Perhaps they'll come back again one day."

"I like flowers. Summer says they were very pretty."

"Yes they were," the woman said in a voice blurred with melancholy.

Marcus and Summer had been so caught up in their conversation and with her rush to dig up the ring, neither of them remembered to include Sasha, nor did they notice that she was no longer in the garden. Marcus filled in the small hole and stuck the spade in the ground at the exact spot while Summer held the ring in the palm of her hand.

"I remember Rose wearing it." She spoke softly, touching the ring with reverence.

"What do you think about putting a marker right here to denote the place where she was married and for our wedding, too?" Marcus asked.

Her eyes misted with tears. "I'd love that and I know Rose would have, too." She put the ring back into the box. "I can't wait to marry you. You are the sweetest man."

"Don't let word get around. I wouldn't want people to think I'm a pushover."

She laughed and drew him back down onto the bench. "Do you have someone to be your best man?"

"I was thinking I'd like Ted to do the honors."

"Really? I know he'd be very touched, but what about Jonathan?"

"He really is very fond of you, Summer. I'd bet he'd love to give the bride away, unless you'd rather have Ted do that. We can easily switch their roles."

"I'll talk to Ted, but I think he'll be fine being the best man. He believed in you even when I refused to listen. I'll make it even more tempting for him by asking Holly to be my attendant and Sasha can be a junior bridesmaid. She deserves to take part since she's the one who wanted us to be married in the first place."

"She'll be ecstatic." He suddenly swore under his breath and rose from the bench.

"We forgot to let her help dig up the ring."

Summer jumped up. "Oh Marcus, I feel terrible. She was so looking forward to it."

"Hopefully she'll forgive us when she finds out she's going to be in the wedding."

He looked toward the area where she'd been playing. "Now where is that little imp?"

He called her name and walked through the garden with Summer close behind him. She was the first one to spot the open gate and pointed toward it. "Marcus, look."

"That better not mean what I think it does." They hurried through and quickly scanned the area. He stared toward the nearby woods. "I have a bad feeling about this."

She squeezed his arm. "She may have gotten tired of waiting and gone in the house. Wait here while I go check." She left him and sprinted toward the backdoor.

"Any luck?" he asked in an anxious voice, as soon as she returned.

She bit her bottom lip and shook her head. "Sorry, no."

"Damn it! She knows she's not supposed to leave the garden on her own."

"Let's take a few minutes to look around. I'm sure she hasn't gone too far."

"I hope to God you're right."

They walked briskly away from the garden toward the woods. Summer's eyes quickly scanned the area, as fear made her heart pick up its rhythm. "We'll have to call for extra help if we don't find her. It's going to be dark soon and these woods are pretty big."

"Come on," he urged and grabbing her by the hand, broke into a run.

CHAPTER TWENTY-NINE

Sasha walked trustingly alongside the woman, but there were times she wanted to stop and pick up things that caught her eye. "I want to take some stuff home to show my daddy and Summer."

"You will have everything you need later."

"But why can't I have it now?" she asked with a hint of rebellion in her voice.

"Because your father is looking for you and we don't want to keep him waiting any longer. You mustn't fret, Sasha. I'll make sure you have what you want and also some surprises. Go to your back steps in the morning and everything will be there."

"You promise?"

"Yes, I promise and you must in turn give me your promise that you will never go into the woods without your father or Summer until you're older. Do you understand?"

"Uh-huh."

"That's a good girl." They walked on a little further before the woman stopped. "This is as far as I will go, but you must stay right here. Your father is calling for you."

"I don't hear anything."

"You will. He'll be here any minute."

"Will that bad lady come back?" she asked looking around her with new fear.

"Not today." She bent and kissed Sasha on both cheeks. Her hand brushed briefly over the dark curls before she stepped back "Goodbye, Sasha."

"Goodbye. Don't forget my forest stuff."

"I won't."

"Are you going to come back when I go play with the fishes?"

"I'm not sure, but remember you mustn't go there alone."

Sasha nodded and watched the woman disappear into the thickness of the forest. She didn't like being alone and called after her, but it was her father's voice that answered.

"Sasha!" She whirled around just as Marcus burst into the small clearing with Summer right behind him. He immediately dropped to his knees and grabbed Sasha in a snug embrace. "Oh baby girl, you scared your daddy."

She gave a little grunt. "You're squeezing me too tight."

He eased his grip. "What did I tell you about coming here alone?"

"I just wanted to see where the squirrel lived, but he kept running away from me. I won't do it again, Daddy. I promised the lady."

He frowned. "What lady?" he asked, quickly scanning the immediate area.

"The nice lady by the water."

Summer inhaled a sharp breath. "Oh sweetheart, you mustn't go near the stream on your own. The water is much too dangerous now."

"I know. The lady told me. She said you and Daddy could bring me back when the water isn't so fast and I can let the fishes come and kiss my toes."

"Did the lady tell you her name?" Marcus wanted to know.

"No."

"How many times have I told you never to go anywhere with strangers?"

"I know Daddy, but they said they knew you."

His eyes narrowed. "They? Did you see more than one person?"

"Uh-huh. There were two ladies. The first one had mean eyes and she scared me, but the other lady was pretty and nice. She had on funny black shoes and a long dress."

Summer gasped and Marcus gave her a sharp look as he stood up with Sasha in his arms. "Let's get you home, young lady."

Later that evening after they'd tucked Sasha in bed, Summer and Marcus sat drinking coffee. "Thank goodness we were able to find Sasha so easily."

"Amen to that. It felt like a couple of years had been knocked off my life when I realized she was missing. Jonathan must have been misinformed about Rose Cottage being the only house near these woods."

"No, he's right. I take it you're asking because of the women Sasha said she saw."

He nodded. "I talked to her while you were cooking dinner. Apparently the first woman showed up outside the garden and they went chasing after a squirrel."

"What about the other one?"

"Sasha didn't see her until she was at the stream."

"So she didn't see where either of them came from?"

"No, but she said the first one kept making her lean closer to the water even when she didn't want to." Both his eyes and voice were hard with barely suppressed anger.

Summer clutched a hand to her chest. "She could have fallen in so easily."

"Just thinking about it makes my blood run cold. Whoever did this has to be sick in the head to want to drown a child." His hand clenched on the arm of his chair. "Thank God the other woman was there to pull her back in time."

"Yes." Summer cleared her throat. "Um, what happened to the mean one?"

"I don't think Sasha knows. The way she described it, one moment she was there and the next moment she was gone. The good woman took her to the spot where we found her. She told Sasha I was calling her, but Sasha says she didn't hear anything."

Summer raised a brow. "That sounds odd."

"It gets stranger. According to Sasha, the woman knew our names and that we lived in Rose Cottage. Besides the black shoes, she said the lady wore a long white apron over her dress." He wagged his head back and forth and smiled. "It seems my little girl is emulating you and has made up quite a story to add to her adventure."

Summer felt a chill go through her and her hand trembled when she set her cup down. "She may not have made it up, Marcus. There's been talk for years about people seeing a woman wandering the woods dressed like that."

He cocked a brow. "Sounds like someone's been playing an

elaborate hoax. But if there really was a woman who helped Sasha I'd like to thank her, even if she is a kook."

"It's no hoax and it wasn't a kook." She stared at him wide eyed. "It was..."

"One of your fairytale creatures?" he teased, cutting her off.

It made her feel sick and afraid, but she had to tell him. "It was Rose."

He frowned. "If that was meant to be a joke I don't find it very amusing."

"I'm not joking. I bet it was Rose who kept Sasha from falling into the water."

"What on earth are you talking about? The woman died years ago."

"There are such things as ghosts," she said giving him a wary look.

He let out a snort. "Don't tell me you actually believe in that kind of nonsense."

She heard the barely veiled cynicism in his voice and felt the slightest tightening in her belly. "Over the years, there have been too many sightings by different people each giving the same description for me not to believe that it could very well be Rose."

"The hell you say."

"Rose may be dead in the flesh, but I believe her spirit lives on. It makes sense knowing that this cottage and that forest are where she spent all of her adult life," she quickly explained when she saw amusement dancing in his eyes.

"I disagree. Dead is dead and even if what you're saying is possible why hasn't she been haunting the house instead of floating, or whatever it is she does, in the woods?"

She thought about the feeling she'd had that someone was in the bedroom with her and Marcus. "For all we know she may come into the house. Other times she might be restless and stay outside searching for her husband."

"Searching for her husband? I thought you said he died a long time before she did."

"He did, but Rose told me he promised to come back for her. She could be waiting here for his return."

"You mean as one dead person waiting to keep a rendezvous

with another dead person?" He let out a grunt of laughter, wagging his head back and forth when she nodded. "Are you telling me that you've actually seen this so-called apparition?"

She could feel the heat of temper beginning to rise at his belittling tone, but did her best to keep it under control. "No, but I told you others have."

"They sound like a bunch of crackpots."

She clenched her teeth. "They're all completely sane, respectable townspeople."

"Townspeople. Well, that explains a lot. No doubt they all have businesses that would benefit from having tourists believe there's a ghost cavorting in yon forest. I have to give them credit for coming up with the idea, though."

"If you'd believe me then a dozen people lying shouldn't matter to you."

He sighed. "Summer, even if you all thought you saw something it can't have been Rose. It doesn't make sense. For one thing, she was an old woman when she died. Sasha said the lady she saw was pretty. Even a child that young isn't going to mistake pretty for as old as Rose must have been when she passed away."

"Maybe she appears in a form that shows what she looked like when she was younger, rather than the age at the time of her death. She might be the same as she was the last time her husband saw her. She was quite young when they married."

He rolled his eyes toward the ceiling. "I had no idea you were a ghost chaser. But I guess I shouldn't be surprised you'd be obsessed growing up with all this around you."

"I am not obsessed," she denied with anger simmering ever closer to the boiling point. "It was what happened with Sasha today that brought it to my mind."

"Believe what you like, but none of it has convinced me that it was Rose out there today. What about the other woman Sasha said she saw? I noticed you haven't mentioned her. Who is she supposed to be?" he asked.

Summer twisted her fingers in her lap. Perhaps he was right that she was more susceptible because she had lived here all her life and had grown up around the cottage. But she felt certain his stubbornness was partly responsible for clouding his objectivity.

Loathed to accept that the situation was beyond redemption, she plunged on.

"I'm not sure, but it may have been Rose's twin sister."

His eyes narrowed. "What the hell is this? You never said there was a sister."

"I don't know much about her, but apparently she wasn't a very nice person."

He rubbed a hand over his face and grimaced. "She's dead too, I suppose."

"Yes." She was worried about Sasha's safety and wanted to tell him she'd seen Rena, but his sarcasm made it obvious he wouldn't believe her.

"Why am I not surprised? My God Summer, this whole thing is ludicrous and frankly I'm surprised you would buy into any of it. I know you were fond of Rose, but you can't bring her back by believing she's hanging around here."

Realizing that she wasn't going to be able to convert him to her way of thinking, Summer tried another approach. "Did it ever occur to you that Rose may have made it possible for us to meet and have Jonathan come to me?"

"What nonsense are you talking about now? I told you I'm the one who sent him."

"But you didn't know he was Rose's relative at first. She could have arranged for you to meet because of his connection, so we'd get together and marry at the cottage."

He shook his head. "No, Summer. You're trying to make a fairytale out of this, but it won't work. I've known Jonathan for years. It's a fluke that things turned out the way they did. It sounds to me as though you've been making up stories so long you're having trouble separating fact from fiction."

This time his criticism stung too much to be ignored. "So you think I'm crazy?'

A deep flush spread over his face. "Don't be ridiculous."

She practically leaped out of her chair. "Oh, so now I'm being stupid."

His eyes flashed with a sudden fiery anger of his own. "For God's sake, stop trying to put words in my mouth. I never said that."

Frustration tore through patience. "Your words suggested it. I know what's real and what isn't and whether you believe in them or not, there are such things as ghosts and who's to say what rules they follow? You want everything to be nice and tidy. I happen to believe there isn't always a logical explanation for everything that happens in life."

"I realize that, but don't you think you're being naïve about this ghost thing?"

She grabbed her purse off a cabinet. "I may be naïve, but at least I'm not so close-minded that I put restrictions inside my head." She slung the strap over her shoulder and snatched up her sweater that was lying on the back of a nearby chair.

He frowned. "Where are you going?"

"Home!"

He reached her in two quick strides. "I thought you were spending the night."

"I changed my mind." Her eyes had hardened along with her tone of voice.

She started to open the door, but he stopped her by putting his hand over hers on the knob. "I can't believe you're leaving because I don't share your viewpoint. Aren't I entitled to my own opinion without having you go running off in a huff?"

"It's more than an opinion, Marcus. We obviously don't share the same philosophy on something I feel very strongly about. I knew Rose, you didn't."

"I'm sorry if I upset you, but you're asking me to accept a theory that's based on speculation and emotion. You don't have any real facts to justify your position."

"Oh well, how silly of me to think that a hard core businessman like yourself would consider anything that wasn't written down in black and white."

"I said I was sorry. Would you rather I lie and pretend to believe something that I don't? Is that was you want? I was trying to be honest with you, especially when I saw how upset you were that I kept it a secret about knowing Jonathan."

Summer supposed he had a point, but she was still too angry to admit it. "I'm not asking you to lie, but I would have expected a little more tolerance in regard to my feelings on the matter, particularly since you already know how much Rose and this house mean to me. If you can't believe in Rose, the least you could do is believe in me."

"You're not being fair, Summer. We're talking about two different things here." He tried to draw her to him, but she jerked away. "I don't want you to go. Not like this."

The eyes she turned on him were fierce with temper that smothered a deep hurt. "I have to. I need to think about some things and I need to be alone to do it. You know how it is with those of us who suffer from overactive imaginations."

"I jammed my foot in my mouth in the heat of the moment. I didn't mean to sound so callous in expressing my opinion."

"Didn't you?" she asked keeping her tone cool.

"No!" Temper skidded around the edges of his voice. "We had a dispute. You had your say and I had mine. I can't understand why you'd want to open up old wounds."

"I'm not trying to open them; I'm trying to heal them."

"No matter what the cost to us? You need to stay, so we can work this out."

"I'm not in the mood." She stormed outside slamming the door behind her.

Marcus hesitated a few seconds before grabbing the door handle intending to stop her, but the door refused to open. He stood there yanking and swearing, unaware of the ghostly white face with its leering grin watching him through a window.

CHAPTER THIRTY

The argument had upset her more than she liked to admit. Marcus's unwillingness to consider her viewpoint bothered Summer because he had seemed so enthralled with the idea of finding Rose's wedding ring and being married at the cottage. She could only hope he hadn't been humoring her just to make sure she went through with the marriage. She shook her head knowing that attitude wasn't going to help anything. As far as she was concerned, false starts made for false endings.

Although they hadn't spent a lot of time discussing her, Summer was worried about what may have been Rena's part in luring Sasha to the stream. It was too disturbing to think about and too upsetting not to. There was definitely something going on. She'd experienced some kind of force and suspected the storm hadn't been totally responsible.

Summer felt this was all the more reason why it was imperative for Marcus believe it had been Rose who had protected Sasha. She felt certain if he'd heard the voice inside his head pleading for help he wouldn't be so quick to dismiss Rose's ghost. Rose might be waiting for their wedding to take place before she could be at peace. That might also be the only way she could be free of Rena. It was as though things could not come to a complete circle until they played their parts. Summer couldn't explain why she felt this way, but something inside told her Rose wouldn't be able to join her husband until she and Marcus had their wedding ceremony in the garden.

But somehow she knew it wasn't enough that Marcus married her. He also had to genuinely believe in all the rest or Rose would be left to wander endlessly waiting to be reunited with her beloved. Summer couldn't explain why she knew this and if she couldn't offer tangible proof, it was unlikely Marcus would ever accept her theory. Without his acceptance, she feared she would never be able to close the gulf between them.

She wondered if she'd been wise to rush off. She hated that they'd fought so soon after their reconciliation. It wouldn't be easy for anyone to accept the things she'd been telling him about. No one could agree with what another person said one hundred per cent of the time unless he or she wanted to be a total doormat. Poor Marcus, he was probably beginning to think he'd gotten himself tangled up with a hellcat.

She stopped the car and leaned her forehead against the steering wheel. She didn't know which one of them to blame for their argument. Should she be infuriated with him for not believing her? Or was she the one at fault for bringing Rose up to him in the first place? She blew out a heavy sigh wishing for the normality in her life she'd once taken for granted.

She wasn't sure how things were going to turn out, but she did know it was time to stop running away. The adult thing was to learn how to properly communicate with Marcus. How could their relationship ever hope to stand the test of time otherwise?

Marcus had tried to go after Summer when she'd slammed out of the house, but the lock had jammed and by the time he'd finally gotten the door open, she was gone.

Frustrated, he poured himself a of couple fingers of Scotch. He had a nasty suspicion he was going to need it to dull his senses. He drained the glass and slumped down onto a chair trying to pinpoint how things had gone wrong.

He leaned forward and pressed his fingertips to his eyes. He wished he could accept what Summer told him if only to appease her, especially now that he realized how she'd used anger to blanket what he was certain had been fear that he had seen in her eyes. But when people died that was the end of it. Surely, if that wasn't so, Sasha would have seen Diana's ghost. God knows, the child had certainly grieved enough to evoke such a phenomenon.

He huffed out a breath and got to his feet feeling sick with disappointment that things had gone so badly tonight. God help him, but the possibility that he might have driven Summer away for good terrified him. The only thing he could do was to wait and hope she'd call him. If not, it looked like he was going to end up on his knees after all.

He was just reaching over to turn off the lamp when he heard a car drive up.

His heart leaped at the possibility that Summer may have changed her mind and come back. He hurried to the door and stepped outside as she scrambled out of the car. He met her halfway and she literally threw herself into his arms.

"I don't want us to be apart. I can't stand it." Her cheeks, pale ovals in the moonlight shimmered with tears. "I keep saying the wrong things. Forgive me."

"No, no it was my fault," he rushed to reassure her while raining kisses over her face. "I was being pigheaded. I didn't understand how important this is to you. I promise I'll try to be more sympathetic in the future."

"But you do have a right to your own opinion. I was being too sensitive. I don't want to be the cause of more unhappiness for you. You've had enough in your life already. I hate myself for hurting you. I want to stay here tonight if you still want me."

His answer was to swing her up into his arms and carry her to the bedroom where he laid her on the bed and quickly stripped away their clothes. The adrenaline that had kicked in during their argument was back in full force. Seduction, hot and sweet sizzled in the air lending a charged energy to their lovemaking.

Passion escalated. Need built. Their bodies literally sank into each other. They moved together with a ferocity born of sheer desperation to tame the emotions that roared through them. They moaned in unison, as lust gradually swelled to a mutual crescendo until the sound burst into a duet of pleasure that echoed around the room.

Summer snuggled contently against him. "I thought you might come after me."

"I tried, but the damn door jammed on me."

She frowned and looked at him. "Really? That's funny, it opened okay for me."

"I know and it was working fine again as soon as you'd driven out of sight."

She wondered if Rena was responsible, but quickly buried

the thought. "I'm starving. Want to wrestle for who gets us something to eat." she said keeping the mood light.

"You bet I do." He nipped her around the waist and pinned her to the mattress making her squeal with laughter.

Several minutes later, they lay panting and he surprised her by bringing up Rose. "I'd like you to hold off on eating if you don't mind and tell me how Rose had us meet."

"Really? Are you sure you want to discuss it so soon after our quarrel?"

"It's important to you. I want to understand. Besides, if we fight again I like the way we make up." He brushed her lips in a kiss. "How was she the catalyst?"

"It's just some thoughts I had."

"Tell me," he urged.

She sat up. "Okay, but if you don't like it, remember this was your idea. The smallest detail might be important, so we can't leave anything out. Let's start with Jonathan. How did you meet him?"

"At a cocktail party given by his law firm."

"I guess you used to go to a lot of those kinds of things."

He made a face. "Not if I could help it. I usually found them to be boring."

"Then why did you go?"

"Unfortunately they were necessary to make new contacts for my business. I wasn't actually planning to go to that particular one, but the person I had slated to attend had to cancel because he broke out in hives from eating too many strawberries. The crazy thing was the guy had never been allergic to them before."

"Really? That's interesting. Rose used to get hives from strawberries."

"That's just a coincidence."

"Maybe. Anyway, so you went to a party you didn't want to go to. How did you get into a conversation with Jonathan and what was it that caused you to become good friends?"

"I was standing next to him in a group when one of the men told him about an estate sale that included quite a large library. The conversation led to a discussion on limited editions. I mentioned that I had been collecting since I was a kid. Things took off from there. I found out later that he had a special interest in fairytales, which was quite helpful when I wanted him to hear your tape. But none of this explains how Rose was involved in our meeting," he reminded her.

"I'm getting to that," she said with a smile.

He pulled himself up into a sitting position and stared at her. "Why do I get the feeling you're about to drop one of your little bombshells?"

She laughed. "Well, it's nothing as momentous as Jonathan being related to Rose, but it does have a kind of serendipitous quality to it. Remember how I fell and knocked you back into the pool on the Disneyland trip?"

"How could I? It was one of the most significant incidents of my life."

She let out an unladylike snort. "Nice job trying to make me forget I was such a klutz. Do you recall how it was I happened to fall?'

"You said you tripped on your towel."

"Not just any towel. Do you remember what it looked like?"

"No. I was too busy concentrating on your sexy body." He leaned over and kissed the soft skin above one breast.

She frowned at him, distracted for the moment. "What do you mean sexy? There was nothing sexy about that rag of a bathing suit I had on. It barely covered my boobs and butt. It's a wonder I wasn't arrested for indecent exposure."

"Rag or not, you were a real turn on. I was especially aware of these beauties," he said and buried his face between her breasts.

She choked out a laugh and pushed him away. "Will you stop that? I'm trying to conduct some serious research here."

"So am I." He growled and drew a rosy tip into his mouth making her shiver.

"You continue to do that and we're never going to get to the facts."

He sighed and pulled away.

"Back to my towel. Since you can't seem to remember this vital clue, I'll remind you. It wasn't one of the hotel towels. I was using one I'd brought from home."

"Is this towel thing leading up to something?" he asked.

She ignored the exasperation in his voice. "Yes. Guess who gave it to me?"

He went very still. "Are you going to tell me it was from Rose?"

"Give the man a gold star. It was a birthday present and I loved it so much that I've always used it sparingly, so it wouldn't wear out."

"That's just another..."

"Coincidence? Let's go over how many flukes we have here." She held up her fingers and began to tick each incident off one by one. "A guy has an allergic reaction to a food that's never bothered him before, which makes you have to go to a party you wouldn't have gone to otherwise."

"People sometimes develop allergies to different things as they get older."

"True, but isn't it interesting that this should have occurred at the very same time as Jonathan's cocktail party? You might never have met him otherwise and it's doubtful you'd have become such good friends if you hadn't discovered you both enjoy old books. And of all the men at that party he's the one who just happens to be related to Rose."

"There's always the possibility we'd eventually meet at a book sale."

"But you didn't. Then you have how we met. You took Sasha to Disneyland for her birthday. I was there because Buster's birthday happened to be at the same time."

"Parents take their kids there all the time."

"That's true, but don't you think it's odd with all the hotels available that we were staying at the same one?"

"I suppose." He wasn't about to tell her the first two he'd called were booked.

"Plus, we wouldn't have been at Disneyland at the same time if it wasn't for the fact that both Sasha and Buster were celebrating their birthdays, and there's also my towel."

He leaned back and closed his eyes. "Rose's towel."

"That's right. Do you want to know a couple other interesting tidbits about that?"

He opened one eye. "No, but you're going to tell me, aren't

you?"

She patted his cheek. "That's what I'm here for, sweetie. I think Rose somehow arranged it, so I'd fall in the pool right in the spot where you'd be." He rolled his eyes, but Summer ignored him and went on. "That's not all. I almost didn't take it because it took up so much room in my suitcase. I was trying to shove it back on the top closet shelf when a tote bag fell out and landed on the floor."

He groaned. "Don't tell me, the bag was from Rose, too."

"No, my sister-in-law gave it to me."

Marcus opened both eyes. "Are you saying this involves two ghosts in cahoots?"

"I'm not ruling it out. Rebecca and I were very close and she knew Rose, too. I understand you have reservations and I don't blame you. But if you look at this logically there is somewhat of a pattern to everything that's happened. That should appeal to you."

"You mean like an orderly sequence?"

"Why not? How many coincidences does it take before a person begins to believe that maybe, granted a big maybe for you, some events simply can't be explained?"

He sighed. "I don't know. I'll have to get back to you on that one."

She yawned and closed her eyes. "You'll feel better about it in the morning."

Despite Summer's theory, he didn't trust coincidences. He had to find more concrete evidence to the mystery, especially if he'd put Sasha in danger by coming here.

CHAPTER THIRTY-ONE

They awoke the next morning to Sasha's excited chatter, as she came running into the kitchen carrying a bucket. "Look! Look! The nice lady didn't forget."

Summer turned from the pan on the stove where she'd been stirring eggs. Marcus set his coffee cup down and frowned. "What do you have there, Sasha?"

"The lady from the woods said she'd leave me some stuff I wanted." Little hands dove eagerly into the depths of the bucket and held up flowers, acorns, and pebbles.

"Where did you get those things? Do not tell me you went back into the woods."

"No Daddy, I told you, the nice lady I saw yesterday got them for me."

Summer made a sound in her throat. Marcus gave her a sharp look. "What?"

"That bucket was one of Rose's favorites."

"How can you be so sure it's the same one? It could have been left by one of the workers during the remodeling. Those buckets have been standard for years."

"I know because I gave it to her. See where I scratched my initials on the side?"

"Can I go look at my stuff now, Daddy?" Sasha cut in.

"All right, but take it outside and don't wander off; breakfast will be ready soon." He waited until she left before turning back to Summer. "Maybe it is the same bucket, but I'm going to have to talk to Sasha about making up another story about that woman."

"You don't believe it was Rose who gathered those things for her, do you?"

He ran long fingers through his hair. "To tell you the truth, I don't know what to believe anymore."

Summer didn't miss Marcus stealing glances at her throughout the morning. She knew he was struggling with her latest claim. He'd questioned Sasha in great detail, but the child never wavered in her assertion that the filled bucket had been left for her.

She looked out the window and watched him walking around the garden and just outside the gate picking up and examining bits and pieces similar to some of the things in Rose's bucket. He seemed determined to find concrete evidence to disprove her claim and she couldn't help feeling a little annoyed that he continued to be so stubborn.

He brought several different examples into the house and laid them on the counter. "I think this explains where Sasha obtained her treasure trove."

He sounded so satisfied Summer hated to dispute his claim. "I know how important it is to convince yourself that Rose had nothing to do with the things in that bucket, Marcus." She pointed to the items he'd collected. "These things were easy enough to find close to the cottage, but the flowers in the bucket only grow deep in the woods and those multicolored pebbles Sasha showed us can't be found anywhere else except in that stream. Those things are exclusive to their particular spots."

"Sure you're not making that up?" he said, his tone only half teasing.

Her eyes clouded with hurt, stung by his persistent skepticism. "I wouldn't do that just so I could prove you wrong. If you can't take my word for it go to the local library. There have been several articles written about them."

He shook his head. "Never mind."

"I wish I could make things easier for you, but I thought you believed me."

"I'm trying and it would help if you'd stop putting a stranglehold on me."

She pressed the heel of her hand to her forehead and closed her eyes for a moment before looking at him again. "Let me see if I can explain something to you." She inhaled a deep breath. "The wind blows. You feel and hear it, but you don't allow yourself to experience anything else. As for me, that same rush of air holds a potpourri of possibilities."

His brows drew together in a frown. "Like what?"

She licked dry lips. "Voices; sensations."

His eyes widened with unmistakable shock. She rushed to apologize, but he waved her efforts away with an impatient shake of his head. "Give it a rest, Summer" he said in a voice filled with warning. "I've obviously got a long way to go before we find equal ground here, but that's my problem and I'll have to deal with it on my own."

Summer left with a heavy feeling inside and could only hope it would pass. She went directly to her store and started on the many tasks that needed taking care of, as she tried to block out the worry that gnawed at her. There was mail to go through, bills to pay, shelves to stock, and stories to select for her next tape. Not to mention a wedding to plan.

Summer looked at her watch and realized she only had a few minutes to get ready for her weekly story time with the children. She'd just slipped into her robe when the first of her audience arrived. She greeted each one by name and a personal comment. As soon as they had all gathered, a hush fell over the group and she opened a book while children and adults alike waited patiently to be transformed into the world of fantasy.

It was a busy day, which meant she hadn't been able to finish all the things she needed to do by closing time. As much as she hated to, Summer called Marcus and begged off joining him and Sasha for dinner. He not only accepted her decision, but suggested she not worry about coming at all that evening. The fact that he didn't bother to put up a token protest and actually sounded relieved took a large bite out of her ego.

Despite having promised Ted she wouldn't work late at the store, Summer knew it was the best time to get the most done. Once she'd completed all the chores for the store, she allowed herself time to concentrate on the wedding. She decided she needed to make a list, so she wouldn't forget anything.

She pulled out a tablet and wrote: WEDDING at the top. It didn't take long before the page was filled. Who knew there would be so many little details even for something as small as she was planning? She was reading over the list when the telephone rang echoing loudly around the quiet room and making her body twitch in response.

She braced herself in case it was Ted calling to lecture her about working late, but hoped it would be Marcus inviting her to come back to the cottage for a nightcap.

"Hello?'

"Twice now you've failed to protect Sasha. You aren't fit to be her mother."

Her hand gripped the receiver and her heart leaped into her throat. "What?" She slid off the stool on shaky legs. "Who is this?"

"Someone who cares about that sweet child. Call off the wedding and leave Marcus be. He belongs to Diana. Always has; always will."

Summer didn't think it sounded like Patrice or Mrs. Gwen, but either could be disguising her voice or having someone else phone for them. She took a deep breath and gathered her courage. "I'm not calling off anything and for your information, Sasha is safe with me. Also, in case you've forgotten, Diana is dead."

"Call off the wedding," the raspy voice repeated. "Or suffer the consequences."

"I have every intention of getting married, so you can just..."

The voice cut her off. "Don't say you haven't been warned."

The line went dead.

Although she tried not to feel intimidated by the strange call, her heart was beating much too fast and she was shaking. Her eyes nervously scanned the room as though she expected someone to appear out of nowhere. Shadows began to take on menacing shapes making her feel alone and defenseless. Her cozy store suddenly didn't feel so secure.

She rushed to lock up and looking fearfully over her shoulder, wished she had a can of Mace as she fled to her car. She drove home, rushed upstairs, and bolted the door. Her answering machine was blinking. She hesitated a few seconds before pushing the play button. But whoever it was had hung up without leaving a message. She pressed a hand to her churning midsection certain it was the same person who'd called the store.

She had to let Marcus know. Her hands shook as she punched in his number, but no one answered. She looked at her watch and saw that it was almost midnight. He'd probably gone to bed. Her stomach muscles clenched with anxiety and her head pounded with nerves. She crawled into bed fully dressed with the bedroom light burning bright.

After spending a restless night. morning couldn't come soon enough for her. Desperate to talk to Marcus, she'd barely left her bed when the phone rang with another warning. This time the voice threatened harm to Ted and the boys if she didn't give Marcus up. Shock and fear warred with anger now, as she fought the sick feeling whirling around inside. She picked up the phone to warn Ted.

"Jesus," he breathed. "Have you contacted the police?"

"No. I called Marcus, but he didn't answer."

"Better let the authorities know and don't go anywhere until you talk to them. Try Marcus again. He's going to want to know about this. Be careful, Sis," he urged.

"You, too. The boys..." She swallowed down the panic. "I'm afraid."

"We'll be fine. Anyone cowardly enough to make threats over the phone is probably too chicken to do much else. Would you feel better if I came over?"

"No, no. You take care of the kids. I'll be okay as soon as I contact the police."

She hung up and made the call. They promised to send someone to question her.

She called Marcus and this time he answered. She repeated her story.

"My God, are you all right?" he demanded in a tense voice.

"Yes, other than being a little unnerved."

"Why didn't you let me know last night?"

"I called, but you didn't answer. It was late. I assumed you'd gone to bed."

"I must have been in the shower. I'm very sorry about this, Summer."

"I'm more concerned for Ted and the boys than myself.

Could it be Patrice?"

"I seriously doubt it. She's found herself a man and the last I heard they were honeymooning abroad. This time for real," he added.

"It could have been Mrs. Gwen."

"Mrs. Gwen? What are you talking about? Why would she do such a thing?"

Summer told him about her conversation with the housekeeper and receiving the defaced magazine article. She heard his quick hiss of breath. "Before you jump all over me for not telling you, I didn't say anything because I assumed that she was protecting your wife's memory."

"You should have told me anyway. Do you think I would have allowed her to get away with saying something like that in my own house?"

"No, but Mrs. Gwen belonged there more than I did."

"What nonsense. She was just the housekeeper for God's sake."

"That may be so, but it doesn't change the fact that she hates me. She feels I'm trespassing on Diana's domain and obviously the person who made the call agrees."

"I appreciate your discretion, but damn it Summer, you should have let me know. In view of what you've just told me, Mrs. Gwen could very well be indirectly involved in these phone calls. What did the woman's voice sound like?"

"Um...kind of raspy with a hint of an accent."

He was quiet for a few seconds. "Listen to me. I want you to stay with Ted as a precaution until I say otherwise."

"I'd rather come and stay at the cottage with you."

"I'm afraid that won't be possible, as I'll be going away for a couple of days."

"Going away?" She frowned. "Isn't this kind of sudden? Where are you going?"

"To see a friend." His voice had gone dangerously quiet.

"I don't understand. The police will need to question you. You can't go off now."

"I'll deal with them when I return."

"But Marcus . . ." she started to protest, but he'd already hung up leaving her staring at the humming receiver and her head buzzing with unanswered questions.

CHAPTER THIRTY-TWO

Summer was in Ted's living room that night sharing a pot of coffee with him after they'd put the boys to bed. "I wish Marcus had told me what he was going to do."

"From what you've told me, I have a feeling he knows who called you."

She nodded. "I think he does, too. He said he was going to see a friend. It doesn't make sense. What kind of a friend would make threatening phone calls for heaven's sake?"

"A jealous one."

"Oh God, not that again." She kneaded her temples. "I'm getting pretty fed up with all these people that insist on trying to keep me from marrying Marcus."

"Yeah, but the best way to hit back is to go ahead with the wedding."

Summer took Ted's advice and filled the hours with work and wedding plans, but underneath all the busyness she felt a sense of unease. It wasn't only the phone calls that disturbed her. Fear for her family's safety and anxiety over Marcus's reaction had her stomach tied in knots. By the time he finally called and said everything had been taken care of her nerves had left her edgy and short tempered.

"You know who made the calls, don't you? That's why you went away."

"Yes."

She waited for more, but he remained silent. "Are you going to give me an explanation or not, Marcus?"

"I said I've taken care of it."

"Did you now? How nice for you, but I'm the one who's been threatened and my family endangered. I have a right to know what the devil is going on."

He hesitated a moment. "It was Constance, the woman who runs the gallery that displays Diana's work. I suspected as much when you described her voice."

"She doesn't even know me. Why would she do such a thing?"

"Mrs. Gwen had called to talk to Sasha and, Sasha being a child, she couldn't resist telling her about the episode in the woods. Mrs. G. told Constance and between the two of them they decided they should step in and speak on Diana's behalf."

"They must have been very fond of her to go to such lengths."

"She did tend to inspire loyalty in people, but I assure you Diana would not have approved of their tactics."

"Have you talked to the police yet?"

"Yes, but I didn't tell them I knew who was responsible. I'm not minimizing what they did, but I'm hoping you won't file charges. I know I'm asking a lot, but it'd mean a great deal to me if you'd let this go. I'd prefer to protect Diana's name for Sasha's sake."

"What about the threat to Ted and the boys?"

"I talked to him and he said he'd leave it up to you."

"I don't think it's fair that those women aren't being punished, especially for scaring me about hurting Ted and the boys."

"I know and I'm sorry they won't be suffering the penalty they deserve. If it's any consolation, I threatened to pull Diana's work out of the gallery. She's Constance's biggest draw."

"All right; we'll let it go. It's been a difficult time for both of us. Let me come out and cook dinner for you and Sasha. It might help improve our mood."

"I appreciate the offer, but I'm afraid I wouldn't be very good company. I'm still riding some of my anger at Constance and Mrs. Gwen."

Her hand squeezed the phone. "Is that the only reason?"

"What do you mean?"

"I have the feeling something hasn't been quite right between us since the incident with Rose's bucket. I'd hoped by now you would have come to some conclusion about my theory that she brought us together."

"From where I'm sitting your theory is based on an illusion and illusions have a tendency to cloud reality. But accepting your idea isn't the only thing you're expecting from me. Is it, Summer?"

Forcing herself to ignore his comment about illusions, she admitted she thought his willingness to believe was a key factor in helping Rose join her husband. "I wouldn't be pushing it on you except I really do hear and feel things when I'm at the cottage."

He was silent for a moment. "You led me to believe this was a peaceful place."

"It was...is," she quickly amended.

"Yet you claim Rose has actually been communicating with you."

"Yes and I believe if we don't do this properly we may not be happy together."

"Your confidence in me is overwhelming," he replied. "I'm beginning to think you want to marry me just so you can appease the whim of a ghost."

She gasped. "How could you even think that I'd do something so underhanded?"

"How could I not?" He snapped back, his voice edgy with impatience. "I would appreciate it if you'd try believing in me as much as you do in Rose. You don't see me shoving Diana's spirit down your throat."

She squeezed her eyes shut for a moment. "No you haven't and I appreciate that. I shouldn't keep talking about Rose. I'm sorry I've upset you, but I don't know how to resolve the problem without your participation."

"Perhaps it's time for you to work on a solution that doesn't involve me."

As the days went by and there was no word from Marcus, Summer's imagination began to build up reasons for his silence besides her concern for Rose. She started to worry that he was beginning to compare her to Diana. The woman had been strikingly beautiful and obviously very talented. He could very well be regretting his decision to remarry, especially after Diana's friends had gone to such lengths to prevent it.

Summer knew he'd never be able to love her in exactly the same way he had Diana. All she could do was try her best to make him happy. But would it be enough? After witnessing what Ted and the boys had gone through after Rebecca's death, she certainly understood the cruel twist of fate that had cheated Marcus and Sasha from having Diana in their lives. Maybe she didn't have what he needed to fill that void. The very thought brought her close to panic.

She was sitting on her living room floor packing some things that Ted had offered to store when he showed up. "I came to see if you needed any help."

"I'm almost finished, but I could use a hand carrying things out to the car. Do you want some coffee?"

Ted shook his head and sat cross legged on the floor beside her. "I'm good."

Summer picked up a section of newspaper and began wrapping it around a vase. "I never realized how much stuff I've accumulated."

"I told you all those yard sales were going to catch up to you."

"Yeah, but they're so much fun."

He looked over her shoulder at her open bedroom door. "I see you're still sleeping here. I'm surprised you haven't been staying at the cottage with Marcus."

She focused on wrapping. "I got the impression he'd rather I didn't hang around."

He grabbed her hand when she reached for more paper. "What's going on?"

"What's going on with what?"

"You, Sis. What's going on with you?"

"I don't know what you mean."

"Oh come on. You've gone from a happy bride planning her wedding to someone who acts like she's going to her execution. I'm not the only one who's noticed it. Holly said you were distracted at lunch. Have you been getting more threatening phone calls?"

"No."

"Okay, then what gives?"

"Nothing." She started to pick up a picture frame, but he stopped her.

He held both of her hands in his and waited until she looked at him. "It's okay to be scared. That happens to a lot of people before they take on the big M. I couldn't keep any food down for two days before I married Bec, even though I knew I was doing the right thing to marry her."

The memory let a smile slip pass her tense lips. "I remember. You were so nervous we thought you were going to pass out before you could finish saying your vows."

She looked down at their clasped hands and felt her heart thud heavily inside her chest. Ted was more than her brother; he was her best friend, her confidant, and more of a parent to her than their father had ever been. She was never more aware than at this moment of how he loved and cared about her. When she looked at him again tears shimmered in her eyes.

"Ah baby, come here." He pulled her into his arms. "Tell daddy all about it."

Summer sniffled and burrowed her face against his shoulder allowing herself a few seconds to release some tears. "I'm not the one who's having cold feet. It's Marcus, but he won't open up to me."

He began to rub her back in gentle strokes. "Closed the door on you, has he?"

"Locked and bolted."

"What makes you think he wants out?"

"We haven't talked in days, but I'm pretty sure I know what's bothering him."

"What, besides tying himself to a brat like you?" he teased.

She sat back and wiped her eyes on her shirtsleeve. "It's a couple of things. I think he regrets asking me to marry him because he's realized I'll never be able to measure up to his wife. But who can blame him when she was so beautiful and talented?"

"She may have been, but you're not exactly a butt-ugly, no talented waif. Marcus loves you and unless he says otherwise, the wedding's still on."

"Then you don't think he's still in love with Diana?" she asked, hopefully.

"I didn't say that. I can't speak for Marcus. I know I'll never stop loving Rebecca, but that doesn't mean that I can't love someone else. It's just in a different way."

She gnawed on a fingertip and peered at him from beneath her lashes. "That's not the only reason he may want out."

"What else is there?" She told him the things she'd said about Rose. He frowned. "Maybe it wasn't a good idea for you to keep going to the cottage after she died, especially if it's upset you like this."

"The cottage doesn't upset me. I like being there and I think Rose wants me to go."

His frown deepened. "That sounds way too weird, Sis. I realize I didn't know Rose as well as you did and quite frankly I didn't want to. She kind of gave me the creeps the way she lived in the past, barely existed in the present, and longed for the future."

"I never knew you thought that. But it actually sounds kind of poetic."

He waved that away. "Yeah, whatever. What on earth possessed you to lay all that on Marcus, though? You could have at least waited until you were married."

She shook his head. "No. I had to tell him before. I can't get over the feeling he has to accept that Rose's spirit is waiting to be reunited with her husband before Marcus and I marry. It's up to me to make him believe, so we can set her free. I know she's depending on us."

"What makes you so certain it has to be Marcus and you?"

She chewed on her bottom lip for a moment. "It just kind of came to me."

"Came to you?" His frown deepened the lines in his forehead. "Like how?"

"It's hard to explain. I feel things when I'm at the cottage and sometimes I think Rose gets inside my head. I've been bonding with her even more than when I was a kid."

His eyebrows snapped up. "You what? God Summer, you're starting to worry me and I'm beginning to see how Marcus would be freaked out. Give the guy a break. Look at it from his side. How would you feel if he was the one talking to ghosts?"

"I'd probably think he was a nut and run the other way as fast as I could."

"There you go, then. Maybe you should look at all this in a more rational manner before you have a complete meltdown." He hesitated. "I want to say something here and I hope you won't take it the wrong way."

Her mouth tightened. "What, that I need to see a shrink?"

"That'd be your call. I don't like the idea of Rose's ghost using you, but you obviously have things going on I don't see. I'm talking about your reaction to men."

"What are you getting at?"

"I've watched you have crushes on guys, but I know Marcus is the first man you've ever been really serious about. It never bothered me that you didn't have anyone special because I personally believed you would someday. What worried me was the fact that you didn't seem to care. Now that you have a man who matters, don't lose him." He squeezed her hands. "Do what you have to do to make things right with Marcus, Sis."

Her sigh was long and heartfelt. "It isn't only up to me, Ted. I always thought if someone loved you the way they should they would do what's right for you." She rushed on before he could comment. "But I admit I've made things terribly difficult for Marcus."

"Sounds like it."

"The paradox here is that in the process of trying to make him do what I think he should, I've actually pushed him away." She sighed again. "Well, I've been on my own before and I can do it again if I have to." The words rang hollow inside her head while a heavy ache pressed against her chest.

Sadness washed over his face. "That may be so, but one is a lonely number."

CHAPTER THIRTY-THREE

After Ted left, Summer spent the better part of an hour pacing. The situation between Marcus and her couldn't go on like this. The wedding was in two days and for all she knew she could be setting herself up for a no show bridegroom. With a quick prayer, she reached for the telephone. Marcus answered on the fourth ring. "Brennan."

"Hi, it's me," she said striving for cheerfulness despite the slight tremor in her voice. "Did I catch you at a bad time?"

"It is a bit inconvenient, yes." His tone was almost cool.

"I'm sorry, but I thought I would have heard from you by now." She waited for him to reply, but he remained quiet. He had to know he was hurting her and still he let the dreadful silence hang between them. "Marcus?"

"I have a lot on my mind right now. What is it you want, Summer?"

The irritation in his voice made her want to weep. Where was the warmth, the humor she'd come to associate with him? "I was wondering the same thing about you."

"This talking in circles isn't getting us anywhere."

She gathered her pride, determined not to beg. If he wouldn't share his thoughts, how could she ever hope to make things right between them? His reluctance made her come to a painful decision, one she hadn't considered before the call. "No it's not, so I'll make it easy for you. I've decided to go on Jonathan's tour. The wedding will have to be delayed," she said, her earlier decision to stop running away forgotten.

His silence filled the void for several seconds. "I see. Well, that's up to you."

Anger blocked her pain. "No Marcus, it should be up to both

of us, but since you've shut me out, you've given me no other choice. It was my mistake thinking you were trying to understand about Rose."

"I've given you all that I'm capable of right now."

"Which isn't a heck of a lot from where I'm sitting," she blurted out.

"I'm trying to salvage our future, Summer. Did it ever occur to you that you might try to respect my feelings? Or are you the only one entitled to such consideration?"

Her stomach rolled with nerves, as she pushed back the fear that he may be getting ready to reject her completely. "I'm going to leave you alone now before we scrape each other more raw than we already have," she said and hung up before he'd have a chance to hear the tears that clogged her throat. But there was still a part of her that hoped he would immediately call back. She waited, but the phone remained silent.

Summer called Jonathan and told him she wanted to begin the tour immediately, her voice tinged with bitterness.

"Summer, what in the world are you saying? Your wedding is in two days."

"It's been postponed."

Puzzled, he asked no questions, but made arrangements for her to leave in three days. All of her appearances were already set up. He had only to firm up the dates.

A couple of weeks into the tour, Summer and Jonathan were seated in a restaurant, their entrees before them.

"Don't answer if you don't want to, Summer, but may I ask if the decision to postpone your wedding was mutual?"

"It was my suggestion, but Marcus didn't object."

"I see," he said. "Something is amiss, obviously. I know about Patrice's prior trickery in causing the split between you and Marcus, but I also know she's no longer a threat. Now I'm going to infringe on our friendship and ask you a personal question." He cleared his throat. "Is another woman involved here, Summer?"

She thought of Rose. "You could say that."

Jonathan looked at her plate. "You've barely touched a bite.

You're going to be a mere whisper of yourself. Marcus will think I've been starving you.

"I doubt if he'd care. It's been two weeks and I haven't heard one word from him." She didn't realize how the yearning came through in her voice.

"Have you called him?" She shook her head. "May I ask why?"

"Pride, I guess. I thought if I stayed away he might miss me. Guess I was wrong." Summer knew she was feeling sorry for herself, but Marcus's long silence was affecting her appetite.

"You haven't told me why you left. I don't want to pry, but perhaps if you tell me what the problem is I might be able to help."

"It's complicated."

"I'm an attorney, remember? Complicated is what I do."

How could she tell him the ghost of one of his ancestors had come between her and Marcus? To make matters worse, the feeling that she was failing Rose was getting stronger. Nighttime was especially bad when she'd lie in bed trying to ignore the guilt.

"Would you mind if we took a walk?"

He immediately stood up. "I think that would be an excellent idea." He laid several bills on the table, including a generous tip before taking Summer by the elbow.

They stepped outside and walked until they came to the end of a long block. She pointed to a metal bench at the edge of the sidewalk. "Let's sit for a while?"

"All right."

The bottom half of a wooden barrel stood next to the bench with petunias and pansies planted inside. She noticed they needed watering. She switched her gaze to the tall buildings across the street with their endless rows of windows. All the cities they'd traveled to seemed the same to her; busy, crowded places where the air smelled of vehicle exhaust and an overabundance of humanity. She missed the green hills and clear skies at home. There were no chirping crickets or croaking frogs here. She realized she hadn't heard a bird's song or inhaled the sweet scent of freshly mowed grass in all the time she'd been gone. She felt disconnected, lost like an alien who had landed on another planet.

"Do you believe in ghosts, Jonathan?"

"I don't know that I've ever given it much thought. Why do you ask?"

"That's why I left."

His brows knitted together. "Sorry?"

"I left because of Rose." She didn't miss his look of surprise.

"I believe she's haunting the cottage and needs me to marry Marcus to be set free."

"Well now." He stared at her and cleared his throat. "I don't know what to say."

"You think I'm losing my mind, don't you?"

"No, but you obviously feel very strongly about this. Do you have proof?"

He reminded her of Marcus wanting evidence. "I haven't seen her, but I've felt her presence and heard her voice. Sometimes the words come inside my head and sometimes they're revealed in the wind."

He frowned. "The wind is just the wind, Summer."

"Not always. Sometimes it can be more if you listen. I guess I've shocked you."

"A bit. I wasn't prepared for something like this."

"Who would be? Certainly not Marcus."

"In all fairness can you blame him, my dear?"

"Not entirely, but I've done my best to explain myself to him. Maybe if he had a ghost doing brain-twisters inside his head he wouldn't be so quick to deny me. He said he wanted to understand, but now he won't talk. What kind of a man does that make him?"

"An honest one. Marcus won't go blindly into anything he doesn't understand. My guess would be that he's trying to make sense of the things you've told him."

"Sometimes we just have to accept that some things don't make sense. Why does he have to be so analytical about this?"

"Because that's his way." Jonathan's eyes filled with sympathy. "Sometimes certain people or events come along that can be difficult to prioritize in our lives. I understand your frustration, but please don't put yourself in the position where you're forced to choose between Rose and Marcus."

She slumped back against the bench. "I'm afraid I already have."

Marcus and Sasha stood in the kitchen looking in the food cupboard. She had become pale and thin over the last few days with that familiar aura of distress clinging to her that he'd come to dread. She had started waking up sobbing during the night again. He knew it was his fault and he hated himself for it.

He stared at the assorted boxes and canned goods and tried to infuse some enthusiasm into his voice. "Well, let's see what we have here. There's chicken noodle soup, macaroni and cheese, or baked beans. It all sounds pretty good to me. What do you think?"

"I don't like that stuff. I want Summer to come back and cook something for us. When is she coming back, Daddy?"

He didn't miss the anxiousness in her voice and the slight quiver around her mouth. "I've told you I don't know." He barely managed to control the sudden leap of guilt. "How about we check the freezer? I think we have fish sticks in there."

She wrinkled her nose. "I don't like them."

"You used to not be able to get enough of them. Come on Sasha, you have to eat and I've given you several choices."

"I don't like this stuff."

"How about a peanut butter and honey sandwich with a glass of chocolate milk? That's one of your favorites."

"I want Summer to fix me something to eat."

He slammed the cupboard door. "Well she's not here and I'm all you've got, so choose something or I will." Tears gathered in her eyes and he instantly regretted his harsh tone. He ran his hand lightly over her hair. "I'm sorry, baby. I'm not mad at you, but it worries me when you won't eat anything. Please, will you try for me?"

"Can I have a bowl of cereal?"

"That's my girl and I'll have one with you."

He hid his inward groan when she chose one that was so sugary sweet he had visions of gagging trying to get it down. It wasn't much of a dinner, but he supposed he should be happy she was willing to eat something despite its dubious nutritional value.

He filled their bowls with cereal and milk and carried them to the table before pouring himself a mug of coffee. Hopefully the strong brew would help to drown the taste of the brightly colored flakes he was about to bombard his digestive system with.

Sasha sat eating obediently. He took a mouthful from his bowl, grimaced and washed the food down with a couple large gulps of coffee. They ate in silence. He missed her childish chatter. He saw the shadows beneath her eyes and felt the weight of his guilt press down harder. He could see the fatigue and something else that dwelled in her face. He recognized it because he'd seen it every time he looked in his mirror. Loneliness.

"Would you like to watch a little television before bedtime?"

She shook her head.

"I'll read you a story if you'd like."

"I want Summer to read me one of her stories."

"All right. I'll play one of her tapes."

"I want her to come here. You said we were going to marry her. You promised."

The last was spoken through trembling lips that flooded his system with such compassion it made his heart ache. Marcus pushed his chair back from the table and held out his arms to her. "Come here, honey."

She slid off her chair and onto his lap. He held her close and pressed her head against his chest. Light and shadow filtered through the small windows into the room carving out odd shaped patterns. A moth fluttered around the ceiling light dancing ever closer to its fateful end. He watched it thinking how easy it was to be drawn to something you couldn't resist even if you didn't know what the result would bring.

He'd given a lot of thought to Summer's obvious irresistible tug toward Rose. Researching information on the paranormal had provided him with interesting tidbits, but hadn't given him the answers he sought. He still considered the whole business to be a bunch of nonsense and could easily dismiss it as being as insignificant as a pimple on the universe if it wasn't so important to Summer.

But he had a feeling their relationship wasn't going to survive if he didn't come around to accepting her ideas soon. The thought of losing her made his insides grind with tension. Their last telephone conversation still echoed inside his head and had gnawed at him until he felt increasingly troubled.

Her anger and hurt had come through clear enough for him not wanting to risk getting in touch with her. He'd picked up the phone half a dozen times to call Jonathan, but ended up backing away from that conversation as well.

Sasha stirred and lifted her head bringing his attention back to her. "Why did Summer go away?"

"I told you, she went to read her stories to children who are sick in hospitals."

"To make them happy?"

"Yes."

"Will she come back when they feel better?"

Marcus saw her anxious expression, but didn't want to make a promise he might not be able to keep. He held her close in an effort to gain comfort for them both. "I don't know, sweetheart."

CHAPTER THIRTY-FOUR

Marcus called Ted the next day. "I'm about to go nuts. You're the only one I can talk to about what's going on with Summer. I know this is short notice, but can you leave the office for lunch today? Choose wherever is convenient and I'll meet you there."

"It's Sunday."

"It is?" His grunt was filled with embarrassment. "I guess I lost track of the days."

"It happens. Come to the house. I'll slap together some peanut butter and jelly sandwiches and shove the kids outside to play."

"Thanks Ted, I appreciate it."

"No problem."

Even if he didn't glean anything useful from the visit he knew it would be good for Sasha. The news at the breakfast table that he was taking her to play with Teddy and Buster had brought a smile to her face for the first time in days.

The children had wolfed down their food and were outside playing while the men sat at the kitchen table nursing their beer and keeping an eye on them through a window.

"You look like you're down for the count," Ted said.

Marcus heaved a sigh. "Being emotionally blackmailed by a ghost will do that."

Ted wished he could mention Diana was mixed up in there. "That's a tough one."

"Doesn't this whole paranormal thing Summer has going bother you?"

"I don't like it, but I don't have the burden of being part of the solution."

"Yeah. Your sister punches a hole in my heart every time I'm with her. I need her, but I keep letting her slip away. I've mocked her ghost theory. Even when I heard her tears and saw them, I didn't stop. The words are etched in my brain and probably hers, too." His eyes filled with misery. "I don't think I could stand losing another woman I love. I'm not sure I'd be able to climb out if I sank back down into that pit again."

Ted saw the need and recognized the all too familiar pain behind the words. "I hear you. What can I do to help?" he asked.

"How about talking to Rose for me?"

"Sorry, that's not one of my talents. But maybe you ought to try it yourself."

A scowl marred Marcus's handsome features. "I'm a little too close to snapping right now for jokes, Ted. Come on, I'm dying here. I screwed up and let Summer take off on that damn tour. I need to rectify my mistakes if I'm ever going to get her to return."

"I wasn't joking. Think about it. You want to work it out with Summer so she'll come home and in order to do that you've got to find a way to get on the same page."

"Hell, we're not even reading from the same book. I thought she'd appreciate my honesty, but I ended up raising her hackles." He scrubbed a hand over his unshaven face. "She's obviously not about to deviate from her path when it comes to helping Rose."

"Then, again I suggest you try a little man to ghost talk with Rose yourself."

"Jesus Ted. How does one go about something like that? Dial a ghost service and make an appointment or do I just start babbling and hope she'll answer?"

"I don't know about the first, but you might try the second idea." Ted shrugged and took a swallow of beer. "I know it's nuts, but I haven't noticed my sister being in any hurry to return the way things stand now. What do you have to lose?"

"Only my sanity, such as it is."

"If Summer's right about Rose hanging around the cottage and communicating with her, maybe the old girl will reach out to you, too."

Marcus rolled his eyes toward the ceiling. "You're beginning to sound like your sister. Give me a break. I get enough of that crap from Summer."

"It isn't crap to her. She's convinced you've got to agree with her way of thinking to make everything fall into place. I think it's kind of creepy myself, but she's made up her mind. If you fail, you can at least tell her you tried."

"I don't suppose there's any chance she'll forget about Rose."

"Not much."

"Maybe I can make up some story about seeing her."

Ted shook his head. "Not going to happen, buddy. Summer would see right through you. The way I see it your only option is to try and make contact. You asked for my advice, well, that's all I've got."

"No offense, but it sucks."

"So is sitting around waiting for Summer to come back."

"Why couldn't she just go get her hair done or buy something like women do when they're ticked off? Why the hell did everything have to get so complicated?"

"That's probably the same thing Adam asked himself after he took the bite out of Eve's apple. Why don't you let Sasha stay here tonight? Holly's bringing Miles over later and I'm barbecuing hotdogs. Go back to the cottage. Give yourself the time alone and see what you can do."

Marcus drank deeply from his bottle. "I'm beginning to regret I ever bought the damn place. Why doesn't Rose show herself to me if she's so anxious to have my help?"

"I don't know. Maybe she can't unless you really work for it."

"I'm going to feel like an idiot trying to talk to a ghost."

Ted drained his beer and grinned. "You've been married. Have you forgotten we men have to do the idiotic now and then to keep our womenfolk happy?"

Marcus stood at a living room window, the mug of coffee forgotten in his hand, as he watched the dawn creep into a new day. Huge trees silhouetted against the sky pierced the pearl gray light with their jagged tips. His gaze moved to the empty field that divided the cottage from the forest.

He studied the delicate mist that hovered over the grasses shrouding the ground within its diaphanous veil. He continued to watch as the filmy vapor shifted making him wonder if Summer's ghosts lingered there watching the house. Or were the answers he sought secreted beyond that curtain somewhere deep in the woods?

His nostrils flared at the fanciful thoughts, as irritation bled its way into his mind. It wasn't as though he hadn't been trying to follow Ted's advice. He'd gone into the garden thinking his best chances would have been there, especially around the area where Rose had taken her wedding vows, but he'd been met with disappointment.

He'd lain awake most of the night straining to pick up any clues until the effort had made him break out in a sweat. It was no use. No matter how hard he tried he hadn't been able to make her appear, as she'd supposedly done with Sasha. Nor had he felt so much as a whiff of any presence, as Summer claimed to have experienced.

His lack of success intensified his belief that Summer was wrong about all of it. But he wasn't going to feel any joy in pointing that out, knowing she probably wouldn't accept his opinion now anymore than she had before. He set the mug aside and rubbed the back of his neck. He felt so frustrated standing there staring at the familiar scenery that even the clock's soft ticking scraped against his nerves.

Although he'd already gone to the stream where Sasha said she'd encountered the mysterious women, Marcus decided to give it another try. He'd convinced himself it would be a waste of time to go back, but realized since he had nothing else going for him, he had nothing to lose.

"I didn't know what I was doing before and here I go again," he muttered before heading for a shower that would hopefully help to clear his head.

He waited until the sun had burned away the mist before setting out. If he hadn't been so intent on what may or may not lay ahead he probably would have enjoyed the walk. The air was pleasantly cool and filled with the aroma of fresh earth and the strong aroma of pine. Light forked its way through the forest canopy laying pockets of molten gold along the ground while giving teasing glimpses of blue sky overhead.

Leaves rustled softly in the breeze flashing silver mixed with assorted shades of green. The older trees seemed to emit deep rumbling groans as they settled themselves more firmly into the ground while young saplings fluttered with whispered sighs of their own. His footsteps crunched through the carpet of fallen leaves and pine needles spread over the forest floor.

There was no set path to follow, so he skirted around clusters of lacy wild ferns and bushes nature had sculpted into unique patterns. Wild flowers dotted the area with splashes of bright color woven among the greenery. He recognized them as some of the ones Sasha had pulled from Rose's bucket. He bent down on an impulse to touch the delicate petals seconds before a squirrel darted across his path.

The little animal stopped a short distance away and twitched its bushy tail while lifting a tiny pointed face to give the air a nervous sniff. It lingered for a moment longer before scampering up a tree to disappear out of sight. A bird's song rang out somewhere overhead and another instantly echoed an answering call.

Marcus trudged on until the sound of rushing water made him quicken his pace. He entered the small clearing where his eyes were immediately drawn to the log where Sasha said she'd sat with the woman. He reluctantly lowered himself down after taking a quick look around.

One hand brushed a bristly clump of pale lichen while the other felt the scrape of rough bark. Except for the rhythm of moving water, this area was eerily quiet. Marcus did his best to erase his mind and block out everything but thoughts of Rose. Despite Ted's suggestion he couldn't bring himself to actually speak out loud to her.

He hoped by sitting still and concentrating it would be enough to somehow make her understand he was in his own way trying to reach out to her. But whatever Ted thought might happen was turning out to be another disappointment. More so, because he loved Summer enough to know he needed to make a connection for both their sakes.

Discouraged, Marcus shoved himself up and walked restlessly over to the water.

Old timers in town claimed the stream was keeping its height a lot longer than they could remember in recent years. Word got around that it was best to stay away until the level dropped back down to normal and the current wasn't so dangerous. Thinking how easily Sasha could have fallen in made his gut clench.

He felt the cold spray whip up wetting his face, as he stood listening to the music of the moving water. It became almost hypnotic watching the rivulets dance and bubble their way along in a ceaseless rippling flow. The surge bit greedily into the embankment leaving fresh exposed cuts where the current eroded small chunks of earth.

The water reminded him of liquid silver and was clear enough to show off the colored pebbles on the bottom sparkling like precious gems. He bent to pick up a small stone and tossed it into the water. The current snatched it away. He wondered how anyone could manage to scoop anything off the bottom amid this treacherous surge.

He stepped nearer to the edge for a better look and suddenly felt a blast of frosty air before a distinct pressure shoved at his back making him lose his balance and pitch forward. Startled, he shouted out in alarm and instinctively made a frantic grab at the muddy embankment.

His fingers clawed desperately at the ground while his feet made futile attempts to dig into the slick earth, but his efforts weren't enough to stop his downward momentum. Gasping from shock when his body slid into the icy stream, Marcus fought against the water's force, as it pulled and tugged at him dragging him into its swirling depths. The last thing he heard above the roar of rushing water and his pounding heart was the distinct sound of a woman's ruthless laughter.

CHAPTER THIRTY-FIVE

Summer lay on her bed trying to rest. One look at her pale face and lackluster eyes and Jonathan insisted on canceling the morning readings. She'd given in knowing her lack of energy would spoil her performance for the children. How could she brighten their spirits when hers were wallowing somewhere down in the basement of her soul?

She'd gone to her room like an obedient child and lay stretched out on the bed fully clothed willing herself to create a serene setting. Thoughts of Marcus had to be blocked if she hoped to get any rest. She closed her eyes and was just sliding into a world of soft colors and gentle music when the telephone rang making her body jerk in reaction.

She roused herself and snatched at the phone. "Hello?"

"Sis?"

"Ted! Is something wrong?"

"Why do you always think something is the matter when I call you?"

"No I don't."

"Then why do you sound so jumpy?"

"I was half asleep."

"Oh shoot, I'm sorry. I didn't expect you to be in bed this late. In fact, I wasn't sure if I'd catch you at all."

"I've been up and had my breakfast, but I was tired and came back to lie down."

"I take it that means you haven't been sleeping at night. Why not?"

"Different beds and strange surroundings, I suppose. How are the boys?"

"Driving me up the wall more often than not like kids are supposed to do at their ages, fine otherwise. How's the tour going

213

if you're having trouble sleeping?"

"Not bad, but when Jonathan saw my eyes looking like a raccoon's he suggested canceling my readings this morning while I try to catch up on some sleep."

"You know what I think your problem is?"

"Assuming I have one, what is your diagnosis, Dr. Gabriel?"

"You're homesick."

"A little," she admitted. "But I still have several places to visit."

"Reschedule them. Come home, Summer. It's time. Marcus needs you."

"No he doesn't." The words sounded wobbly.

"Oh yes he does and from the sound of you, the feeling is mutual."

"I sound the way I do because I'm tired and I told you I was half asleep."

"Uh-huh, right. I thought women in love were supposed to be intuitive."

"Did you call just to harass me?"

"No, I called to let you know it's time for you to listen to your heart, baby sister."

Summer started to protest to, but he'd already hung up. She replaced the receiver and sat brooding. Had Marcus asked Ted to call her? Her hands clenched the bed quilt. He was a miserable coward if he had. If Marcus really was anxious to see her, he could pick up the phone and tell her himself.

She lay back down, but her mind was so filled with thoughts of him that it took sheer willpower before she managed to drift off again and even then his image was the last thing etched on her brain. Time ticked by and she gradually fell into a deep sleep.

It was peaceful in the beginning, as she wandered in and out of dreams too vague to be disturbing until suddenly her body began to twist uncontrollably. The sensation that she was submerged in cold water became so strong she began to tremble. Fear, sharp and quick plunged deep. She thrashed about, choking. She flung her hands out reaching into empty space while she continued to gulp for air. Her legs kicked in a desperate attempt to control the sensation that she was being swept helplessly along against her will. She fought her way through layers of sleep and bolted up into a sitting position.

She gasped for breath while her heart hammered out its protest at the abuse. Her eyes darted around the room, confused and full of fear. Sweat beaded her body leaving her skin clammy to the touch. Was this what a panic attack felt like? She'd never had one, but had heard people talk about them.

She sat trembling trying to control her breathing, as her hands fluttered around her face and throat. Summer reminded herself it had only been a nightmare, but the experience had seemed so real every muscle in her body felt strained. She pushed the hair away from her face and felt a sigh shiver through her.

Exhausted, weariness laying on her like a heavy weight, she flopped down on the bed and closed her eyes. Moments later she slipped back into a dream world filled with a strange combination of icy water, pine trees, and the scent of roses.

When she awoke again, Summer rolled over and looked at the bedside clock. Surprised to see that she'd slept through the lunch hour, she sat up and swung her legs over the edge of the bed. The memory of her nightmare came flooding back, swamping her with renewed unrest. She tried to block it out, but couldn't. Giving into defeat, she let the details work their way back into her mind.

Water; there had been water so cold it had taken her breath away. It felt as though icy fingers were grabbing and pulling at her body sapping her strength and leaving her helplessly in its grip. She remembered fighting against that invisible force until her body ached with the effort. She flexed her arms and legs now, testing their stamina.

She recalled the scents that followed. They'd been so vivid that even now her nostrils twitched. Those aromas reminded her of home. She stood up and headed for the bathroom thinking she must be more homesick than she thought.

At the sound of knocking, Marcus and Sasha looked toward the front door together. "Who's that, Daddy?"

"Maybe it's some fairies coming to call."

Sasha had been in a better mood since her visit to Ted and the boys, and Marcus had been trying a few of what he liked to think of as Summerisms to keep the good humor going as long as possible.

She giggled. "Fairies don't knock at doors; they come in through the windows."

"Ah, I see." He followed her to the door and reached over to help her when she fumbled with the handle.

"Summer! You came back," she cried and surged forward.

Summer used one hand to balance a large pizza with a smaller box of brownies stacked on top while she returned Sasha's hug with her free hand. "Hello, sweetie."

The smile she gave Marcus was strained with nervous tension. "I took a chance you haven't eaten yet."

"Oh, goody, pizza! We were going to have icky fish sticks."

"Sounds like I got here in the nick of time."

"I wasn't expecting you," Marcus said.

"Surprise." Her hands shook where they gripped the box. "Aren't you going to invite me in?"

He stepped back, but it was Sasha who took her by the hand and tugged her over the threshold and into the kitchen. Summer set the boxes on the table and let Sasha lift the pizza lid. "Pepperoni! My favorite."

Summer pointed to the dish cupboard. "May I?" she asked.

Marcus shrugged. "Suit yourself."

Without Sasha's chatter the meal would have been taken in complete silence. Marcus continued to maintain his earlier reserve and barely touched his food while Summer only picked at hers.

"Did you make the sick kids feel better with your stories, Summer?" Sasha wanted to know between bites of a brownie.

Summer smiled and reached over with a napkin to wipe some crumbs off Sasha's mouth. "I hope so. I know I tried."

"Does that mean you'll stay here now, so you and Daddy can get married?"

Summer held her breath and swallowed hard at Marcus' deep frown. Ted had obviously been wrong about him needing her. It had been a mistake to come. She felt crushed by the idea that he didn't want her here. A quick rush of tears wanted to come, but she forced them back and stared at her plate.

He drummed his fingers on the table for a few seconds before turning his gaze toward Sasha. "Finish up that mess. It's getting late and you need your bath before bed."

"But, Daddy..."

"You heard me." He stood up and took his plate to the sink.

Summer had hoped to talk to him after Sasha went to bed, but now all she could think about was escaping as soon as possible.

Escape. How sad that she'd think of her departure in that way. The thought of leaving the cottage and the life that she'd pictured here was breaking her heart. But the little house was a cauldron of turmoil for her now rather the haven of peace she craved.

She would have left right then, but Sasha begged her to stay for her bath and a story. Summer looked at Marcus and risked seeing the disapproval she was sure would be reflected in his expression, but he merely shrugged. Since this would probably be the last time she'd tend to the child, Summer gave into her plea.

"Let's clear the table first." She started to pick up her plate.

"Leave it. Go with Sasha."

"All right." She held out her hand to Sasha. "Come on sweetheart, let's get you your bath."

With her nerves fraying, listening to the child happily babble on about the wedding, having a new mommy, and the baby brothers and sister she wanted, Summer held her smile in place. But she felt her dreams slowly begin to shatter like delicate glass.

CHAPTER THIRTY-SIX

Marcus came into the bedroom to bid Sasha goodnight as Summer kissed her on the cheek, held on a little too long for the hug, and stepped by him without a word.

She was already at the front door when he returned to the living room. "I'll be going now," she told him, careful to keep her voice steady. She felt like a coward running out like this and imagined a yellow streak a foot wide going down the middle of her back.

"Not a good idea, Summer."

"What?"

"You need to hang around for a while." He shoved his hands in his pockets. "We both know you didn't come here just to deliver pizza."

She was tempted to lie to protect her pride, but instead, "You're right," she said. "I didn't. It would have been a lot easier if I had been invited. But I'm not going to apologize for showing up unannounced."

"I'm not asking for an apology. And for the record, how was I supposed to invite you when I didn't know you were back?"

"You would have if you'd called me. Do you have any idea how difficult it was for me to show up here after hearing nothing from you the whole time I was gone? Two weeks, Marcus, and not so much as a lousy text message." She knew she sounded resentful and she didn't care. She was tired of pretending otherwise.

"You were never far from my thoughts."

"Is that so? It would have been nice to know that."

"I was under the impression you wanted time to work some things out...alone."

She shook her head. "You were the one who needed his space. It's pretty hard to work anything out when two parties are involved and one of them refuses to take his part in the discussion."

"True, but right now I'm not the one getting ready to bolt."

"I thought it was the best thing to do given the lack of warmth in your greeting."

"The unexpectedness of your visit caught me off guard. You have a right to be angry, but running away isn't going to solve anything for either of us."

"Am I supposed to pin a medal on you for acknowledging I'm entitled to my anger when you've been so oblivious to everything else that I feel?"

"I told you before I'm not unaware of your position, but I won't be forced into something I cannot make sense of. You shouldn't leave here until we've had our talk."

The seriousness in his tone sent an arrow of alarm straight to her heart. She had a feeling he was going to tell her that he'd made a mistake in thinking he could ever truly love her. She wanted to run away and weep her heart out.

"Do you still want to get married?" she asked.

"Do you?"

"I asked you first."

"Well, this conversation is certainly starting off in a mature manner."

Summer felt the pressure against her temples push harder. Her pulse pounded with a maddening beat while he stood there quietly staring at her. She held up her hands. "Oh never mind, you don't have to answer that. It's all right. I understand you've had a change of heart. You don't owe me any allegiance."

"If you really believed that you wouldn't be here." He pointed to a chair. "Sit."

But she shook her head and stared at the door.

"You want to run away and wallow in pity, fine, but before you go you might ask yourself why I stayed here in a house that's supposed to be haunted and where my child has been exposed to danger?"

"I'm sorry, I don't..."

"You know why," he cut in. "I stayed because I've been wait-ing for you to come back. Now stop acting like a scared rabbit and sit down."

She sensed a raw efficiency about him now. But as much as she wanted to get away she was beginning to feel lightheaded from tension. She sank down onto the nearest chair.

"Would you like coffee?" he asked.

"No thank you."

"A brandy, then? You've gone very pale."

"I'm fine."

He sat in a chair across from her, raising his ankle to rest on one knee. "If you're fine, then why are you shaking?"

She resented his composure. It made her feel inferior in comparison that she wasn't doing a better job of hiding her feelings. "I'm trying to be civilized about this, but I guess I'm not as ready as I thought I'd be."

"What is it exactly you think you need to ready yourself for?'

"Stop toying with me, can't you?" She dropped her purse on the floor and shot to her feet, pacing. "Must you deliberately act so obtuse? You know very well I'm talking about your wanting to dump me."

He stood, folding his arms across his chest. "Is that what I'm doing? I don't remember saying anything about walking away."

"Oh, you needn't pretend to be so surprised. I've seen it coming. I just wished you would have had the courtesy to say something before I'd gone ahead with the wedding plans. I still had hope, you see. But then what's a little embarrassment compared to being married to someone who doesn't want you?" She whirled to face him. "Right, Marcus?"

"Summer, I never..."

"I realize you got caught up with your daughter's needs and tried to convince yourself that because she wanted me, you would try to love me, too. I don't blame you, really. Given the circumstances, I probably would have done the same thing if she were my child. She's suffered enough already. But I understand even Sasha's needs weren't enough to make you accept me as your wife once you began comparing me to Diana."

Unfolding his arms, he frowned at her. "Whatever gave you that idea?"

"It wasn't too difficult. You couldn't possibly want to marry me after you'd been with someone as lovely as your wife?"

"Did you have help reaching these conclusions, or did you come up with them on your own?"

Ignoring him, she plunged on, "I realize Diana isn't the only person standing in the way. There's also the Rose issue. I know you don't believe me, but she does need our help." Summer stopped and stared at him with a pleading look. "It hasn't been easy having her intrude into my private thoughts."

"I don't imagine it would be."

She started to pace again in short agitated steps. "I shouldn't have mentioned anything to you. I made you turn away from me. God knows I didn't want to, but I couldn't stop even when I saw what it was doing to us because I can't ignore her pleas. I'm sorry, but I can't."

"Which puts us on two very different wavelengths. Let me ask you this, why do you suppose all this has come up now when Rose has been gone for so many years?"

"I'm not sure, but maybe she had to wait for me to reach adulthood and also because..." she stopped.

"Because?"

"Because I love you," she said in a rush.

"Well, that's certainly nice to hear."

"But how I feel hasn't made you believe me about all the rest." She sank down onto the chair and buried her face in her hands when he didn't dispute her statement.

He frowned, reached out a hand, but pulled it back. "I wish you wouldn't cry."

Her head snapped up and she made a quick swipe over her face. "You think I enjoy having you see me like this? It's just one more humiliation. You can't accept that Rose needs us to work together and I can't let it go. It hurts, but I can't really blame you for ending things between us before you went ahead and made the mistake of marrying someone you believe is touched in the head."

"Don't say things like that."

"Well, it's true isn't it? Summer paused. "I am worried about Sasha, though. I assume you'll be moving back to Vegas, but I'm hoping you'll let me visit her whenever it's convenient. I'd also like to make arrangements to rent the cottage from you if you've no objection. You've gone to so much trouble and expense to fix it up, I'd hate to see it stand empty again. Will you talk to Jonathan or would you rather I did?"

He sat quietly watching her fidget in her chair. "Are you finished now?"

Her hands gripped both arms of the chair.

"I asked if you were finished because I have a few things I'd like to say if you'll allow me to get a word in. You did say you wanted a two-way conversation."

Her face took on a rosy hue. "I tend to run off at the mouth when I get worked up and all this has been pretty upsetting for me."

"I noticed, but you have no need to be ill at ease, Summer. That's the last thing I want you to feel when you're with me."

"Well, what did you expect? I'm no mind reader and without knowing what you were thinking I couldn't help but feel you were drifting away from me. You must admit you've been about as communicative as a lamppost."

"I realize that and I'm sorry to have caused you so much stress. I didn't mean to shut you out, but I've been preoccupied trying to work out some things on my own."

"What kind of things?"

"That's what I'm about to tell you. But first I'd like to address that very vivid, very wild imagination of yours."

"Look, if you're going to start in again about my making everything up about Rose I don't want to hear it. I've already told you that I..."

He held up a hand. "Just stop for a few minutes, will you? You've had your say, now it's my turn."

She clamped her mouth shut.

"Better. I've said your imagination is a wonderful gift, but clearly it can also be a bane to you at times." She glared at him, but remained silent. "I wasn't talking about Rose. I was referring to your comments about Diana."

"Oh."

"Diana was an extraordinary person and I loved her very much, but I'm sitting here looking at an equally amazing woman. I'm not asking you to take Diana's place, nor do I want you to try and emulate her. I'm sorry if I ever gave you that impression."

"Thank you for that, Marcus. When I was at your house and saw her photo and how beautiful she was I felt totally intimidated. Add that to the art she'd created and I knew I'd never be able to compete with her. But I want you to know despite all that I couldn't stop myself from falling in love with you."

"I think deep down I knew that," he said softly.

"I should have said these things to you sooner, but I was afraid of what your reaction would be. It's obvious you had a very fulfilling life with Diana. Mrs. Gwen told me what a remarkable person she was. Can you honestly believe you'll be able to leave all those memories behind?"

"I did have a wonderful marriage while it lasted and Diana's death stripped me to the bone at the time. But I had to let her go and get on with my life. The day I marry you will signify a new beginning for me. You've filled in all the dark empty spaces and when I thought I'd lost you it was as though everything had drained out of me again."

"Oh, Marcus I..." He held up his hand and she bit her lip to silence herself.

"It nearly drove me into the ground when you went away so soon after I'd found you again. But we have to make things right for both our sakes and that isn't going to happen so easily for me." He touched a fingertip lightly to her cheek before drawing away. "I love you for exactly the person you are and I don't want you to ever forget that."

Tiny beads of tears lined her lashes. "I see that I was hurting both of us with the things I'd dreamed up, but you scared me when you became withdrawn."

"Understandable, and again my fault."

"Are you usually a moody person? Don't get me wrong, we all have our quirks that we try to hide but which sometimes sneak out. I can deal with moody if you're willing to deal with my imagination."

"I don't think I'm any moodier than the next person, but I admit to feeling pretty edgy lately. As I told you earlier, I've been more pensive than usual because I was trying to work through some very confusing emotions."

"About me, right? No matter what you said earlier you have to admit you must have been worried about the state of my mental health, especially for Sasha's sake."

"You're going to have to learn to have more confidence in yourself. This time I was referring to Rose."

"Oh. Have you come to any new conclusions, or do you still believe she's dead and you wish she'd stay that way?"

"I believe she paid me a visit."

CHAPTER THIRTY-SEVEN

"What! Oh my God." Her hands flew to her mouth and her eyes instinctively darted around the room as though she expected Rose to suddenly appear. Of all the things Summer expected Marcus to say that definitely was not one of them. "Did she talk to you? Was I right about her being with Sasha and putting those things in the bucket? Did she mention anything about us getting married here and needing your help?"

He held up a hand. "You're worse than Sasha with all your questions. Am I going to have to put a muzzle on you to finish my story?"

"Sorry. I'm just so..." she waved her hand in the air. "Never mind. What happened?"

"I didn't actually see her and no words were exchanged, so I can't answer your barrage of questions the way you'd like me to. But something did happen."

"In the house?"

He shook his head. "At the stream. I tried to believe as you did, but it wasn't coming through for me. I did everything I could think of to try and open myself to her here in the house and the garden, but nothing worked."

"So you went to the stream?"

"Yes. I didn't possess your acceptance of the supernatural, but I realized I needed to try harder to get some kind of understanding before I went slowly out of my mind." It was his turn to stand and pace. "It was difficult for me to know what to do in a case like this where there were no guidelines to follow. I wasn't even sure where to start looking."

"Maybe it's been easier for me because I grew up hearing the stories about the woman in the woods and because I knew Rose so

225

well," she added.

"I'm sure that has a lot to do with it. Plus, I think you're more naturally accepting of the unknown without the burden of having to have everything laid out in detail."

"You mean I'm like a child because I trust too easily?"

"Call it what you will, but I've come to realize that's not such a bad thing."

"I think there might be a compliment in there somewhere."

"You could be right. Anyway, I took Sasha to the stream and had her show me the exact spot where she'd seen the women. We stayed there quite awhile, but nothing came of it and I began to feel that Sasha was actually starting to become a deterrent for me."

"What did you think Rose would do if she had you there by yourself?"

"I had no idea, but I felt it was worth a try to go back without Sasha to see if it would make a difference."

"At least you were willing to show up, so she could see that you were genuinely interested. The fact that you were trying should have accounted for something with her."

"That's what I was hoping in my own clumsy way. I sat there on Sasha's log and waited, but once again nothing happened. I'd just about run out of patience by then and had decided I was wasting my time...until this morning." He stopped.

She saw the intensity in his eyes and swore she could feel every muscle in her body stiffen. Her mouth went dry. She licked her lips and looked at him with a mixture of anticipation and dread. "I think I could use that brandy now if you don't mind."

He nodded and went over to a cabinet where he splashed the amber liquid into a couple of bubble shaped glasses. He handed Summer one and sat down across from her cupping his between his long fingers. The first taste made her cough. Wary of its potency now, she paused and took another, more cautious sip.

The evening had turned cool while she'd been with Sasha and Marcus had started a fire in the small fireplace. Summer stared at the golden flames, watching them dance over the logs. The liquor and the fire helped her to relax. She was about to ask him to continue with his story when the clock on the mantel chimed the hour. Rose's clock. She recognized the sound from her childhood.

"I thought vandals had probably stolen that clock. Where did you find it? It wasn't there the last time I was here."

"The workers discovered it in an old trunk under the house when they were doing the renovations. It wasn't working and I only recently had it repaired. Why?"

"Bear with me here for a moment. What made you put it on the mantel?"

He shrugged. "I don't know. What difference does it make? It's just an old clock, but I liked the look of it, so I had it fixed." She lifted her eyebrows at the hint of impatience in his tone. He sighed. "I swear woman, you'd squeeze the last drop of blood out of a skeleton if you could. If you must know I thought it would please you to have it in the house."

Touched by his thoughtfulness, she reached over and squeezed his hand. "Thank you, it does please me, but I think it probably pleases Rose even more." She rushed on when she saw him frown. "I'm curious as to why you happen to put it on the mantel."

He scraped a hand through his hair. "Summer, for God's sake, I thought you said you wanted to talk about Rose."

"This is about Rose."

"What the hell is that supposed to mean?" When she took a sip from her glass rather than answer him he continued. "I put it there because that's the only place it would stay."

She smiled. "It sounds like you're talking about an ill-behaved dog."

"What I meant was that's the only place I could get it to stand up right. Every time I put it anywhere else I'd come back to find it laying face down. It's a wonder it didn't break. Why this sudden intensive interest in some old clock besides the fact that it obviously belonged to Rose?"

"It was very special to her. Rose told me it was a wedding gift. She always kept it there in that exact spot."

He sucked in his breath and looked warily at the timepiece. "That means she must have..." He shook his head, unable to finish.

Summer continued for him. "She must have kept laying the clock down, until you finally put it where she wanted it to be."

"Ah Jesus," he mumbled and took a swallow from his glass.

"I have a feeling since she hasn't shown herself to you that may have been her way of letting you know she really is here."

"A lot of good it did me. It would have helped if I'd known the story behind the clock. I kept looking for some sign and there it was all this time. I should have guessed something wasn't quite right when the damn thing wouldn't stay put." He shook his head. "I don't think I'll ever fully get the hang of all this mumbo jumbo stuff."

"At least you're trying. Tell me what happened at the stream."

"I was feeling unsettled. I was finally willing to open myself to accept Rose, but there was always this void. I'd begun to feel fed up with the whole damn business and knew I had to prove or disprove your theory once and for all or go crazy."

Summer knew she shouldn't be surprised after what Jonathan had told her about Marcus needing to make sense of things. But she had to ask, "What were you going to do if you couldn't prove anything?"

"Haul you back and ghost or no ghost I'd make myself accept whatever was going to happen because I wasn't about to live here without you."

Her mouth swept up into a big grin and her heart did a little jig. "Good answer."

"But there was still the thing with Sasha. I really wanted to find a way to thank Rose in case it actually was her who kept my daughter safe. I'm sure you'll agree the simplest way to do that was to speak my gratitude out loud, but I couldn't make the words come." A rush of color stained his cheeks. "The whole concept made me feel foolish."

"I know what you're saying, believe me. Talking to a ghost isn't exactly an every day normal occurrence. So what did you do when you decided having a little chitchat with Rose wasn't in the works for you?"

"I sat on Sasha's log and tried to empty my head of everything, so I could concentrate on nothing but Rose. I hoped she'd somehow know that and reveal herself."

"Where was Sasha?"

"I had left her with Ted and the boys. It was his suggestion.

He felt that if I were going to go searching for ghosts I might have better luck on my own."

"I wonder why he didn't tell me."

"He probably thought it best not to in the event I came away empty handed, which was a real possibility the way things had been going for me." He gave her a warning look. "I don't want you giving Ted any grief about not saying anything to you."

"I wasn't planning to. So what did you do next?"

"I don't know how long I sat there and when nothing happened I became restless and walked over to the stream. I stood staring at the water looking at the pebbles like the ones Sasha had in her bucket."

"I suppose you didn't believe me about those, either."

"I wasn't accepting a lot of things at that point if you'll remember. That's why I went searching for some answers that would hopefully help me to understand what was going on. I stood there wondering how it was possible that anyone could get such little stones out of such a swiftly moving current. My mind was fogged up with thoughts of Rose and I guess I wasn't paying attention when I..."

"Oh my God, please don't tell me you fell in."

"More like I was pushed. I'm a strong swimmer, but it happened so fast I went under like a box of rocks."

"You were pushed? I don't understand."

"Someone wanted me to drown and they nearly got their wish."

"I know. I felt it. That's why I came back tonight. The water was so cold I couldn't stop shaking. I thought I might be having a panic attack." She looked at him with haunted eyes. "But it was you."

He leaned forward and grabbed her hands. "What are you saying?"

"I felt as though I was there with you." She told him what she'd experienced in her hotel room and even now fought to steady her breathing. He put the glass of brandy to her lips and made her drink until she pushed it away.

"What the hell is going on here?" His voice wasn't quite steady.

"I'm not sure, but I had the sensation that I was drowning at the same time you were in the water."

"Jesus God! That's just not possible."

"Maybe not, but it felt real enough."

"I need to say something here. I wasn't going to tell you, but I've been doing some research on paranormal activities."

"You have? Well, that's certainly a surprise. I never expected you to bother."

"I know, but I did tell you I was trying to work all this out. One of the things I learned was that there are certain limitations on how far a spirit can travel. Rose is probably restricted to the cottage, the surrounding grounds, and the woods here. So that's why I think you were probably having a very vivid nightmare and with your, don't bite my head off, imagination that's not out of the realm of possibility."

"Nevertheless, the chills, the sensation of being submerged and unable to breathe at the exact same time you were in the water have convinced me that we've both become so connected to Rose she somehow made me feel that I was there with you."

"A ghost with mental telepathy?" He snorted out a strangled laugh and looked as though he was ready to debate with her, but she held up her hand cutting him off.

"Let's not get into an argument over this, Marcus. I know how you hate hearing it, but I have a feeling it was another one of those inconvenient coincidences that you don't like to talk about."

He dragged both hands through his hair. "Anymore of these flukes, or whatever the hell they are and I'm going to commit myself to a mental ward."

"I know this is very hard, but we've come too far to stop. Did you see who pushed you?" She held her breath waiting for his answer.

He shifted uneasily on his chair. "No, but I heard a woman laugh."

Summer suddenly felt cold inside, fearing what he would say next, but needing to know. "What kind of laugh?"

He paused, as though he might be trying to select a word to best describe what he had heard. "Fiendish," he said at last. "It was the kind of sound that makes the hairs on the back of your neck stand on end." A muscle bunched in his cheek. "And I knew something that sounded that bad, couldn't be good."

CHAPTER THIRTY-EIGHT

Summer closed her eyes for a few seconds and when she opened them they were glazed with concern. "It sounds like the one I heard here in the garden," she whispered.

"When was this?"

She shook her head. "Finish your story first. How long were you in the water?"

"Long enough. By the time I managed to pop to the surface the water had already carried me quite a way downstream. I was fighting to get to the bank, but the current kept pulling me back. I could feel myself tiring and the water was so cold I was beginning to go numb when suddenly someone was there swimming next to me."

She felt as though the blood had drained down to her toes. "Helping or hindering?"

"Helping; definitely helping. I'm not sure if I could have made it on my own at this point. I couldn't see anyone, but I swear to God I felt as though hands were guiding me to the embankment and actually pushing me back onto solid ground."

"What did you do once you were out of the water?"

"My first reaction was to jump up and get the hell out of there, but I was too exhausted. I felt my own fear as though it were a living thing. I've never experienced anything quite like that before."

"I doubt if you've ever come close to dying before, either."

"Got me there. I looked around and I still couldn't see anyone, but I had the distinct impression that I wasn't alone. There was a presence there with me. It was very strong, almost tangible. I know I felt something, Summer."

She rose from her chair and knelt before him laying her hands on his thighs. "I believe you. Besides hearing the awful laughter there have been times when I've sensed a presence, too."

He gripped her fingers. "I have to ask you. Do you think there's a possibility that it might have been Rose's sister who was responsible for my falling into the water?"

"Yes, I'm afraid so." She told him the things Sandy had related to her. "She intimated that Rena may even have been responsible for Rose's husband drowning."

"My God. Now she's come after us and what's worse she tried to harm my child." His hands clenched into fists. "We can't go on like this, Summer, never knowing when or where Rena will strike. How in the hell are we supposed to protect ourselves?"

"Remember we have Rose on our side. I'm sure she's the one who got you out of the water. I believe she's been trying to reach you all along by saving Sasha, the things she put in the bucket, and through the episodes with the clock. I know in my heart that Rose is as caring in death as she was in life. I hope you can come to accept that."

"It's pretty hard to think otherwise after what happened."

"Do you accept it was Rose who was with Sasha?"

"Yes and not only because of my impromptu swim, but I experienced something else."

She felt her pulse race again. "What?"

"Every other time that I've gone to the stream the scent of pine was always very strong, but today as I lay there I swear to God I smelled roses. The fragrance was unmistakable."

"I'm sure it was," she said.

He lifted a questioning brow.

"Rose may not appear with bolts of thunder or flashing lights and swirling smoke. That wouldn't be her way because she was a very subtle person."

"But did she ever wear a rose scented perfume?"

"Always."

"Figures."

"What did you do after that?" Summer asked.

"When I was finally able to pull myself into a sitting position I sat there for a long time. I was pretty sure I was alone again because the floral scent was gone. I assumed Rose had decided I was going to be okay and it was time for her to leave me. I stayed for quite a while. I needed the time to think about what had happened while everything was still fresh in my mind."

"I'll bet. But you must have been freezing sitting there in your wet clothes."

"It wasn't too bad. I'd stripped off my shirt and the sun came through the trees. I was shaking, but it felt more like it was from adrenaline pumping through me than the cold."

"You were probably experiencing a delayed reaction to the shock of what you'd just been through. You may even have been so focused on what had happened you weren't aware of anything else."

"It was probably a combination of the two. I've been giving it a lot of thought since then and I've come to the conclusion that I've been too cerebral about all this. I think it's because I felt the need to try and pigeonhole everything into nice neat slots. I thought if I couldn't explain what was going on with a bunch of solid facts, then all this ghost business couldn't be real. It's taken me a while to catch on, but I think I've finally learned to listen with my heart as well as with my head."

"Are you talking about intellectualism vs. emotionalism?"

"Something like that. I think every action has a pattern and some are more difficult than others to follow. But certainly less intriguing," he added.

"So, how do you feel about Rose now?"

"Confused. Intrigued. Maybe even a little vulnerable. It hasn't been easy for me to give into any of this, but the longer I sat there the more I decided it wasn't going to kill me to accept that something quite unusual had taken place. It definitely felt strange, but I was determined to accept whatever the hell it was."

She smiled, understanding. "You'd just exposed your soft underbelly. Men don't like admitting to that kind of thing."

He gave a snort of disgust. "Women do, I suppose."

"Not necessarily, but I think we handle it better. You asked me once if I'd ever actually seen Rose's ghost and I told you I hadn't."

"I remember."

"I still haven't. Apparently Rena was the flamboyant one and insisted on upstaging Rose in life and now in death. But I really have felt Rose's presence."

"It makes more sense to me now. When did it happen for you?"

"More than once, actually. The first time was right after Rebecca's death and again after I'd made that first tape for Jonathan's grandson. I've always felt she was the one who'd inspired me in my storytelling and I suddenly felt the need to go to the cottage and soak up some of its atmosphere." Summer decided it wasn't the time to tell him she thought Rose may have been in the bedroom when they'd made love.

"Were you too nervous to mention it because of the way I'd reacted before?"

"A little," she confessed. "But that wasn't all. I also didn't want to tell you I was missing you so much I was in the garden on my knees crying to Rose about never finding anyone to love like she had. Especially since I'd grown up witnessing my parents' loveless marriage and vowed I'd rather be alone than be in a relationship like that."

He cupped her face and looked at her with regret shining in his dark eyes. "Forgive me. I never wanted to make you cry."

"I don't think I was the only one. I had the feeling that Rose was there with me that day shedding some tears of her own because things had taken such a bad turn for us, Marcus." She gave a little shrug and worked up a small smile. "So now you know that I talk to ghosts on top of all my other idiosyncrasies."

He pulled her onto his lap and buried his face at the side of her neck, then raised his head and looked into her eyes. "I'm sorry I hurt you and I deeply regret all the harsh words and the times I shoved you away. I stomped on your feelings and risked tearing your love to shreds because I was being a big dumb male. I guess that's why women often refer to men as beasts."

"Beasts can be tamed, especially with love." She smiled. "I forgive you." A lot of important things had been aired between them and she hoped he felt better because of it.

"Well, that's a relief." His grip tightened. "Do you realize I've yet to kiss you since you walked through that door?"

"That can easily be remedied, but before we do anything else, I want you to know I'm glad you shared your experience about

Rose with me and talked about your feelings for Diana. I know none of it was easy, but I'm very grateful that you did."

"Just how grateful are we talking here?"

She saw the sudden gleam in his eyes and gave him a sassy grin while pushing a heavy wave of hair off his forehead. "That depends. Are we using a one to ten kind of scale because I think you should know that I'm way off the chart." She wiggled suggestively making him draw in a breath.

"You might want to be careful. I'm a man on the edge right now."

"And I'm a woman on a mission."

Her mouth swooped down onto his lips with such speed she barely gave him time to take a breath. But he recovered quickly and fisted one hand in her hair while pressing the other into the hollow at the base of her spine and kissed her back. She dug her fingers into his shoulders before moving to lace them behind his neck.

The kiss swelled with passion too hungry to tame as heat begin to build and boil to the surface. Teeth nipped and tongues danced while hands stroked and gripped. He lifted her sweater seeking the alluring flesh beneath. She pulled his shirt away from his jeans ripping buttons off in her haste. They moaned into each other's mouths before he pulled back, chest heaving like a sprinter. "No man should want a woman as much as I want you," he murmured in a voice gone thick with raw lust.

Love and longing raced along her veins. "I'm only half alive without you, Marcus. These last couple of weeks away from you has proven that. Make love to me," she pleaded. "Make all the pain and loneliness go away. I need you so much."

His eyes darkened to ebony. "Summer. Will I ever have enough of you?" he groaned before his mouth ground down onto her willing lips.

She tasted the impatience and the intense desire that rippled through him spilling over, taking her with him. She shuddered, as nerve endings stirred and came alive. It became all greed and reckless demand. Their hands were everywhere struggling to remove clothing. He pushed to his feet and she wrapped her legs around his waist.

He staggered his way to the bedroom and nearly tripped getting them to the bed. Moonlight flowed into the room bathing their bodies in a pool of soft pearly white, as they tossed the last of their clothes to the floor. The air seemed to shimmer around them flooding the room with a gentle glow that chased away dark shadows.

Muscles taut and skin burning with fevered passion, they rolled in a twist of limbs craving more; needing more. Summer felt his heart beating strong and steady against her breasts and shivered, as his tongue slid down the vulnerable cord at the side of her neck. Desire, hot and slick tore through her pulling her down into an eddy of whirling emotion and obliterating all inhibitions.

She cried out in a primitive plea for release and he answered with a primordial groan of his own. There was no time for gentleness, as they slammed into each other, found their rhythm, rose and fell again and again until she gasped out his name one last time and he answered with a roar of pure male satisfaction before they plummeted and fell together.

CHAPTER THIRTY-NINE

Time slipped away. Summer lay in a sexual haze, too replete to work up the energy to move. Her arms were still locked around Marcus, legs entwined, and bodies glistening with sweat. His face was buried in the wild tangle of her hair that spread across the pillow they shared. A lazy smile played around her mouth and she pressed her hands into his back enjoying the weight of his body.

"Give me a couple of months and I might be able to move again," he groaned.

Her eyes were half closed and thoughts of drifting off to sleep were appealing when the air around the bed seemed to move in a slow humming vibration. She opened her eyes wide and strained to see in the semidarkness. The scent of roses hit her with such intensity she instantly felt dizzy.

"Marcus, there's something...a fragrance."

He raised himself on his elbows. "I know, I smell it, too." He glanced over at the open window. "I suppose it'd be too much to hope that the rose bushes have suddenly decided to burst into bloom after all these years."

"I kind of doubt it."

"Damn, I was afraid of that." He rolled away from her.

"I never thought she would..." Summer's voice trailed off and she felt her body flush with embarrassment. "You don't think Rose was actually watching us, do you?"

"How should I know? But as long as she thinks she has the right to come and go as she pleases who knows what to expect? I don't mind accepting the existence of Rose's spirit, but that doesn't mean I appreciate her having a ringside seat every time we make love. It's enough to put a man off his stride," he grumbled.

"Well, when you think about it, this was her bedroom."

"So? We've got squatter's rights and we're the ones heating

up the sheets now."

She laughed. "I'd have to agree with you. I'm willing to help her, but that doesn't include having her critique our bedroom performance. It's all the more reason we'd better get her reunited with her husband before Rena decides I should share you."

He shuddered. "I'd rather sleep with a snake."

"Yuck! That's disgusting," she said wrinkling her nose.

"So is the prospect of sharing my body with a dead person," he retaliated.

She inhaled deeply, but could no longer smell roses. "I think Rose is gone."

"About time," he mumbled.

"I don't think Rena can come into the house; it was Rose's domain. But she'll probably be outside trying to stop our wedding like she wanted to stop Rose's."

"I still don't really get why she's so against us or Rose getting married."

"Sandy told me that despite Rena's jealousy of being twins, there was a bond between the sisters. I'm beginning to think Rena didn't want Rose to marry because she thought it would break that bond. She's got to be desperate now. God knows what she'll try next."

Their wedding day dawned bright and beautiful, but the weather wasn't the only thing that made it so perfect. When Summer awoke and looked out the bedroom window she couldn't hold back her gasp of delight. Much to her amazement and joy every rose bush in the garden had burst into glorious full bloom for the first time since Rose's death.

Marcus, hearing her cry of surprise jumped out of bed and nearly stumbled in his haste to reach her. "What is it?" He ran his hands up and down her arms in an automatic soothing gesture.

She pointed a shaky finger toward the window. "Take a look."

He leaned closer toward the window. "Well, I'll be damned. Did you have any idea something like this would happen?"

"Not a clue, but oh, aren't they a beautiful sight?"

"Can't argue with that," he said. "Kind of puts the others to shame."

"They always did." She wrapped her arms around his waist and laid her head against his bare chest. "I believe it's a good omen for us, Marcus."

He held her and kissed the top of her head. "Maybe this is a gift from Rose and it's her way of letting us know the wedding's going to go off without any problem."

She leaned back and looked at him. "What a lovely thought. I think you're starting to understand the mumbo jumbo after all." She moved away from him. "I'm too nervous to eat, but I'll fix you and Sasha something as soon as I shower," she offered.

"Cooking on your wedding day?" He shook his head. "I should say not. I'll just grab a cup of coffee and give Sasha a bowl of cereal."

"I thought it was your wedding day, too." She brushed his lips in a soft kiss.

"It is, but I think the bride probably needs more time to primp."

"You're a wise man, Marcus Brennan."

The morning seemed to fly by in a flurry of activity. Holly and her mother had arrived early to help Summer and Sasha dress before they began preparing food for the reception. Ted and the boys came soon after with Jonathan following close behind. The minister wasn't due yet, which gave Marcus plenty of time to dress and visit.

The children became bored waiting for the festivities to start and were allowed to go outside with dire warnings about keeping clean and not leaving the confines of the garden. But the boys continued to complain there was nothing to do and in an effort to impress them with her new home, Sasha began to talk about her trip through the woods and the fish that inhabited the stream.

"I get to go back there when the water's not so high. I'm going to touch the fish then 'cuz they won't be swimming so fast. They'll come right up and tickle my feet," she added importantly.

Buster's eyes lit up while he hung on her every word, but Teddy made a face. "Fish don't do that."

"These will," she assured him.

"Who says?" he challenged.

Sasha looked over her shoulder toward the house as though she wanted to be sure they were alone. "I'm not supposed to tell you," she said lowering her voice. "But there are two lady ghosts who live here and one of them is friends with the fishes."

Teddy scowled at her. "You're making that up."

"No I'm not. She's really nice. Her name is Rose. This used to be her house."

"You said there were two ghosts," he reminded her. "Who's the other one?"

She wrinkled her nose. "I don't know her name, but she's mean. I like Rose the best because she brought me lots of good stuff from the forest."

"What kinds of stuff?" he asked in a dubious voice.

"I keep it in a bucket in my room. Do you want me to show you?"

He shrugged. "I guess so." He turned to Buster. "You wanna come, too?'

Buster shook his head and watched them go. His body quivered impatiently until they were out of sight. He rushed over to the gate Sasha claimed she'd used to start her adventure. A quick look around assured him that he was alone. He had to see those fish; he just had to and if he hurried no one would even know he'd been gone.

Holly's mother frowned, as Ted swiped a canapé off a tray. "Those are for later."

"Well, I'm starving right now. Got anything else around here to eat?"

She shoved a cracker into his hand. "Here, now go away."

"What? Do I look like Polly the Parrot?" He snatched another canapé and grinned, as she slapped his hand. "Is Holly still with Summer?"

"Yes, she's doing her hair."

"It's certainly taking long enough to get ready," he grumbled.

"She's entitled on her wedding day. Now go swap manly stories with the others."

"I'm going." He went out the backdoor thinking he may as

241

well check on the children, but after walking around the cottage he didn't see them. He opened the door again and stuck his head in. "Did the kids come through here? I don't see them outside."

"They must have used the front door. They're probably in Sasha's room playing."

He nodded. "I should have thought of that," he said and went out again.

"You look like a man on a quest," Jonathan remarked when he saw Ted come in through the front door.

"I guess you could say that. I'm looking for the kids."

Marcus looked up from a book he'd been showing Jonathan. "They're outside."

"Not anymore. Mind if I check Sasha's room?"

"Go for it."

He couldn't help thinking how cute Teddy and Sasha looked studying the brightly colored pebbles spread out on the floor. Teddy looked up. "Aren't they neat, Dad? Sasha says they're from that stream that's back in the woods here and there's lots of fish, too."

"Yes, I know. I remember seeing them when I was a kid."

"You did? How come you never took me and Buster there?"

"I guess I never thought about it. Speaking of Buster, where is your brother?"

"He wanted to stay outside."

Ted passed a hand over his face. "Oh great. He must have gone into the garden shed. He's probably full of dust and cobwebs by now. Aunt Summer's going to have my hide." He gave them a warning look. "You two stay put while I go get him," he said, but their attention had already drifted back to Sasha's treasures.

When a thorough search of the shed, another trip around the garden, and calling Buster's name didn't bring results, Ted began to feel his first twinge of concern. He knew about Sasha's experience at the stream and was also aware of Rena's part in luring her there. Was it possible the same thing had now happened with Buster? A sick sense of dread suddenly settled in his stomach.

He turned on his heel and hurried into the house where Jonathan and Marcus still stood in the living room. They looked up as Ted jerked to a halt. "I can't find Buster."

Marcus's brows snapped together. "What do you mean?"

"He's not in Sasha's room with her and Teddy, and I've checked outside twice without finding him," he explained trying to stifle his rising unease.

"Perhaps he's with Summer," Jonathan suggested.

The very idea brought a measure of relief. "You could be right. I'll go see."

"Any luck?" Marcus asked as soon as Ted returned.

"No and don't worry, I didn't say anything to Summer."

"I appreciate that. There's no sense in upsetting her today of all days."

Ted gripped the back of a chair, strain etched on his face. "Sasha told the boys about the stream."

"Jesus."

"We both know what happened there. I have a bad feeling about this."

"So do I. I hope Rose is out there somewhere," Marcus murmured under his breath.

"What did you say?" Ted asked, frowning.

Marcus shrugged. "Nothing." He turned to Jonathan. "The three of us are going to have to search for him without letting Summer know what we're doing."

Ted nodded. "Let me tell Holly's mother we're going to step outside for a while and ask her to be sure Teddy and Sasha don't leave the house."

Jonathan turned to Marcus as soon as Ted had left the room. "I have the feeling there's something going on here besides the missing boy."

"I'll fill you in on the way, but right now we need to find Buster as quickly as possible."

CHAPTER FORTY

There was so much for a small boy to see that it was impossible for Buster to take in his surroundings all at once. Sometimes he ran and other times he walked or stopped altogether to examine something new that caught his eye. It was exhilarating being on his own and each step brought him closer to things more wondrous, more intriguing than he could have imagined. It reminded him of the enchanted forests in Aunt Summer's stories.

He looked up and could only guess what it would be like to build a tree house in one of the tall trees or have the animals that lived here be his pets. But the thought of finding the stream drove him on, guided by an unseen voice like a traveler following a beacon through a strange and mysterious land.

His body was literally quivering with excitement by the time he finally came to the water. Forgetting about the need to keep his clothes clean, he dropped to his knees and looked down delighting at the sight of several fish swimming by. The three men burst into the clearing just as he was about to reach into the water.

Ted was the first to react. "Buster, no!" He rushed forward and grabbing Buster around the waist pulled him into his arms. A tremor of relief went through his body, as he held his son to him. "What were you thinking running off on your own?"

"I wanted to touch the fishes. Sasha said..."

"Don't you ever do anything like this again." Ted scolded and gave him a little shake. "Do you understand?"

Buster's bottom lip wobbled. "I'm sorry. Don't be mad, Daddy."

Focused on Buster, they failed to notice the woman until she stepped out of the shadows. The sun suddenly slid behind a newly formed cloud coating the thicket in a gray gloom and chilling the air. Buster whimpered and buried his face against Ted.

"Who's she?" Ted asked, instinctively tightening his hold on his son.

Marcus would have lunged forward, but Jonathan grabbed his shoulder. "Wait."

Muscles tense, adrenaline spiking, he shoved Jonathan's hand away. "It's got to be Rena. Do you think I can just walk away and not try to confront her?" Fury showed on his face and sounded in his voice. "She caused Rose's husband to drown and tried to do the same thing to me and the children. By God this time she'll answer for her actions." Anger pounded through him matched only by the violent roar of rushing water.

"I understand how you feel, but you need to back off."

Marcus paused and looked around him. "Are you expecting Rose to step in?"

"I don't know, but I have a feeling you have to trust me or you may never be free of this."

Temper warred with reason until Marcus finally managed a curt nod. "I don't know what you think you can do, but you've got five minutes," he snapped before spinning on his heels to stomp away.

Jonathan gestured for Ted to follow and waited until they'd moved out of the clearing behind some nearby bushes. He turned toward the woman. "Hello, Rena."

Her eyes, piercing and red glowed with suspicion. "Who are you?"

He sat on Sasha's log. "You know who I am. The same blood flowing in my veins once ran in yours." He pointed to the sky and swept his arm around the clearing. "Very impressive, but being an actress you'd want to set the stage. Come, sit. You need to talk to someone and I'd like to try and help you."

She hesitated for a few more seconds before moving closer, but she continued to stand. "What makes you think I need help from anyone?" .

"I know because you're still here and you shouldn't be. After all these years you're still here," he repeated causing her to glare at him with renewed fire.

"How dare you tell me that!" she snarled, causing the air to crackle around them.

"Lucky for you that I do dare or this will be how you'll spend eternity and I don't think that's what you want." He sounded calm despite the pulse hammering in his throat.

"You don't know what you're talking about."

"Oh, but I do," he said gently. "Every child has the right to be loved by their parents. It's the first love we experience and need. When that love is rejected it often shapes the way we handle our emotions for the rest of our lives."

Her eyes narrowed to mere slits. "What are you getting at?"

"I know the pain of rejection that burns within you, but hurting others, especially the children won't change the fact that your father loved Rose best." She hissed, but he continued. "It's not your fault, nor is it hers. Trying to fill that void by making other men fall in love with you never worked, did it? It only made you feel more alone."

Her lips quivered for a moment. "I thought if I kept looking there would be a special one just for me." Bony fingers tightened into fists." But Rose, Daddy's perfect daughter never had to grovel while I had to beg for whatever attention I got from him."

"So you wanted to take Rose's fiancé away from her to get your revenge."

"I hated her for being so happy, but I didn't kill him. I planned to seduce him when I followed him here, but I didn't kill him. He tripped. I didn't kill him," she repeated and sank down onto the log next to Jonathan.

"What about Sasha and Marcus? You deliberately tried to harm them."

"I wanted to frighten them, so they'd go away. I was jealous because he'd found love. I wanted him to think it was Rose pushing him, so he wouldn't marry Summer."

"They could have died, Rena."

She shook her head. "No, I wouldn't have allowed that, especially with the child. I didn't intend for him to fall in. It was just supposed to be a warning. The ground was softer there than I realized and when he did fall I had every intention of saving him, but Rose intruded and pulled him out of the water before I had the chance."

"Well, fortunately for all of us, she did. I know how unhappy you are, but it's time to stop allowing your anger and jealousy to rule your actions."

"It's always been my way and I don't know how to change."

"Yes you do. Make peace with Rose and let Marcus and Summer have their wedding. Then step through that portal to the other side, so your sister can, too."

"Why should I?"

"There are others who loved you and the fact that your father chose to give up the gift of you loving him was his loss. You've gained nothing by taking it out on Rose. If you had," he said before she could interrupt, "You wouldn't be so unhappy now."

"I don't remember ever being happy. Perhaps if I go I'll discover what it's like."

"I do believe you will." They stood up together and she smiled at him.

It was a lovely smile and for the first time in years it was filled with genuine joy instead of malice. Her smile slowly began to fade along with the rest of her until she simply was no longer there and as she disappeared the sun once again warmed the air.

The others stumbled from behind the bushes and rushed back into the clearing. Marcus stared at Jonathan, his mouth agape. "How did you know all those things?"

"I started going through some old family trunks in the attic and found Rena's diaries. Everything was there. I just wish I hadn't waited so long. It might have saved all of you a lot of heartache if I'd gotten to them sooner."

Ted hitched Buster higher on his hip. "My God, I wouldn't have believed this if I hadn't seen Rena with my own eyes." He looked at Marcus. "Man, when you set your mind to summoning ghosts, you really don't mess around."

Marcus ran a hand through his hair. "I certainly never planned to make contact with Rena." He looked at Jonathan. "But considering you were here when she did appear I hope she'll take your advice and let us get on with our lives."

Jonathan nodded. "Only time will tell, but I have a feeling she'll not bother you again. I think she just needed someone to steer her in the right direction."

"I hope to God you're right because I'm tired of paying the

price for her unrequited love. I want her to leave Summer and me the hell alone and Rose too, for that matter."

Jonathan clapped Marcus on the shoulder. "Well, let's get you married and see how things go from there."

That afternoon, as Summer and Marcus stood reciting their vows, a gentle breeze swirled the scent of all the different colored roses throughout the garden. Rose's husband had left nothing to chance when he'd planted the flowers for his bride.

Red for love, yellow for joy, pink for happiness, cream for thoughtfulness, orange for admiration, and white for purity. Summer carried some of each in the bridal bouquet she'd put together shortly before the ceremony. She felt certain Rose had been there guiding her to select the perfect flowers from each bush.

As soon as Marcus slipped Rose's wedding band on Summer's finger, she glanced over the minister's shoulder and caught a sudden movement by the edge of the forest. There standing in a long old-fashioned flowered dress she saw a woman. Summer caught her breath realizing it must be Rose. She nudged Marcus and nodded toward the forest as Rose turned and gestured. They held their breaths when a man stepped out of the shadows. He stood straight and tall in his military uniform. They both looked young and made an attractive couple.

Rose held out her hand and he reached over and took it in his. They smiled at each other and then at Summer and Marcus, nodding, letting them know they approved of what was taking place in their garden. They lingered a few more seconds and waved as the man slowly led a beaming Rose away.

Summer felt Marcus's grip on her hand tighten, as they stared after their unexpected wedding guests. The minister completed the ceremony a few moments later and invited Marcus to kiss his bride. She lifted her face and felt how his body's trembling matched her own. It was easy for Summer to forget that Ted and the others were watching until they started cheering and offering their congratulations.

Once the good wishes had been played out, they all wandered into the cottage to enjoy the lunch Holly and her mother had prepared for them. The newlyweds cut their wedding cake with its rose trim, accepted the champagne toasts with happy smiles, and laughed at Sasha's enthusiastic announcement that she liked weddings very, very much.

Summer and Marcus had already agreed they wanted to spend their first night of marriage in the cottage before embarking on the Caribbean honeymoon he had planned on a private yacht. Despite all their careful planning, they worried how Sasha would take having them away for two weeks.

But when they'd kissed her goodbye and told her they'd be away for awhile, she happily climbed into the backseat of Ted's car with the boys and gave a cheerful wave. Holly assured them she'd be checking on her every day. Apparently knowing Summer was finally married to Marcus and officially going to be her new mother was all Sasha needed to ease any anxiety.

After everyone had left and they'd gone into the bedroom, Summer stopped just inside the doorway and stared at the yellow rose petals sprinkled across the pillows. She smiled at Marcus when he came up behind her.

"Now that's what I call a lovely touch. It's romantic enough to make me want to get you naked and put some serious sexual moves on you to show my appreciation."

He raised both brows and gave her a big grin. "Well now, I'm happy to oblige you, but what exactly have I done to deserve such an exciting prospect?"

She pointed at the bed. "The rose petals. I love that you did that."

He peered over her shoulder. "I wish I had thought of it considering your reaction, but regrettably it wasn't me. Maybe Holly sneaked in here when we were busy shoving cake into our mouths."

She walked to the bed and picked up one of the delicate petals and touched it to her cheek. "I don't think so." Her voice rasped and her eyes became misty. "It was Rose."

He came to stand by her. "Knowing what I know now, I won't even begin to contradict you. I assume she chose yellow because as you told me it stands for joy."

"That's not all. It also signifies friendship and freedom," she whispered around the lump lodged in her throat.

"Freedom." He nodded. "Makes sense when you think about it. She has you to thank for breaking the shackles that kept her here and for setting her free, so she could go on to the next life."

He'd asked Jonathan not to say anything yet about his part in sending Rena away. For now he wanted Summer to have all the credit. "You should be very proud of yourself for accomplishing so much."

"I couldn't have done it without your help."

He shook his head. "It was your doing because you had the courage to believe even when I refused to accept it. I nearly wrecked everything with my stubbornness."

"Are you sorry? Even though you said you've accepted everything that's happened I hope you don't feel you've had to concede your principles to please me."

"No I'm not sorry and I haven't forfeited anything, so stop trying to dig up old misunderstandings on our wedding night," he scolded in a teasing voice.

"I wasn't. I just didn't want you to have any regrets." She twisted Rose's wedding band.

He and pulled her into his arms. "If I did I wouldn't have put that ring on your finger today," he murmured before nipping her bottom lip with his teeth.

CHAPTER FORTY-ONE

Summer snuggled against Marcus and began rubbing a foot up and down his calf. His body was still slightly damp from their lovemaking. She pressed her lips to his chest and tasted traces of the soap he used along with his unique male scent.

"Marcus?"

"Hmm?"

"Are you asleep?"

"Yes. You wore me out, woman," he mumbled with his eyes closed.

"Are you complaining?"

He opened his eyes and gave her a lopsided grin. "Not a chance."

"Good, because there's plenty more where that came from. I wanted to thank you again for choosing the Caribbean for our honeymoon. I can't wait to see the islands."

He shifted his head on the pillow to look at her. "Do you mind that I didn't discuss it with you before I made the plans?"

"No. I like surprises; when they're good ones," she added.

"I'll see what I can do for the next fifty years or so to give you more."

She smiled and kissed him. "Speaking of surprises, did you have any idea that Jonathan was going to give us the deed to the cottage for our wedding present?"

He shook his head. "Not a clue. I didn't find out until I handed him my check and he tore it up. He said the house belonged to you more than to him and he looked so pleased with himself I didn't have the heart to refuse."

"He's such a sweet man. I think I might have ended up asking him to marry me if you'd turned me down," she teased.

251

He gave her bare bottom a playful slap. "Stop trying to make me jealous." He tucked a curl behind her ear. "He told me he felt very privileged having the honor of giving the bride away today."

"When I said I wished I could have had a father like he would have been, he told me that now I do. It was all I could do to keep from blubbering all over his suit coat."

"I'll bet."

They lay quietly for a few more minutes. "Marcus?"

"Still here."

"Do you think we'll ever see Rose and her husband again?"

"His name was Mark."

She frowned and raised her head trying to see his face in the darkness. "Who?"

"Rose's husband. His name was Mark."

She gasped in surprise and struggled to brace herself up on his chest. "I never heard that before and as far as I know no one around here knew what his name was."

"Jonathan told me while I was trying to give him my check. He'd been doing some digging in the family tree and there it was."

"My God," she whispered. "Your names are so similar it staggers the mind. That's got to be more than just a coincidence by anyone's reckoning."

He nodded. "You'll get no argument from me there. I'm surprised you never knew. Didn't Rose ever mention it?"

"No. She always referred to him as her 'beloved.'"

"Well, he was obviously all that and more to her. Their love was so powerful that it transcended two different dimensions."

She smiled to herself, pleased to hear him talk like that. "I hope we get to see them again."

"I don't know if we ever will, but I'll never get over what happened today."

"That makes two of us. I'm just thankful that we both saw them together. It made it more special for me, Marcus."

"Same goes, believe me. I would have hated missing out on sharing that with you. It's kind of strange that no one else noticed them, especially Sasha considering what had happened at the stream."

"Maybe they wanted their appearance to be only for us."

"Could be. Why do you think Rose never showed herself to either of us before?"

"I don't know." Summer frowned for a moment. "Maybe she couldn't until she was reunited with her husband."

"Are you going to figure out how to use this as one of your new stories?"

She shook her head. "No I wouldn't feel right doing that. It's too personal."

"I'm sure you're right, but when you think about it, it's her story, too." He held her hand in his and touched the ring. "I'm amazed it's such a perfect fit. I never asked you, but had you tried it on before the wedding?"

"No. I just always knew it would be all right."

"You had such faith in all of this. Even as a young child I think Rose knew you understood things that most children wouldn't. I'm sure that's why she wanted you to have her ring and be married here."

"I'll never stop believing that she was the one who brought us together. I'm more convinced than ever now that I know your name is so close to her husband's. She chose you for me, Marcus. She wanted me to be happy. She looked after me in her own way."

"It would appear so."

She laughed. "I think it was a bit of whimsy on her part that she had us meet in Disneyland because she knew how much I loved a good fairytale."

"I suppose she got a kick out of that because it's a place filled with fantasy."

"I also think she wanted to prove that fairytales sometimes come true in real life."

He pressed his lips to her ring. "Well, at least we know they do at Rose Cottage."

EPILOGUE

The predawn silence at Rose Cottage was suddenly shattered by the lusty cry of an infant. Summer's eyes instantly snapped opened and she lay listening for a few seconds before her mouth tipped into a smile. At two weeks old Marcus William Brennan, Jr. had a very distinctive sound and at the moment he was letting the entire household know that he was awake and wanting immediate attention.

Summer nudged Marcus causing him to grunt and tighten his arm that lay across her waist. She pushed harder eliciting a low groan from him. "I'm trying to sleep here," he grumbled. "Why are you poking me at this hour?"

Her mouth twitched in a smile. "Guess."

Another wail cut through the silence. "Sounds like our prince is awake." He moved away and put his hand on her shoulder as she started to get out of bed. "I'll go."

"You'd better hurry before he disturbs his sisters," she warned.

Marcus nodded and rushed to the new wing that had been added onto the cottage.

He entered the room where two cradles stood silhouetted in the dim morning light. "All right, all right I hear you, son. In fact, I'm sure the whole countryside can hear you," he said in a gently scolding voice.

He reached into the small blue trimmed bed and gently scooped out the red faced infant whose tiny fists were flailing about. The baby stopped crying, as Marcus lifted the agitated little body. Father and son stared at each other. Marcus felt his heart swell with love, as his lips brushed the small head covered in dark hair so like his own.

He cradled the baby carefully in his arms before walking over to the pink trimmed bed to peer at his still sleeping daughter. There was no question that his son favored him in looks, but his twin was the image of Summer. That same love burst in his chest at the sight of her.

"Good morning, little princess," Marcus whispered. He turned to leave when something made him stop. He stood there breathing deeply absorbing the sensation. "I'll be damned," he muttered after a few seconds and, a smile on his face, carried the baby into his mother.

Summer held out her arms and took the whimpering baby from Marcus as soon as he came to the bed. She immediately opened her nightgown and put the hungry infant to her breast where he began to nurse with such eagerness she had to chuckle. "Is that better now my little man?"

"Greedy little devil isn't he?" Marcus said with amusement twinkling in his eyes.

"Hmm, reminds me of his father. Is Rebecca Rose still asleep?"

He sat on the side of the bed. "Yes, but she has company."

"Is Sasha awake?"

"No. I have the distinct feeling that Rose decided to have a look at her namesake."

She grabbed his hand joining their fingers. "Oh Marcus, are you sure?"

"Either that, or I imagined the scent of roses in the nursery just now."

"She called babies little miracles. How sad there weren't any for her."

"Well, there are now. Miracles and fairytales. This really is a magical place."

Summer bent her head and kissed the baby at her breast. "Yes it is."

Olivia Claire High

Olivia Claire High was born in Waukegan, Illinois and raised in San Francisco, California. With a B.A. in Liberal Studies and a Multiple Subjects teaching credential, she was a public school teacher for nineteen years.

A member of Romance Writers of America, she is now concentrating on her passion for writing romance. This is her third published book. Her first romantic suspense novel, *The Crystal Angel,* is available from www.firesidepubs.com.

Olivia lived on Guam for a year, but currently resides in northern California with her husband, Joe. They have three grown daughters and four grandchildren. She is working on her next novel. If you care to contact her, she can be reached via email directed to firesidepubs@comcast.net.